I0713659

CASTRUM LUCIS

Castrum Lucis

Book II of
The Chameleon Sagas

J.E. Marriott

Wyrdwood,
Canada

THIS BOOK IS PUBLISHED BY WYRDWOOD,
OTTAWA, ON, CANADA

Issued in print and electronic formats.
ISBN 978-1-988332-10-9 (paperback)
ISBN 978-1-988332-11-6 (ebook)

First trade paperback edition May 2015
Second trade paperback edition July 2023

DEDICATION

This book is dedicated to all my family in England, not a day goes by when I don't think of you and send you my love.

FORESIGHT

He caught a reflection of himself in the glass door as he walked into her room; the quick blur of rainbow colours never failed to please him. They made him feel superior. Hell: he was superior. He was a more advanced being than those worthless mortals that usually surrounded him. They were nothing but blood and meat sacks. They existed for his benefit, and they were only allowed to remain alive in this place by his own choosing. This delicious thought made him smile to himself. It was the outward smile of a handsome man, but it hinted toward the darkness that hid within. It revealed the depth of someone who had embraced evil into their life and fully revelled in it.

The door swung silently open, revealing her, her body limp and strangely pale for one of such dark skin. She appeared lifeless though he knew she wasn't. Oh yes, he knew. She was trapped both in body and mind and had no place to run. Even if she could, she would never escape him with either her body or her mind. She was his and his alone.

His smile remained. He loved the power he had over her; it made him gloat, and even though fate had brought her to him, it had all happened because of an accident on the other side of the world.

Are there truly any accidents, when one is of the superior race? he wondered. His mind distinctly said 'no' back to him and his smile deepened, crinkling his face into the face of a very handsome, cruel monster.

He stepped closer to her bed and checked the chart hanging at the end of it. Nothing had changed: she remained in a coma, utterly trapped and defenceless. He recalled his reason for being there in the middle of the night when he had more pressing issues to be concerned with, and his anger rose as he looked down at her.

"Bitch," he said, spitting the word out. "Why did you not see that Kate was still alive? And that the Marston boy had healed her?"

He was now by her side, his hand crushing her wrist, feeling her bones break under his fingers with his enormous strength. He hoped she could feel it, every excruciating second of it.

"Our cause was almost lost in Croatia because you couldn't see. You have one more chance to show me what I want or I will take your heart in my hand and drain the last of your life from you, do you understand me, Ramla?"

Silence, of course. What could she truly say with a body that was no longer controlled by her mind?

Nothing about the young woman's inert body indicated that she'd felt or heard him, or even knew he was there at all. Her face remained serene. The bed covers came up just above her small chest, her pale green hospital gown showed above and the soft colour of it only reinforced the darkness of her skin, which shined gloriously in the bright lights, but her aura was muted and blanched, barely visible.

Jonas placed his hand on her cheek and began to drain the life energy from her, carefully and slowly. He didn't want to kill her yet, but he would soon, especially if she gave him nothing this time. He could feel her weak energy creeping into him: not unpleasant, but not wholly satisfying either.

Several quiet moments ticked by.

Still he waited, without moving, knowing 'it' would come very soon.

Suddenly, his body jerked as the vision passed from her mind to his, making him twitch. Once his body had settled down again, he waited. He knew it would be like watching a silent movie once the darkness in his mind cleared.

The only sound that could be heard was in his head, and it was Ramla constantly screaming as he took her energy and vision into himself. At last, the vision became stronger in his mind, Ramla's screams evaporated like smoke in the wind and the darkness cleared as the scene came into focus.

He was standing in a large, long, stone room where lit torches lined the walls. He recognised the room from a brief visit many, many years ago. He knew he was looking at the inner sanctum of the Council of Nine. The room that only the Council were usually allowed to enter, it was where they plotted and ruled over the entire Chameleon society through deceit, fear, and killing all who opposed them, just as they had for thousands of years. It was the private throne room of the immortal tyrants.

He looked around the empty stone room, save for the nine ornately carved thrones spaced equally apart at the far end, upon a wooden dais. The lit torches attached to the wall sconces in between gave the room an eerie glow. The walls were dark with no windows and no fire burned in the giant fireplace to lend a note of cheer. Behind every third throne stood a massive stone pillar, each one rising up and becoming a buttress holding the vaulted stone ceiling high up above them. It was a cold and desolate place, filled with memories of dark deeds and death.

A noise behind him drew his attention around to the opposite end of the ancient room. He watched the huge wooden doors creak open and the Council file in reverently. He watched them cross the room in their dark red, hooded cloaks as each one sat on their own throne.

Jonas recognised the newly appointed members of the Council, who hadn't even been announced to the society they ruled yet. He was displeased and surprised by what he saw; he would not have picked those weak Chameleons to rule, but then he would slay all the Council if he had his way.

He smiled.

He knew this foreknowledge would be useful in some unknowable ways in the weeks to come as he now knew who to intimidate and get control of so he would have pawns who sat on the Council of Nine. His heart swelled with excitement; he knew this power would get him much nearer his goal.

He watched the Councillors carefully as they discussed something passionately, exaggerated hand movements punctuated a heated conversation, and some Council members stood and paced around the room to argue their point. For the hundredth time, he wished Ramla's visions came with sound. He could do so much more with the knowledge, if he knew ahead of time what was being said.

Suddenly, the doors in the Council chamber burst open, banging violently against their frames, and the personal guard of the Council rushed in and spread themselves in a line protecting the Council members. The new head of security stood in front of the guards, willing to give his life for the Council. A tremor of shock rippled through Jonas as he recognised the man.

Ramy, the leader of The Council of Nine, stood and called for silence as chaos erupted around him. Jonas saw himself walk into the Council's inner sanctum, bloodied and armed with a sword.

He nodded at the vision because he knew the sword was the ideal weapon to kill a Chameleon: slow enough to penetrate any shield of energy, and yet sharp enough to detach any head from its body. It was the only way to kill one: by separating the head from the heart, and it was the only thing that a Chameleon couldn't heal from.

He noticed his sword had been used already; it was gruesomely covered with blood and gore, which dripped onto the stone floor, like a gentle red rain. Jonas saw that his own right hand, the one with which he so loved to feel the dying beat of a human victim's heart, hung loose and damaged by his side.

However, a huge smile of victory glowed on his face, both in the vision and in reality.

The images faded from his mind all too fast.

He wanted more.

He needed to know what happened next and who would win the battle. He removed his hand from Ramla's cheek and looked into her emotionless face, knowing, from sharing her visions so many times before, that this was all he would get for now.

"You have shown me my destiny, for that I will let you live. In fact, I may still have use of your visions. It's a shame you fell into this coma just before you became truly useful to me, but I may just have a way of resolving that," he said, and smiled to himself in his cleverness, not caring if she could hear him.

Jonas walked out of the room, closing the door behind him. He paused and stood with his eyes closed, remembering every single detail of the vision. He recalled the look on the Councillors' faces as they realised their immortal enemy had been able to break through their many defences and get inside their most hallowed ground. The sheer horror that showed on each and every one of them expressed when they realised he would actually succeed in killing them all

Now, he knew he would finally win and get his long overdue revenge.

HOME

The drive home from the private airport with some of the Marston family was a quiet one. In fact, the whole trip home from my 'holiday' in Croatia with them was subdued. It was not surprising, after all that had happened, but I tried not to think too hard on everything. I could do that when I reached home and was in the peace and quiet of my room.

Our other friends and companions on the journey, Moira and Michael, had taken their own transport home. Tara and Wil, Joshua's brother, were travelling back in Tara's car. That left me in a car with my beloved, Joshua, whose hand I was holding tightly, and, of course, his parents Daniel and Helena or Lord and Lady Marston as they were also known. Now, for any normal teenage girl that would be awkward enough, but I had much bigger worries to think about. Far, far bigger ones, and I nibbled on my lip in apprehension of what was to come.

I watched out of the side window as the street lamps flashed past in blurs of light in the darkness, and found myself wishing for more time, a lot more time. The events of the last couple of weeks had barely sunk in for me; how on earth was I going to be able to explain it all to my mum? So much had happened to me, and my life had been utterly changed forever. Indeed, how could I tell her that I was no longer even human, but a Chameleon, and about all that that truly entailed? What if she ran away screaming? What if she no longer loved me? I desperately thought about all these terrible outcomes as I blindly gazed into the semi-darkness of the passing streets.

My heart raced in my chest when I started to recognise the outskirts of Shipton-under-Wychwood, the little English town we now called home. This was the place we'd moved to, just a couple of months ago, so I could attend The Marston School of Performing Arts and Sciences. The same school I'd only attended for eight weeks and would be unable to return to for at least a year. A whole year! My mind whirled at the thought and at how my life had changed so abruptly and so permanently.

"Everything will be fine," Joshua said, as he squeezed my hand.

"How can you be so sure? What if she'll have nothing to do with me?" I turned to look at him, tears welling in my eyes.

"Well, admittedly, I don't know her as well as you do, but she seemed a sensible person to me, and you say she always thinks on the positive side of things. I'm sure once the shock wears off, she'll be able to handle it," he said, and smiled encouragingly, "Are you sure you want to do this on your own?"

"Yeah." I moodily went back to looking out the window, trying to order my thoughts. Not even Joshua's good looks could distract me, this time, from the dread I could feel inside me.

How do I even start to explain? I wondered. Perhaps I could try: 'Hi Mum, yes, I had a great time on holiday in Croatia, thanks for asking. Oh, and by the way, I'm no longer human.' I cringed against this thought and the coming conversation. I could feel the nervous butterflies in my stomach build and reach a thrashing point as my breathing became short and shallow.

"Kate, I am sure this will be unnecessary, but just in case, if your mother does have... an odd reaction to the news, you know you are always welcome to come and stay with us. I am sure we could find a spare room for you," Helena said, and half laughed.

A feeble attempt at a laugh escaped my lips, as the thought of the Marstons having difficulty finding me a room in their thirty-two roomed mansion was rather ridiculous. I realised Helena was only trying to make me feel better and lighten the mood a little, but that the offer of a room was actually a very serious one.

"Thanks, I hope I won't need it though," I said and continued to nibble my lip.

"I am sure you won't, my dear," Daniel said from the driver's seat.

I found his soft, silky voice comforting. There was something about it I'd always liked. It was like hot chocolate: deep, smooth and relaxing. Sadly, not on this occasion. This time not even his voice could calm my fears.

At last, we drove down the lane beside The Green Man pub and I could see the familiar row of cottages ahead. In the dark, I could make out the old apple tree as it stood outside the house I called home. I looked at its green, softly glowing aura and realised that even our apple tree had changed to me now. Would anything ever be the same again?

"Thirteen, wasn't it?" Daniel asked.

"Yes, please," I said as my breath came quicker again because of nerves.

Daniel pulled the car over to the curb in one smooth movement.

"Thank you for the lift." My heart began to pound faster again, almost in triple time to my breathing as I reached for the door handle. "Oh, and thank you for allowing me to come on... holiday... with you."

"You are most welcome, my dear," Daniel said.

"It was lovely to spend some time with you, Kate. Perhaps it would be nice to have a little more of a restful holiday next time," Helena said, and smiled.

"Yeah, I would like that. Thanks again," I said as I climbed out of the deep blue coloured Mercedes.

"I'll get your suitcase," Joshua said as he climbed out of the car too, retrieved my suitcase from the boot and watched as his parents drove away.

Joshua stood silently beside me as I looked upon the small, stone cottage that my mum and I lived in. It was the centre house of a row of old cottages built for farm labourers back in the mid 1800's. It had been modernised, and was, luckily, up for rent when we came to the village only a couple of months ago. On the inside, it was just big enough for the two of us and felt cosy and warm. It felt good to be home, but then I wondered if it would remain my home after tonight.

I looked at the front door and had just a few seconds to regain control of myself as we walked up the path towards it. The living room curtains were closed. A light was on and I could hear the TV, so I knew Mum was home.

I concentrated hard on calming myself down with my new Chameleon body, and no sooner had I thought of it that a wonderful feeling of bliss spread through me like a wave caressing a sun-kissed beach.

I stopped mid-step. "What if I feed on her?" I

whispered, suddenly panicked again.

"You won't. I'll stay with you until you think you're okay, then I'll give you both some privacy, okay?" Joshua reached forward and gently kissed me on the lips. "Don't worry, everything will be fine. You can do this," he said, and smiled a half smile.

It was so sexy, it melted my insides.

What a great distraction technique he has. I thought to myself.

"Okay," I said, and nodded, trying to convince myself. I took a deep breath and opened the door. "Hello? Mum? I'm home!"

"Kate!" Mum leapt out of her chair, rushed to the door and hugged me before I could say another word, never mind take my coat off. "I missed you," she said.

Before I could reply, I felt the energy of her aura around her. My awareness expanded as I began to draw in her energy without even thinking about it.

"Nice to see you again, Mrs Henson," Joshua said, intentionally interrupting us and making her end the hug.

I staggered a little from the massive jolt of Mum's energy I'd just unwillingly stolen, and instantly felt sick to my stomach. I knew I was going to vomit at any moment, and, with my hand over my mouth, I rushed upstairs to the bathroom without another word.

I just made it to the toilet before retching. There

was no actual vomit, considering I'd not eaten for several days. There was, however, a lot of dry heaving. The feeling of nausea soon passed, but I knew it would be the last time I ever drained a human. It felt, tasted and smelt disgusting, like rotting food. Ugh... I shuddered, repulsed by it.

As horrible as the experience was, I was happy now because I knew I would never hurt a human nor drain them during my new and very long existence. I went to the sink and rinsed my face, looking at myself in the mirror. The beautiful rainbow colours swirled around my skin, showing me to be the Chameleon I had become, and I was glad that only those of my kind could see them.

By the time I'd gotten downstairs, Mum and Joshua were sitting in the living room, talking.

"There you are Kate. Are you feeling better? Joshua was just telling me that you had been suffering from travel sickness." She smiled and patted the sofa. "Come and sit down, tell me all about your holiday. What was Croatia like? And the Marston's villa, what was that like?"

I sat next to her, but not too close, just in case I might accidentally drain more energy from her. It would take me a while to control it, but now that I knew I didn't like it or crave it, I was sure control would be much easier to attain. Easier than I'd first thought anyway.

"I'm fine, thanks. Just felt a bit queasy." I looked at Joshua meaningfully, and silently thanked him for giving me an excuse for my behaviour. I looked back at Mum and I could see the blue colour of her energy floating around her. It was such a beautifully happy colour for an aura, and it meant she was at peace now that her daughter had arrived home, safe and sound. I could easily have been mesmerised by the depth of colour in it. It was amazing to watch, and I was sure I'd never get used to seeing such a lovely insight into human emotions. What was even more fascinating was that I knew it would change with her moods, and I would be able to see my mum in a whole new light, quite literally.

"Well, it's time for me to go. It was nice to see you again, Mrs Henson." Joshua stood and put his coat back on.

"Please Joshua, call me Caroline," she said.

"Thank you, Caroline."

He flashed one of his lovely smiles at her; the smile that would make anyone's heart melt, and then he turned it on me. "Kate, would you see me out?"

"Of course."

I grinned back at him, happy knowing that I wouldn't lose control and feed off my mum or any other human for that matter. Or maybe even kill someone unintentionally, which had been something I'd been absolutely dreading and worrying myself sick about.

Outside, with the front door closed behind us, I

held him close. I felt much braver now that I knew I could sit in the same room with Mum and not be driven to feed on her like some crazed animal.

"Will you be okay, now?" Joshua said, the concern showing on his lovely face.

"Yes, but that was a horrible reaction to her energy. Human energy is revolting. I don't know how some of the others can crave it so much. I'm amazed it made me feel sick, I had no clue I would react like that, did you?"

"No, but at least you know it will be safe for your mum now. I'll go home, but if you need me, for anything, just text me and I'll be here quickly, okay?"

I pulled away from him and kissed him gently on the lips.

"Okay... and thanks... for everything."

"You're welcome. I'll be back first thing in the morning, if that's okay?" he said.

I nodded.

With one last encouraging hug, he turned and as he ran towards his home so inhumanly fast that his Chameleon colours blurred.

At last, I was finally left alone with the task of telling my mum the whole truth of what I was and how it had all happened. I took a deep breath and bravely walked back into the house, closing the door firmly behind me in my determination to do his right.

EVIDENCE

Mum looked me in the eye, "So, you're telling me that you're no longer human?" Mum said. Her voice rose at the end of the sentence and her eyes opened wide as she glared at me.

"Yes. I have evolved from human to Chameleon. Here, let me show you." I blurred across the room to the fireplace and glanced back at her seeing her face full of shock. I walked at a slow pace back to the sofa and sat down again. I wanted to reach out and touch her or hold her hand, but I didn't want to frighten her. The expression on her face could easily have been amazement or terror. "Think of it as the next evolution of mankind," I said, trying to make it sound like more of a positive thing.

It took a moment for her to find words again.

"How did this happen: was it an infection? Did you catch it off someone?"

"They don't know how it happens. Some people just evolve while others don't. It usually happens between the ages of fifteen and twenty, although I've been told there are occasionally some that evolve older than that. No one is sure why it happens at all," I said.

"Who is we? How many more are there of you?" Mum nibbled at her fingernail and shifted in her seat. She was definitely starting to look more than a little nervous.

"I'm okay Mum, I promise."

I tried to smile encouragingly.

She breathed out deeply. It seemed as if she was starting to relax after the initial shock, and I began to feel hopeful and started to relax a little too.

"I don't know how many of us there are as I am new to it all," I said. "The entire Marston family are, which is very unusual. Rarely does a whole family..."

"The whole family are?"

"Yes. Joshua evolved this summer, and his brother, Wil, evolved last winter. Their parents have been Chameleons for many years."

Now, of course, it was an understatement, considering his mother evolved in the 1930's and his father in 1899, but I thought it best to keep that information quiet for now.

"Oh," she said and looked thoughtful. "So... do you do anything, human, anymore? Like eat or drink? Breathe? Go out in sunlight?"

I grinned, I remembered saying something similar when Joshua first told me what he and his family were only a few weeks ago. I smiled to myself again, remembering how awkward he'd seemed while doing this exact thing with me.

"What's funny? What did I say?" Mum's eyebrows rose.

"When Joshua first told me he was a Chameleon, I thought he was a vampire too," I said, and laughed. I really couldn't help myself, it was ridiculous, it all sounded so crazy. It was like something from a bad movie plot.

Mum laughed, but not wholeheartedly. I could see she was still confused and felt edgy.

"Are you sure you're not making fun of me, this all seems so unbelievable."

"I promise, Mum. I promise on Grandma's grave," I said with my hand on my heart.

Mum nodded knowing that I would never tell a lie on her mum's grave. I had adored my Grandma and it was an unbreakable promise we had used since she died.

"We can eat in public when we have to, but otherwise we don't need to very often, we feed... on other... energies. As for breathing, yes, we do that, we are still alive after all. As for the whole sunlight thing, that's rubbish told by Hollywood in their vampire movies. There's one other thing though... we don't really need to sleep."

"Not ever?"

She looked shocked.

"Well, rarely. We can, so I am told, shut down so

it looks like sleeping or so we can fake death but we can do neither...well, at least not like before anyway."

"You can't die?"

"They said the only way we can die is to have our heads separated from our bodies, otherwise we are immortal."

"What? Have your head chopped off?" She said with a lopsided grin, "Now you have gone all 'Highlander' on me. Are you sure you're not making all this up?" She laughed nervously and moved a lock of hair behind her ear.

I laughed at her reference to her favourite old movie. "I'm sure, Mum."

There were a few minutes of silence and I watched her trying to digest everything I'd told her so far.

"Tell me about how you feed," she said.

"Well, I've not really done it properly yet."

I ignored the memory of stealing some of mum's energy when I came home.

"There are three types of Chameleon. One type is called 'Hippies' as they take energy from plants, trees and animals..."

"Oh, very droll," she said and looked amused.

"I know... tree huggers, right?" I grinned and rolled my eyes jokingly. "Then there are 'Feeders' who feed on human or animal energy. You need to understand that we can see the energy or aura around everyone and everything and some Feeders like certain colours caused by your emotions." I explained.

"They actually feed on humans?" She looked shocked again.

"Yes, some Feeders drain a little and the human doesn't notice, while others..." I didn't finish the sentence on purpose, I knew she would get the idea.

"Oh my God! Please tell me you are not one of those. Tell me my little girl is not a murderer." Her face suddenly showed shock and I could hear panic in her rising voice.

"It's okay Mum, I am a Hippie. I could never hurt anyone." She didn't need to know about the episode at the front door and the real reason why I was sick to my stomach. Also, that my feeding habits hadn't been tested yet and I was most definitely not interested in contemplating if I was one of the third kind of Chameleon, a Bleeder.

"Oh, thank God." She reached out her hand to touch mine without thinking and pulled it away.

"It's okay, Mum, I won't hurt you. I love you." I could feel tears in my eyes as I looked at her.

I had to finish what I was saying. I had to tell her the worst of it. "You have to know everything..." I said, and took a deep breath. "There are also the 'Bleeders', they are Chameleons who hurt humans on purpose as they drain them to death. Some even like to punch through the chest cavity and hold the victim's heart in their hands as they drain them

dry, and feel the heart stop and die in their hands."
I stopped speaking, I had said the worst bit, now I
cringed as I waited for her reaction.

"Dear God!" Mum stood and began pacing.

"I had to tell you, I can't keep anything from
you. I am sorry, if you want me to leave... I... I will."

I looked down at my hands on my lap, not
wanting to see the horror and disgust that was
fighting for prominence on my mum's face. I sat,
silently crying, my tears dripping onto my hands,
waiting for her answer. It was unbearable, and I felt
like I couldn't breathe. If only there was an easier
way to do all this, I thought desperately as I waited.

Suddenly, I was pulled into a hug as Mum sat
down next to me and took me in her arms.

"It's okay baby, don't cry. It's okay. I still love
you, I will always love you. You are my child and
nothing you do, or turn into, will change my love
for you. Please don't cry, it's okay."

She stroked my hair as she used to when I was
little.

"It's just a lot to take in at once. I mean, an hour
ago everyone on the planet was human and now...
well... that doesn't matter...just as long as you are
safe and okay."

I sat huddled in her arms for quite some time,
feeling her energy press against mine, but if I
concentrated on creating a wall between us, one
that her energy couldn't seep through, I was able to
be next to her and not drain her. I continued doing

this for a while and it became easier the longer I did it. Now, I knew I'd be able to touch and hold Mum whenever I liked; it was such a huge relief to me, to say the least.

"I'm... so glad... you feel that... way still." I sat up, sniffed and wiped my eyes. "I have to tell you more...I'm sorry."

"It's okay, tell me everything. I think I need to know about it all as much as you need to tell me it."

Mum placed her hand on mine and left it there, no longer afraid to touch me.

I explained about the murders in Oxford earlier in the year, and how they'd been caused by a group of Bleeders, led by a Chameleon called Jonas. I told her how those Bleeders were using a seer to find newly evolved Chameleons, and those who refused to be Bleeders were being killed by them. I told her about how I'd died at the hands of one of these, Sebastian, and how Joshua had been able to bring me back from the dead by giving me some of his energy. I told her about how the car accident with her had been aimed at me, that they were trying to kill me again, and that Joshua had brought her back from the dead too and had healed her. I told her about the Council and how they ruled the Chameleons and how Jonas and his group were trying to form an army against them and take over via a coup, and how my evolving in Croatia had led to their exposure and eventual escape.

Mum sat, stunned, listening to everything,

occasionally nodding or gasping as the facts unfolded. I had one final thing to tell her and I hated to do it, but I had to: there was simply no other way round it.

"Now you understand who and what Jonas is."

"Yes, Kate I do. He has a lot to answer for."

I could hear grim determination in her words, each one laced with steel. I remembered I'd heard once about how unwise it was to threaten a woman's child, for she will be a ferocious lioness against you. I now began to understand what that meant.

"I am sorry Mum... but... Jonas is... Nathan."

I cringed again, waiting for her reaction. It was not every day that someone told you your wonderful, loving boyfriend was the most evil Chameleon on the planet. The same person who had tried to kill your daughter a few times and had successfully managed to off you once already.

"What? My Nathan? You can't be serious! He is a lovely, kind and a very charming man. You must be wrong," she said, disbelief on her face.

"It's true, I promise. Tara and I saw him in Croatia. I told her it was Nathan, your boyfriend, and she confirmed it one hundred percent... He is not Nathan, his name is Jonas... *the* Jonas. Later, in front of the Council, I saw who he was for myself. I'm so sorry, Mum."

I could see she was shaken; she had truly fallen for the guy. "Are you okay?" I reached out and held her hand again, automatically putting back up the wall between our energies.

"I will be," she said grimly. "No thanks to him, the bastard."

Mum didn't often swear, but when she did, she meant it. I snuggled up to her and held her for a long time, and neither of us moved nor spoke. Both of us needed and wanted the comfort the closeness brought.

It was Mum who eventually broke the silence.

"You said Joshua healed you and that Nathan... I mean Jonas... had a seer. Do you all have 'super powers'? Do you have any?"

"We can all move fast and hear from great distances, some have extra gifts like being a seer. Joshua's healing is very special: they've never heard of a Chameleon having the power to heal humans before. Others, like Tara's friend Moira, can tell when Chameleons are lying, whilst her ex-husband..."

"Ex-husband? I thought she was only your age."

"Tara is actually much older than me. She evolved in 1848, but age doesn't mean anything in the Chameleon world, you can look as old or as young as you like. I have no clue how though... I have so much to learn," I said with a small sigh. "Michael, that's Tara's ex, can create an area around a group of us so we can't be heard by anyone, Chameleon or human, outside of it. Very useful it is, too. As for me, I don't know yet if I have any, it is too early to tell. However, we discovered that before I evolved, I was having dreams that were really visions. I was dreaming about what was actually happening elsewhere, but now I don't sleep... so I don't know what I can do, if anything at all."

"Well, I'm sure we will figure it all out, and it does seem like you do have a lot to learn, certainly from what you've told me about the others. Will the Marstons help you?" she said.

"Oh yes. Joshua's coming round in the morning and hopefully we'll get started. I'm looking forward to learning new things about myself now I'm back home."

"Talking about being back, what about school?" Mum frowned.

I grinned. Mum was as practical as ever and I took this as a good sign. "Well, the Marstons thought I may have to take a year out while I learn how to deal with this... with... what I am now. I think perhaps it won't need to be that long, I seem to be able to handle it far better than I first thought. I'll talk with them tomorrow and see what they think," I said. I was hopeful that I might be able to go back to school sooner rather than later.

"I see." Mum yawned.

I glanced at the clock on the mantelpiece and saw it was 2.36am. I wasn't feeling even slightly tired; it was strange to think I had so many more hours in the day and night now to do whatever I wanted. "You should go and get some sleep, it's Monday tomorrow, I mean today, and you have to work."

"I think I will, although I can take a day off and stay here, if you need me to," she said.

"Thanks, but I'll be with Joshua and his family anyway, they said my lessons can't start soon enough."

"Okay, I'll call school and let them know you have a tummy bug or something... normal."

"Thanks Mum, you're the best."

I gave her one last big hug and watched her as she wearily got off the sofa and headed for the stairs.

"Goodnight, hon." She smiled sleepily, "It's good to have you home, no matter what and thanks for trusting me with all this craziness. You are very brave."

"It's good to be home and thanks for not running away screaming." I smiled at her, "I love you very much."

"I love you too, hon. Will you be okay down here on your own?" She was almost at the top of the stairs.

"Yup, gonna watch some TV and then might go read a book on my bed. I'll try not to wake you. Night, Mum."

"Night, hon."

I heard the creaky floor above me as Mum made a brief stop in the bathroom and then headed for bed. I switched on the TV and flicked through the hundreds of channels until I came to the movies channel. I knew they would be showing movies all night and welcomed the distraction. It would be nice not to think for a while.

I was a little way into the first film when I heard a noise. I concentrated on tuning out the TV and tuning in the noise with my new and very sensitive Chameleon hearing, when I suddenly realised what I was listening to.

Mum was crying softly upstairs.

I had no way of knowing if it was because of me and how I'd utterly changed or because of Nathan really being Jonas: either way, the sound was truly heartbreaking. I quickly tuned her out and I listened to the movie more intently. It felt like I was intruding on Mum's privacy and it made me feel guilty and incredibly sad too.

***

After my early morning shower, I was sitting on the sofa reading when the first rays of sunlight came through the front room window, sending pale streams of light across the room and onto the carpet. It was then that I heard the gentle knock on the front door. Knowing who would be waiting when I opened it, I smiled to myself. At last, we could spend some quality time together, hopefully without either of us being in danger of losing our lives.

I pulled the door open to find Joshua standing there with a worried expression on his face.

"How did it go?" He whispered and stepped into the hall.

"Fine... difficult in places... but okay in the end, I think." I smiled at him. Closing the door behind us, we walked back into the living room and sat down on the sofa together. "Have you been worrying about us all night?"

"I have to admit, I was. I know how difficult it is to tell someone you love, what we truly are." He looked at me with that sexy half smile that I adored. I knew he was thinking about the time he told me he was a Chameleon and *I* was the human on the receiving end of the life changing news.

"I think she'll be okay, although she's very upset about Nathan and very angry at him too for wanting to hurt us, especially me."

"Never mess with a lioness that has cubs," he said thoughtfully.

"Exactly! That's what I was thinking earlier."

"It's so great your talk went well. How did your control do?"

"Actually, it's much easier than I first thought. I just put up a mental wall between my energy and hers and that was it."

"Wow, that was fast. Not sure I know of anyone who got it under control so fast." He looked surprised and proud. "How are you feeling today?"

"Dunno... a bit odd, actually. Kind of like I need to rest or sleep, even though I don't. Like I'm tired or something," I said.

"Hmm... sounds like you are starting to need to feed. We will have to show you how to do it today. We can head out to my place, lots of things to feed on and lots of privacy there. How does that sound?"

"Great," I said and cuddled up to him.

"Morning you two." Mum called as she came down the stairs in her bathrobe. "I guess there is no point in offering either of you breakfast." She walked into the living room.

Joshua stood up. "Good morning, Caroline. I understand Kate has explained about us... I mean... about everything," he said, looking at her nervously.

"She has and don't worry, I won't run away screaming, well, not in my bathrobe anyway." She smiled and winked at me.

My heart soared to know that Mum was okay with everything and was taking it in her stride. I guess she had cried out what she'd needed to last night and was more focused today. I was amazed at how easy it had all been. Far easier than I'd imagined it would be. I was amazed, happy and very, very relieved.

Joshua laughed at Mum's joke. "I am very happy to hear you are not afraid of us now you know the truth," he said.

"Me too." I grinned. "Let me make you a cuppa,

Mum." I rushed off to the kitchen before she could reply.

"Wow, I see what you mean about moving quickly. You just turned into a blur right in front of me, Kate," Mum said as she followed me into the kitchen.

"I did? Oh, sorry, I didn't even think about it, I just did it. At least you believe me now," I said and laughed.

"It does help to see it, but I believed you anyway. You had better not do that in public, though." She pulled out a chair and sat down at the kitchen table.

"That'll be one of the things we'll be teaching her, how to fit in with... erm... everyone else. It's one of our laws that we don't allow humans to know of our existence. Except in very special cases when it is unavoidable to tell someone, like yourself, of course." Joshua smiled.

"Very sensible too, I think if the general public knew, they might panic, especially when they would realise they were no longer at the top of the food chain." Mum looked thoughtfully between us.

"And those people are called our 'Trusted Humans'. They hold a place of honour over normal humans," Joshua said.

"Thanks, I think," Mum said. "Yes, I think it's best to keep it all hush-hush."

The kettle boiled and I poured Mum a cup of Earl Grey tea, her favourite. I passed it over to her as I sat down next to her.

"Exactly, and we also don't want to end up as lab rats," Joshua said as he pulled out a chair and sat down too.

"Good point. You had better learn to be very careful, young lady," Mum said sternly. "I will not have you chopped up and put in bottles full of formaldehyde," she said with an utterly serious face.

"Yes, Mum." I tried to hide my smile. "I promise, I'll be extra careful."

"Good. Now get off with you both and go learn everything you need to know to be safe, while I enjoy a very large bacon and mushroom sandwich... are you sure I can't tempt either of you with human food?" Mum grinned impishly.

Joshua and I shook our heads, said thanks but no thanks, and headed for the door and my first real lessons on how to exist as a Chameleon.

NEWS

We walked into Marston Court, the huge Elizabethan mansion that the Marston family called home, to the smell of a cooked breakfast. It was not something I was prepared for, considering that only Chameleons actually lived in the house. Although, the estate workers were all human and could sometimes be found having a warm drink in the kitchen, if they needed to discuss farm matters with the family. We followed our noses to the huge modern kitchen to find it full of people. Joshua and I looked at each other, puzzled. He had no clue what was going on either.

Everyone stopped talking and turned to greet us. I was pleased to see that not only were Joshua's parents and his brother, Wil, there, but also Tara, Moira and Michael, as well as several of the Marston's trusted humans who worked their estate.

"What's going on?" Joshua said, looking around

him.

"Ah... Joshua, Kate, good morning to you both," Daniel said and smiled brightly.

"Oh, Kate, how did it go?" Helena asked as she rushed over to hug me.

"Actually, very well, thanks. Mum seems to have accepted everything quite easily," I replied. I looked expectantly at the others in the room and then I recognised George, the head stockman of the estate, looking very proud with a huge smile on his face. He was Daniel's closest human friend, and was standing against the central kitchen counter with his wife, Rosie, next to him as were his two sons Joe and Peter.

"Oh my God, Peter!" I suddenly realised what I was looking at, and Joshua peered around me to see what was going on with his best friend.

Peter's handsome face turned towards me, his smoky grey eyes bright and his long hair tied back as usual, as he stepped out in front of his family with his full Chameleon rainbow colours showing vividly.

Joshua, for a brief moment, stared in disbelief and then rushed to his friend's side and hugged him, "Way to go, mate!" His voice rose in surprise. "When did this happen?"

Peter grinned. "This morning. We came straight over to tell you and you missed it." He playfully slapped him on the shoulder.

"Sorry, Pete. I had no clue."

"Neither did I 'til I got up and jumped in the shower. I thought at first it was the water in my eyes making everything funny colours, and when I went to wipe the steam off the mirror, there it was: the Chameleon aura. Blew my mind," Peter said and grinned.

I stepped around Joshua, "Welcome to the club, Peter." I grinned.

"Bloody hell, you too? When?" Peter's eyes widened in surprise and he moved forward to hug me.

"A couple of days ago," I said as I hugged him. I realised that the food I could smell, as we came in, was not cooked here but back in the kitchen of Peter's home, a cottage on the estate. My nose was so much more sensitive now that I could smell it on him and his family. How bizarre it all seemed.

"Wow, this is so cool," Peter said.

"I guess there will be two of you learning the ropes today, as they say," Daniel said and laughed.

"Good, I never did like being the odd one out," I said and turned to the other Chameleon visitors who were all sitting around the large dining table. "What brings you all here? Not that I'm unhappy to see you, of course. I just didn't expect it again so soon."

"We were just getting to that as you arrived. Moira and Michael only got here a few minutes before you did," Tara explained. "Daniel wanted us all together for an announcement, and luckily Peter arrived just in the nick of time." She grinned and winked at him.

Tara looked radiant in a green sweater with her long red hair tumbling down over her shoulders. Her green eyes were glowing with joy. I looked down to see that she and Wil were holding hands and sat so close together that you couldn't slip a piece of paper between them if you tried.

I remembered Michael was also there. I glanced across the table at him and recalled he was Tara's ex-husband. Sometimes, he looked at her like he was still in love with her. I could see him occasionally glancing at the new lovers now, but he was forcing himself to look away. As much as I felt sorry for him, I was very happy for Tara and Wil. They had both become close friends of mine and I wanted them to be happy.

Daniel cleared his throat and the room fell silent, everyone looked at him with expectation.

"The Council of Nine has made a declaration," he said, sounding very official. Daniel pulled out a piece of paper from his pocket.

I could see that it was an email from Ramy, or, Ramses II to quote his proper title, who belonged to the Council of Nine, the Chameleon governing body. I don't know why an email surprised me, I guess it shouldn't have really. Somehow though, when a body as ancient and as powerful as The Council of Nine made an announcement, I sort of expected it to be hand written on parchment and closed with a wax seal.

Silly, I know.

Daniel waited for silence and then began reading aloud, "The declaration reads as follows: 'The Council of Nine has reconvened at Castrum Lucis and shall be conducting all business from there for the foreseeable future. As such, all newly evolved will be tested at Castrum Lucis under the protection of the house guard and the securities of the building. Previous to the ten day testing will be a three week compulsory residential training of all newly evolved, without exception. This training will be held during August each year without fail, unless there are no newly evolved within that year. All newly evolved are to report to Castrum Lucis by the 1st August. They must be presented by their sponsors and then left in the capable hands of the Council until the Evolution Ball thirty-one days later, which will be held in the castle's ballroom. Sponsors will only be able to return to Castrum Lucis at the time of the ball to collect the successfully evolved members of our illustrious Chameleon society. At such time the three newly elected members of The Council of Nine will be announced. By order of The Council of Nine and my hand, Ramses II.'" Daniel laid the sheet of paper back down on the table. "That's everything. It seems that the Council is taking no chances now that the Bleeders have hived off under the control of Jonas."

"Bloody Hell," I said, "That is a lot different to how it was done in Croatia."

I sat down on one of the spare chairs around the kitchen table. I remembered that when Joshua evolved, he had a day of training, then ten days of interment before the ball. I couldn't help but wonder why the testing was now so long.

"We have never had a civil war before, but now everything is different. Most of the Bleeders are siding with Jonas and those that aren't are under suspicion from the Council and are now being rounded up as a precaution. I had expected everything to change quickly but the compulsory residency of three weeks was a surprise to me too," Daniel said.

"Why would they extend the testing for such a long time?" Joshua asked.

Tara leant forward on the table. "The only reason, I can think of, is to make sure that every newly evolved Chameleon knows they have a choice of what they can feed on and do not just have to be a Bleeder as Jonas would have them believe. But, what I want to know is, what they will do with someone who is one already?" Tara said.

"Good point, Tara. I am not sure why they are doing it this way either, but I have the feeling this will divide the Chameleon society even more than it already is. I can understand them wanting to prevent Bleeders from joining Jonas but at what cost?" Daniel said, and a worried expression appeared on his face.

"Three weeks though? Not really liking the thought of spending three weeks alone with the Council," I said.

"You won't be alone, Kate, I will be there too," Peter said.

"That's true. You can look after each other," Tara said.

Joshua looked at Peter meaningfully but didn't say a word.

"I wonder what they'll teach us for three weeks?" I said.

"I think it will be more about them observing you than teaching you. I think they will try to weed out the Bleeders," Daniel said.

"Surely, if you were a Bleeder you wouldn't go, given what's happening," I said.

"The Council will still expect every newly evolved to be there and they will hunt them down, as usual, if they are not," Daniel said.

I glanced nervously at Peter; there was no way of knowing what type of Chameleon he was until he needed to feed. He could easily be a Hippie, Feeder or Bleeder. What if he was a Bleeder? What would happen to him? Would he be safe? Hell, what if I was a Bleeder?

Everyone fell quiet, we were all lost in our own thoughts.

George was the first to speak, and said that he and the rest of his family had work to be getting on with and made their goodbyes, leaving Peter with us.

I noticed Peter staring at everyone in a kind of daze.

"Those rainbows are mesmerising, huh?" I said with a smile, remembering how I couldn't drag my eyes away from them when I first evolved.

"No kidding," he said, still staring at the colours around everyone.

"Wait until you look at rugs and sand and so many other things, you can easily get lost in the colours and details," I said.

"My worst one was an oil painting in a museum, the depth of colour and shades and the trail of energy... astounding," Michael said with a half-smile of remembrance on his face.

"I get endlessly fascinated with plants. Did you know that the older varieties have different energy patterns to the modern ones?" Helena said with a smile.

"I have never really thought about it before, but that kind of makes sense though." Peter said, "This is all so cool." He grinned impishly.

"Well, I guess we had better get to work on your control," Daniel said to both Peter and I.

"Tell Father what you told me about your control, Kate. With your Mum, I mean." Joshua stood next to me and placed a warm hand on my shoulder.

Joshua gently squeezed my shoulder and

brought me back to the present conversation.

"Yeah, well, my control around my mum was much easier than I'd expected. She hugged me when we got back last night and I felt her energy flow into me..."

"Oh my!" Helena looked horrified, and held her hand over her mouth.

"No, it's okay. I only had a little, but felt so ill I thought I was going to vomit on her feet, and I rushed to the bathroom. I wasn't sick, of course, not having eaten for days, but the feel, taste and smell of human energy was disgusting, and I will never drain another human as long as I live."

"Oh, I am so pleased to hear you say that, Kate," Helena said and smiled at me, relief written all over her face.

I glanced at Michael. He was the only Feeder in the room, except for Peter, of whom we had no clue about yet. Thankfully, Michael did not look bothered by the conversation. I remembered that Tara told me he'd learnt many years ago to keep his feelings to himself regarding being a Feeder; when he was married to Tara it was one of their main problems, him being one and her being a Hippie.

"So did feeling sick help your control, Kate?" Wil asked, looking a little confused.

"It helped me to relax, knowing that I wasn't going to be a danger to Mum. As I sat next to her and talked, I was able to put up a mental wall between her energy and mine. The longer I did it, the easier it got, and it stopped me from connecting with her energy."

I glanced nervously at Joshua. He looked very proud of me.

I also heard multiple intakes of breath, the sound made me look around the room in surprise.

"How interesting," Daniel said.

"Wow," Wil said.

"That was quick," said Tara.

"She is telling the truth. Kate has found her control already," Moira said with the absolute certainty of her gift, which allowed her to know if Chameleons were lying or not.

"What?" I said, feeling like I had done something wrong as I looked around at everyone.

"My dear Kate, you do continue to surprise me," Daniel said delightedly.

"Why? Did I do it wrong?" I said, worried I'd made a terrible mistake.

"On the contrary, my dear, you have just learnt the ability to control your energy from feeding on a human, which normally takes a Chameleon several weeks to grasp and several months more to perfect. Congratulations, my dear, most impressive," he said, and smiled proudly.

"Are you serious? That was it? That was the control you were all talking about?" I said and looked around at them all in amazement.

"Well done, Kate, well done." Tara grinned.

"Yes, Kate, that was it. We will have to test it of

course, but, if you can do as you say, there is no reason you should not go back to school in a couple of months, perhaps earlier." Daniel smiled broadly, "You really are an exceptional young lady."

"Isn't she?" Joshua said and kissed me on the top of my head.

I was amazed. It had been so easy in the end and yet I'd been preparing myself for weeks and weeks of trial and error, terrified of making a mistake and hurting someone.

"Can you teach me how, Kate?" asked Peter. "I've been afraid to touch anyone at home this morning."

"I would be happy to try," I said, and smiled at him reassuringly.

"First, we have to test her control and then see if she can teach it, so we need a human to test it on," Daniel said matter-of-factly.

"Know anyone that would volunteer, seeing as our usual tester is one of us now?" Wil asked Peter.

"How inconvenient of me to have evolved just when you need a tester." Peter laughed. It was a warm, infectious laugh that made everyone join in. "I guess I could ask Joe, he watched Joshua test on me before, I am pretty sure he would be up for it."

"Get permission from your parents first though, Peter," Helena said.

Peter nodded and walked a little away from the rest of us, pulled out his phone and presumably set about getting Joe, his younger brother, to be our tester.

I was not sure I liked the idea of testing my new control on a human. What if I got it wrong and hurt him? I began to nibble my lower lip nervously.

"Whilst we are waiting to hear if Joe will help us, I wanted to ask what you and your Mother's plans are for Christmas, Kate?" Helena said.

"Erm... nothing out of the ordinary, I would think. It's kind of a bad time for us." I glanced at Joshua and back at Helena, feeling a little uncomfortable. "We were going to have a quiet Christmas. You see, it's when my Mum and Dad split up last year." I could feel the blood rushing to my face and the heat of my cheeks rising. I concentrated hard and felt the flow of blood drain away from my face again as I managed to divert a blush. These new Chameleon abilities were helpful.

"I'm sorry to hear that." Helena reached over and placed her hand on mine briefly, "We were wondering if, now that your Mother knows everything, you would both like to spend it with us?"

"Oh, I... erm... I will have to ask Mum. Not sure she'll be comfortable coming here not knowing you and... well, with everything else."

"Oh, we never spend Christmas here: we like a white Christmas." Helena laughed, "We have a cabin in Canada, which we go to every year. I particularly love lots of snow and log fires at the Yuletide. We were just planning the trip, seeing as everyone is here. Tara, Moira and Michael have already agreed to join us this year." She smiled, her face filling with true joy at the thought of everyone spending it together.

"Oh... Canada... right." I was excited. I would love to go, but would Mum? Would she want to be snowed in with a group of Chameleons, especially when one of them was a Feeder? I looked again at Michael, just as he looked at me.

"Don't worry, I don't drain guests. The host tends not to invite me back again," he said and laughed, several others joined in. His smile lit up his face and made his blue eyes sparkle, and once again I was amazed at how handsome this tall, blond Chameleon really was.

This time my blush at being so obviously worried about him was so fast I couldn't stop it, which made everyone laugh even more when they spotted it. I got the blush under control and said, "I'm sorry, I didn't mean to be rude. It's just... well... it's my mum..."

"Don't worry, I shall behave, and your Mum will be quite safe, I promise," Michael said.

"Thanks," I said to him and turned back to Helena. "Thank you for the invite. I will ask her about it later."

"Good, do let me know, won't you?" she said.

I nodded and smiled at her.

Peter walked back to the table, "Joe is on his way. He's more than happy to help, and Mum and

Dad give their permission."

"Good, thank you, Peter," Daniel said.

"I suppose growing up with Joshua and Wil you know all about the Chameleon world?" I said to Peter.

"Yeah, I was full of questions at first, but now it's normal to me. I know exactly what is to come with the interment, but now with the new twist of the three weeks residency, well... that has me wondering." Peter leaned against the kitchen wall.

I heard a door close somewhere and footsteps walking down the hall, and within moments Joe stood in the doorway of the kitchen. Joe, or Joseph as his parents had originally called him, was similar-looking to his older brother Peter. With thick brown hair and smoky-grey eyes, however, Joe's hair was kept short. Although he was handsome, he wasn't as stunning as Peter.

"I hear you need to torture a poor innocent human." He grinned naughtily.

I gasped, which made Joshua laugh at me.

"Yeah, you know any humans? Horse boy?" Wil insulted him.

"None that would have anything to do with you, vampire." Joe said.

Wil, Joe, Peter and Joshua all laughed out loud, like this was a normal conversation they had with each other every day.

"Take no notice, they are like this all the time," Tara said to me, confirming it.

The laughter died down and Daniel suggested we move to the library where we could sit and begin testing my control.

Daniel led the way as Joshua and I followed, with Joe and Peter walking behind us. The others remained in the kitchen, talking. In the library, I sat as instructed at one end of the sofa whilst Joe sat at the other.

Again, I nervously chewed my lip. 'What if... what if' my brain began, but I clamped down on that kind of thinking. I simply would not allow myself to hurt Joe, that's all there was to it.

"All right, Kate, my dear, reach out and touch Joe's hand, but do the same thing with the wall that you did with your Mother," Daniel said, as he positioned himself kneeling in front of us, ready to take my hand off Joe's, if he showed pain.

I glanced at Joshua, who nodded encouragement, then I looked back towards Joe.

"I'm sorry in advance if I hurt you, Joe," I said.

"I'll forgive you," he said and smiled shyly.

"Concentrate, Kate," Daniel instructed.

I closed my eyes and took a deep breath. An instant calm filled me as I imagined a wall around my body, with my Chameleon rainbow coloured aura inside it. I reached out my hand and gently placed it on Joe's.

Joe looked at me.

I looked at him and then at Daniel.

"Can you feel anything, Joe?" Daniel looked

surprised.

"Absolutely nothing," Joe said. "Although, I have never felt being drained before... I do feel normal."

"Good, very good," Daniel said, "Now, Kate, I want you to let the wall down bit by bit until Joe can feel something, all right?"

"If you are sure?" I said to Joe.

He nodded, but looked a little nervous.

I concentrated and lowered the wall just the tiniest bit, there was no reaction from Joe, so I lowered it a little more and Joe twitched.

"Keep it there, Kate. What did you feel, Joe?" Daniel asked.

"At first it was like a static shock but now I feel like I'm about to fall asleep," he said, and his eyelids began to look heavy, like he was having trouble keeping them open.

I shuddered as I began to feel, taste and smell the human energy, like I had with my mum. Again, it was like eating rotting food: kind of sweet, sickly and incredibly revolting. I raised the wall back up almost on instinct and the revolting sensation went away immediately.

Joe relaxed, "Thanks."

"What happened?" Daniel asked.

"The feeling stopped," Joe said.

"I don't like the energy from humans: it tastes and smells of something left in the fridge. Ugh... I had to put the wall back up. No offence meant, Joe." I took my hand away from his.

"None taken," he said.

"That is extremely interesting, Kate; I believe you have mastered control in an astonishing short time. I have never known anything like it." Daniel smiled, the look of amazement lingering in his eyes as he peered up at me.

I relaxed and glanced at Joshua, who was leant against the fireplace looking handsome, with a huge, proud smile on his face. I had an urge to walk over to him and kiss him, hard, but sadly I had to ignore the urge... for now.

"Well, then I guess it is my turn now," Peter said.

I stood and let Peter sit in my place. He looked nervously at his brother.

"If you really hurt me, you are doing my chores for a week, got it?" Joe said.

"Sure thing, Joe." Peter laughed nervously.

"Kate, tell Peter what you just did," Daniel said.

I nodded. "Try to imagine a wall between you and Joe." I said.

Peter reached out his hand, just as I had, and touched his brother. Joe instantly cried out. Daniel removed Peter's hand from Joe's so fast, that his movement became a blur.

"I'm so sorry, bro," Peter said, his face looked terrified, "Are you okay?"

"Yeah, just a nasty shock up my arm."

"We can stop now if you wish," Daniel suggested.

"No, I'm okay, carry on," Joe said bravely.

Again Peter reached out and touched his brother's hand and again Joe cried out in pain. Daniel severed the connection.

"I can see a wall but it's doing nothing to stop me from getting to his energy." Peter sounded very disappointed.

"It does take practice, Peter," Joshua said.

"I think I have an idea: may I... I... try something?" I said to Peter.

"Sure," he said.

"What do you have in mind, Kate?" Daniel asked.

I moved back over to the sofa and knelt in front of it next to Daniel and said, "I will put up my wall and place my hand between yours and Joe's, that way you might be able to feel what the wall should be like and Joe won't get hurt... I hope." I smiled self-consciously at Joe, hoping he would agree.

"Go for it," Joe said.

"Can you hover just in case you need to sever the connection again?" I said to Daniel.

"Of course. This is an intriguing idea you have, Kate, I will be very interested to see the results."

I took a deep breath and put up my wall, placed my hand on Joe's and nodded to Peter to place his hand on mine, which he did carefully so as to not touch his brother. "Now try to see or feel my wall in your mind, see how it's working, how it's stopping Joe's energy from getting through."

Peter frowned hard with concentration for a few moments.

"I can see it!" Peter said, suddenly excited.

I looked at him, he had his eyes shut, but he had a smile on his handsome face.

"I can really see it; you made a brick wall." He laughed.

"That's it," I said, and I knew he really had seen it because I'd never told anyone it was a brick wall. I closed my eyes and concentrated on my wall and slowly, bit by bit, I could see another wall being built right next to it, almost identical, but it wasn't mine, it was Peter's. "That's good Peter... keep doing that, that's right."

"What's happening?" I heard Joshua say.

"I can see Peter's wall. He almost has it built." I still had my eyes shut and watched as his wall reached the height of mine. "Okay, now I'm going to remove my hand and let you touch Joe. Keep your wall up. Okay, Peter?"

"Okay." His voice sounded nervous again.

I opened my eyes and slowly pulled out my hand from between the brothers and let them touch. Joe didn't flinch this time and, as I watched his face, a huge smile spread across it.

"I can't feel anything," he said.

Peter's eyes flew open, "Really? Nothing?"

"Nothing," Joe said.

"Very interesting," Daniel said, "Now let go and take down the wall, Peter. Then I want you to build it back up and touch Joe again, this time without Kate's help."

Peter did as instructed and again Joe didn't flinch, he just smiled.

"Outstanding," Daniel said as he rose and began pacing, with a thoughtful look on his face.

"It was much easier this time, almost like flicking a light switch on. Thank you so much, Kate." Peter leapt up and hugged me hard. He smelled pleasantly of soil and leather.

"Wow. That was amazing. How did you know to show Peter how to build a wall instead of just telling him?" Joshua asked.

I shrugged. "I don't know, it just seemed like the most sensible thing to do," I said.

"Kate, you are a very talented teacher, well done," Daniel said, as he walked back over to me and laid his hand on my shoulder.

With everyone's eyes on me I knew I was beginning to blush and diverted it again. It was definitely becoming my first Chameleon habit.

"Well, that just saved Peter weeks of study. Do you feel confident with the wall now, Peter?" Daniel asked.

"Oh yes. Everything just clicked into place. I know I can switch it on and off whenever I like now. I can't believe how much easier it was after Kate helped, so much better." He grinned.

I realised that the control had really been bothering Peter. Who could blame him, when his entire family was human. I was very glad I could help and more than a little surprised that my idea had actually worked.

We thanked Joe and let him get back to his chores. He seemed reluctant to go, but was happy to have helped.

"So what's next?" I said, excited by our success.

"Well, I guess we don't need to cover the Chameleon histories and laws seeing as how you will be taught them at Castrum Lucis during the residency. Control is the biggest thing. Let's see what's left... we need to show you how to use your sight, hearing, speed, body control and the feeding process, of course," Daniel said.

"I think Kate needs to feed soon; she said earlier she is starting to feel odd," Joshua said.

"Oh? Kate, how do you feel now?" Daniel asked.

"I'm okay, I just feel a bit... tired I guess, kind of similar to when I was first drained by a Chameleon, but different somehow." I said and frowned. It was difficult to put into words.

"Sounds like it is your feeding time. It is a sensation you will get used to and be able to spot coming. How about you, Peter, how do you feel?" Daniel asked.

"Okay, I guess... a little tired too actually."

"Everyone needs to feed at different times when they first evolve. I fed straight away, and Helena didn't feed for four days," Daniel said, "I think we should try a couple of different things today. I believe that we have a pig ready for slaughter too, so that will be helpful."

I was unsure I wanted to kill a pig but I was willing to try to taste its energy to see if I liked it or not. I hoped I didn't, but only by trying it would I know exactly what kind of Chameleon I had truly become.

LESSONS

Soon, the four of us, Joshua, Daniel, Peter and I, were heading for the solarium in the east wing of the huge house and out onto the now familiar path through the gardens, towards the farm buildings and the rest of the large estate. Helena joined us as we walked down the track-way, past her herb and vegetable garden, which doubled as her business and her feeding ground, and into the main working area of the farm.

With my improved senses, I could hear the chickens clucking in their pens, the horses neighing in their field and workers talking to each other all over the property. Also the smells, oh the smells, I could smell everything, I could tell the difference between horse, pig and chicken droppings and I could smell the cheese in the cheese house as they matured. I could even smell coffee being brewed somewhere on the huge farm. The amount of new sensations I was experiencing in my new life was dizzying.

I looked around me and up at the sky.

The day was bright and sunny despite it being almost the end of November, but there was definitely a chill in the air signalling that winter was approaching, a feeling of nature withdrawing into itself. I smelled the air, filling my lungs with it,, and as we walked, I could taste and smell an electrical storm coming.

Daniel took the lead and took us past some of the outbuildings, to one that was further away from the others. It was the only one with a large, stone chimney protruding from its roof, toward its furthest end. We all walked in, and I noticed how clean it was. I could smell the strong cleaning fluids that had been used recently. I saw there were several pens, all of which were empty, except one, which had a single pig in it, snuffling in the fresh smelling straw.

Daniel asked us to wait for a moment while he went off to find George.

They both soon returned and were able, between them, to move the pig out of the holding pen and into the room at the end of the building. Once it was safely housed in another pen, George had a word with Daniel and left, leaving the five of us on one side of the room and the pig behind the fence on the other.

I looked nervously at Joshua and reached out for his hand. I felt it in mine and it made me feel somehow stronger and safer, as it always did.

Daniel moved in front of the pig and the dividing fence. "The first thing we need to do is to find out if either of you are going to be a Feeder, in which case you will like pig energy as well as human. Peter, when you felt Joe's energy, did it revolt you like it did Kate?" Daniel said.

"In a way, yes. I didn't like it very much, but I did not have such a strong reaction against it as Kate did." Peter looked embarrassed, "I would much rather not feed on humans though."

"Well, as you know, there are alternatives to that. You can feed on animals like I do or on plants and trees like Helena does, if you are a Hippie, or even a combination of them both, like Joshua and Wil do. What we shall do first is just let you both have a taste of the pig. You can take a small amount of energy from it, without causing it harm, and you can decide if you like it or not. How does that sound?" Daniel looked at Peter and I.

"Okay," said Peter, looking hopeful.

"Right," I said, not sure I wanted to do it at all, but I was pleased that I wasn't expected to kill the pig; I just had to taste its energy.

"Ladies first, Kate, if you would like to come over here and stroke the pig as you would a household pet, then let your wall down, just a little, mind, sufficient enough to be able to taste the energy rather than harm the pig in any way. Can you do that?" Daniel said.

I nodded, feeling nervous.

"Excellent," he said and stepped back a little.

I moved forward, letting go of Joshua's hand, and bent down by the fence in the straw and reached in and touched the pig's warm, hairy back. I concentrated on letting my wall down just a little, until I could feel the energy of the pig. It was amazingly similar to human energy and yet something, somewhere, was different. Again I got the taste and smell of rotting food, or rather, rotting vegetation this time, but it was not as strong as with human energy. I wrinkled my nose and pulled my hand away.

"Erm... nope... not my thing either. Not bad, and I am sure I could feed on it if I had to, but I would prefer not. I get a similar rotting food taste, although it was somewhat less than before when I touched Joe and my mum," I said and rubbed the hand I'd touched the pig with, as if it would take the nasty taste away.

"Welcome to my world, Kate," Helena said and clasped her hands together with joy.

"She is all yours, my love," Daniel smiled lovingly at Helena.

"I guess I'm with you on the whole plants and trees thing," I said, as I moved away from the fence and felt a strange sense of relief. It made me happy that I would not have to harm any living being nor animal just to live. It was odd how strongly I now felt about it, considering I ate meat and was nowhere near a vegetarian in my previous life as a human.

"I hope I do like trees and plants, as there is nothing else left," I said as an irrational fear spread through me: what if I could not feed at all? What then?

"I am sure you will do just fine, Kate." She said and smiled encouragingly at me as if knowing my worries and fears.

I gave her a not-completely-convinced kind of smile back and went to stand over by Joshua again, who put his arm around me and held me close. "Well done. You've really got that control thing sorted." He smiled down at me.

"Thanks," I said as I watched Peter take his turn and walk up to the fence, he crouched down and nervously reached out to stroke the pig just as I had.

"Oh!" Peter said, and his face lit up with a mixture of confusion and delight.

I looked at the pig, which seemed to like being stroked and it moved closer to Peter. It also seemed a little calmer, as if it was enjoying every minute of the attention.

"Everything all right, Peter?" Daniel asked as he took a step closer to check on him.

"Yes... it's weird though, I can feel the pig's energy coming into my body and spreading . It feels sort of nice and warm, kind of like stepping into a perfectly warm bath. Definitely not what I'd imagined or expected," Peter said, not taking his eyes off the pig.

"What can you taste?" I asked, amazed that he could stand it.

"It's almost like eating a rare steak, kind of juicy and nice. Sort of metallic too, but in a good way," he said, taking his hand off the pig at last and standing up. He looked down at his own hand in wonder. "I feel stronger and a lot more focused now," he said, shaking his head in disbelief. "How awesome is that?" he said to no one in particular.

"Congratulations, Peter. I do believe you are a Feeder, and will be able to feed on animals during your new life from now onward. We will, of course, try you on the plants and trees too, to see what you think of that energy," Daniel said.

"Welcome to the club, Pete. I prefer animals but the green stuff is not bad either," Joshua said, and grinned at his friend.

Peter seemed much more relaxed now and smiled broadly at everyone.

"It is best, at first, just to drain some of the energy of the pig instead of killing the animal, but, if you find that you can't stop feeding, perhaps if you have been without a feed for too long, then remember to do so gently, not causing the animal any pain, and to let go just as the heart falters. Also, and this is most important, do not feed on anything that is recently dead. I can't stress that enough. When you feed on something recently dead, the energy is changed somehow and can make you very disoriented. In some cases, you might get out of control. Obviously, we cannot feed on anything that is long dead, as there is no energy remaining in the body," Daniel said.

"I guess the movies were right about something then, vampires are not supposed to drink the blood of the dead as it will kill them." I laughed.

Joshua and Peter laughed, Helena and Daniel didn't.

"Ah... well, you may find that amusing, but this is something most serious which you really need to remember. I have seen someone who continued to drain the energy once the... subject... was dead and it drove him crazy, to the point of attacking other Chameleons. He tried to feed on them. It was very unpleasant and the Council had to... deal... with him," Daniel said, his face looking very serious indeed.

I felt somewhat guilty for making light of it and I got the distinct impression that 'deal with him' meant killing the Chameleon outright. I no longer found my comment at all funny either.

Daniel changed the conversation, "This pig is ready to be 'put down' and will be butchered for selling. George and I will deal with it, and I will feed, while you go outside with Helena. She will now show you how to feed on the plants and trees."

Daniel stayed behind as we walked out of the building and headed towards the woods at the far side of the horse field. We all walked in utter silence, subdued after our last conversation and my, as I now realised, insensitive remark. Being a Chameleon might be good in so many ways but it certainly didn't stop you from opening your mouth and putting your foot fully in it without thinking.

"Don't let Daniel get to you, my dear, it was to his close friend that it happened to, and he blames himself for not stopping him. He's right, however, feeding on the recently dead is a very dangerous thing to do and must be avoided at all costs," Helena said as she guided us through the almost leafless woods, "Luckily, we don't ever have that problem with plants and trees."

We followed Helena into a small clearing, which was surrounded by trees of many different species, including oaks, elms and spruce, which formed a natural grove. I didn't recognise the place from when Joshua and I had gone exploring, as we had gone in the opposite direction when he'd brought me out to the house on a date and showed me around just a few short weeks ago. However, even if I was in a different part of the woods from then, I again felt at home in these ancient and wild woods that surrounded their estate. I simply loved it here, no matter the season.

"We are lucky to have so many different species of tree in this grove and so it's an excellent place for you to taste their individual energies. Now, tasting the energy of a tree or plant is slightly different than a pig or any other animal for that matter, you have to do it slowly and steadily so the tree can replenish its energy as you go. Therefore, it never runs out or gets too low for the tree to survive the draining and we never destroy anything," Helena said, proud that she never harmed anything she fed on. "All right, Peter and Kate, choose a tree and place your hand upon it and then gently let the energy in. Remember to drain lightly and steadily. You can move around and taste different trees if you wish. They each have a distinctive flavour of their own."

I looked around the circle and spotted an old oak and walked towards it, raising my hand as I went. Oaks had always held a special place in my heart from being a young child and playing in one at my grandma's house. As I got nearer, I could see the energy of the oak just as I could on other growing things, and it made me smile. I touched its gnarly bark and, for the first time, I drew in some of a tree's energy.

"Oh!" I echoed Peter's exclamation from earlier. I couldn't believe it, a weird and yet utterly wonderful feeling came over me. It rushed through my skin, into my muscles, veins, blood vessels and bones. It soaked into me like nothing I had ever experienced in my human or Chameleon lives so far. The strange sensation was both amazing and so incredibly intoxicating that I was completely drawn into this peculiar connection, and all else around me fell away as if it had never existed. There was just me and the oak tree that embraced me, there was no other way of describing it.

"You ok?" Joshua said next to me.

I nodded but could find no words to speak, my mouth was not connected to my brain at that very moment and it felt so good, so freeing, so... perfect.

Joshua said nothing more and just stood waiting beside me.

The feeling of the tree's energy was nothing like I had expected. The warm gentle flow of the oak's energy softly waved into my body, filling it with a strange warmth and taste that could only be described as sunshine mixed with vegetable soup. The taste had a colour, if that was possible, or perhaps the colour had a taste, I was unsure which, but I knew the energy was green, fluid, warm and utterly satisfying. A huge smile spread across my face as the oak's energy flowed into me and it reached every corner of my being. It gave me such pleasure that I almost got goosebumps. My skin felt alive, my mind became even more clear and my heart swelled with happiness. To say the its energy filled me up would be an understatement.

Eventually, I concentrated on what the tree was doing, rather than how it was making me feel and I discovered that the tree was continuing the cycle. It created more energy as I slowly drained some of it. There was a distinct welcome from the tree, as if it was allowing me the gift of life rather than me taking it. How bizarre, and yet how utterly beautiful the strange sensation was. I stood with my hand on the tree and a smile on my face for several minutes; I felt Joshua's energy beside me and I opened my eyes to look at him.

He looked at me with a look of worry. "Are you okay, you look... strange," he said.

"Hmm..." It was all I could manage to say. I closed my eyes again and my hand remained on the tree. I was not willing to let this feeling go, at least not just yet.

I heard Helena's footsteps on the soft ground as she came closer.

"You should remember what that sensation of the first feed on something that connects with you feels like, Joshua. Especially after the calf incident," Helena said and laughed.

"I do, of course, I was just unsure Kate was feeling that with a tree of all things." Joshua's voice rose in amazement.

"It matters not what the source of the connection is, it is still very profound the first time. Give her a few moments," Helena said.

I could hear everyone go quiet and then I heard Helena softly walk away, presumably to see how Peter was doing. My mind turned back to the tree. There was a change in the feeling, a completeness and yet a breaking away as both I and the tree disconnected simultaneously. I opened my eyes and looked up at the last couple of leaves on the branches above me.

"Thank you," I whispered to the tree. It seemed the right thing to do knowing that it had given me life. I turned back to look at Joshua with what I knew was a look of astonishment and pure joy on my face. "Did you know it would be like that? Did you feel it too?" I said, breathless with excitement.

"Yes, amazing isn't it? When I first fed I was so moved by the connection that I wouldn't let go at all," he said, stepped closer, wrapped me in his warm arms and held me close.

"The calf, I presume?" I said, recalling his mother's words.

"I'll tell you all about it later." He laughed and kissed me gently on the lips.

"Get a room," Peter said cheekily as he suddenly appeared next to us.

Joshua took a moment's pause from kissing me, "We're in it, clear off," he said and went back to kissing me gently.

"I don't know what you see in those trees, Kate. That pig was much, much better...it's weird to say it, but it felt like I had more of a connection," Peter said nervously, as if he wasn't sure he was doing it right.

I broke away from the delicious kiss reluctantly and remembered that Joshua's Mother was standing somewhere behind me, and this thought made me shy of kissing him again.

"I had the same feeling with the tree, too," I said.

"It is the same for all of us when we find our true connection with the energy, it gives us a feeling of belonging to something greater," Helena explained, "And I know the word 'connection' is woefully and deeply understating the feeling."

I turned round to face her. "Will it always be like that? When we feed, I mean."

"For some, more than others. Nothing is ever quite like the first time though, the feeling is still there, even for me, after all these years, but as you continue to feed it will be less so than now," she said, and looked up at the darkening sky. "Well, seeing as the light is now beginning to draw in and I see a storm is brewing, that is all the lessons for today. Well done, you have both managed wonderfully with your control and feeding, I'm so very proud of you. Tomorrow, we shall take a look at speed and perhaps withdrawing from the living world," Helena said.

"May I ask you something?" I said.

"Of course," she said and turned towards me.

"Do you think I would be all right to go back to school yet?"

"I think you would be able to do so soon, you seem very in control of your feeding, which is a great help. Perhaps, after a few more lessons, including the speed lesson as it will cover restraint. We can't allow you to blur in public by accident, now can we?" she said and smiled, "Take it from me, it's not a wise thing to do at all. It can get you into a whole lot of trouble," and winked at me, then she began to walk ahead of us and back down the trail leading back towards her home.

As the thunder rumbled around the darkened sky, I followed behind her, wondering what tales Helena could tell about her early days as a Chameleon and I decided I would get her to tell me them all one day and, by the sound of it, she would have some very interesting tales to tell.

As the first few drops of rain found us negotiating the wildness of the woodland paths, I thought of the oak tree, my oak tree, and my first official Chameleon feed. The thought of that green, deliciously warm energy flowing into me and spreading around my body made me smile, and I noticed there was a lightness in my step and a feeling of strength in my body that hadn't been there before. It was as if I had just eaten a very satisfying meal and had the best night's sleep ever, all rolled into one feeling. I never realised that feeding, something we all have to do whether human or Chameleon, would be an absolute and utter pleasure. More importantly, I now knew what type of Chameleon I truly was, and how I was going to feed for the rest of my very long life.

I was a Hippie and very proud of it.

MOVEMENT

Dawn's pale light shone through the living room window and onto the threads of the carpet at my feet. I had sat reading during most of the early morning until I saw the light shine on the threads and it utterly caught my attention. Now, I watched the light with my new eyesight, seeing so many colours in the light and the carpet that it fascinated me beyond my comprehension. I was convinced I did not have enough names for the colours I saw. I looked deeper into the carpet at the weft and weave of it, at its fibres. The Deeper and deeper I looked into it, the more enthralled I became by its complexity of colours.

I heard the faint knocking on the front door, but I could not tear myself away just yet. I gazed a little longer, hypnotized by its sheer beauty.

The knocking came again, a little louder and a little more insistent this time.

With a struggle, my mind pulled itself away

from the depth of colours and shapes in the carpet. I shook my head, trying to remove the mental images of the fibres, and I looked across the room at the front door.

A third knock came from the other side of it.

Leaping off the sofa, I moved to answer the door. Opening it, I stared at the only person who could make butterflies flutter in my stomach by just standing there. Joshua wore black jeans and a dark green t-shirt, the shirt mostly hidden under his unfastened jacket and above that was his handsome face and almost jet black hair. One look was all it took for my breath to be whisked away. He was absolutely stunning. Even before I had my new vision, his beauty fascinated me to distraction, now it felt incredibly surreal.

"Good morning, Miss Henson. I wondered if you would like to accompany me for an early morning walk on this beautiful day?" Joshua said. He smiled, and his joking good humour showed in his lovely blue eyes.

"My, what a gentleman you are, Mr. Marston." I grinned and laughed. "I would be delighted to accompany you on this fine day."

We both laughed.

"Actually, we're meeting Tara, Peter and Michael in the woods, and I thought we could walk there together."

"Mornin' you two. Off out to practice again?" Mum asked nonchalantly from behind us, as if I were going to swimming practice or something as she walked down the stairs in her pink bathrobe, her wet bob swinging about her face.

"Good morning, Caroline. We're teaching Kate about speed, amongst other things today," Joshua said happily.

Excited, I kissed Mum on the cheek and smiled at her, as I rushed past to grab my jacket from the hooks on the wall between the stairs and the front door. "Hopefully, I can learn how not to blur every time I move." I said, having just accidentally blurred in front of both of them.

"Yes, I think that would be a good idea, especially if you want to return to school sometime soon. And why the jacket? From what you told me, you can control your body temperature too, so why do you need a coat on?" Mum said, looking surprised.

"We do try to avoid acting in an unusual way. It would no doubt seem odd to humans if we were out without a coat in November," Joshua said.

"Ah, yes, good point. Well, good luck in your lessons today and have a great day, you two," she said as she made her way past us into the kitchen for her usual morning cup of tea, leaving us to close the door behind us as we left.

Within minutes, Joshua and I were walking down the narrow country lane that led from my home, down to and alongside the Greenman Pub, and then onward towards the centre of the village.

"I've not been in there yet, what's it like?" I asked, as we passed the pub.

"The Greenman? It's okay, it's a typical village pub. A few regulars and rather quiet. Perhaps we should go for a drink some time, if you want to check it out," he said.

"We could do. I still find it odd that we don't need to eat or drink very often. How strange it feels to not do it regularly like before."

"Remember, we still have to drink water more often than food and we still need to do both occasionally when we are in public. Some parts of us are still human in their functions, so we still need to eat, especially. Perhaps it's just so we, and our bodies, remember how to do it during our long lives. Like a backup plan or something. Also, our bodies are a lot more efficient now, so maybe that's why it needs to be less often. I'm not really sure of the reason, though. Anyway, we would arouse suspicion if we never ate with our friends or had people over for dinner or birthdays. We have to stay concealed, and by not doing these everyday things, it would make us seem very weird, and we'd stand out way too much."

"True. It's just so strange to not eat when Mum does or feel the need for food or even sleep anymore," I said.

"You may feel the need for it from time to time, when you are running low on energy in particular. It can be a quick fix if you are in desperate need, but it doesn't last long with the workings of your new body. Think of it this way: we have to eat so rarely that we can always have our favourites and we never get bored of them," he said.

"Bonus." I grinned and slipped my arm around his waist. He pulled me towards him and held me close as we walked in the pale early morning light, listening to the birds performing their dawn chorus.

We walked through the centre of the village, past the shops and the village green and stopped briefly to watch the ducks on the pond. Of course, very few people were up at this time of day, and so we were in no danger of being spotted by anyone from school. I enjoyed the peace and quiet; it seemed like there was only Joshua and I in the entire world at that moment and I loved the calm feeling as we walked along the quiet paths toward his home.

However, I knew that feeling of being carefree wouldn't last long, and it didn't. I began to feel paranoid that someone would see us and constantly looked around me, checking for people watching us, worried we'd be found out and that everyone would know I was not unwell and I'd been lying to them all.

Once on the grounds of Marston Court, a great relief flooded through me. I was glad that we were beyond the eyes of the general public and our school friends. The walk had made me realise I hated sneaking about and I hated how it made me nervous about the lies we were telling, about why I wasn't in school, but now, at last, I could truly relax. I realised I was afraid of slipping up in public and revealing to the world about the secret society of Chameleons, to which I now belonged. A world that was hidden in plain sight right under the noses of the humans. Of course, I was scared of being the one who accidentally revealed the truth to humanity, and because of this I would lose my life for it. Capital punishment was the penalty for breaking their first law, that of concealment. I tried to keep my mind on the coming lessons of the day and not focus on my fears. At last, we were walking back down the lane leading from the house to the farm buildings and on to the woods beyond.

"Ally rang me last night, wanting to know when I was returning to school and if I was feeling better yet," I said, remembering the concerned voice of my best friend, who had sounded like she was missing me.

"Oh? What did you tell her?" Joshua said.

"I said I should be back soon, when I had fully recovered and had begun to feel more like myself." I grimaced, not liking to lie to anyone, especially not my best friend, and, of course, she had no clue how I had truly changed. Especially since the last time I'd seen her was at school, before my life changed so dramatically. "That's not exactly a lie," Joshua said. "You do need to learn to be more like your old self by mimicking human speed, it's just not the way she'll think you meant it."

"It's not exactly the truth either," I said and sighed. "I wish I could tell her everything."

"I know. Let's hope you can go back to school soon and avoid telling her any more lies, I know you hate doing it to her." Joshua said, understanding my dilemma. He stopped walking, pulled me towards him and kissed me gently on the lips.

Ally was far from my mind as I kissed him back. My breath came quickly as he moved his hands round to my back and held me against him tightly, the kiss becoming more passionate between us. When it ended, it left us both breathless. He smiled down at me with that half smile I love.

"Hmm... that was nice. More please," I said greedily.

"Would love to, but the others are waiting for us. Rain-check?" he offered.

"Anytime." I gave him a small kiss on the lips and we continued walking towards the end of the lane.

We walked along without a word for a while, content in each other's company. It was a nice comfortable silence, as we walked past the field where horses grazed to the edge of the woodland.

"Oh, yeah... Ally said she had something to tell me, by the way, something exciting, but she refused to tell me what over the phone. She said I had to wait until we were face to face. I wonder what it could be?"

"Perhaps she has a boyfriend," Joshua said.

"Nah... well, I don't think so. She never seemed interested in anyone at school that I know of, that's for sure. She's far more into her studies than boys," I said, confident in my knowledge of her.

"I guess you will have to wait and see, then," he said.

"I hate waiting to know about something; it drives me nuts," I said, as we finally came to the edge of the woods where everyone else was standing waiting for us.

"Good morning." Tara smiled and rushed over to hug me, "How are things going at home?" Tara's long red hair was plated and hung down the front of her cream-coloured jumper like a narrow splash of blood.

"Pretty good actually, thanks. Mum seems calm and is being very understanding. I'm so pleased she's not freaking out or running away from me," I said, joking... kind of.

Michael stepped closer and hugged me, "Great to see you again, Kate," he said. His tall, handsome, Nordic looks made me smile. What a striking couple Tara and Michael must have been all those years ago when they were married.

"Nice to see you too, Michael." I smiled up at him and glanced over to where Joshua had walked and was talking with Peter, and watched as both of them burst into laughter. Again, I was reminded just how handsome they both were but in different and subtle ways, and I looked around me. Indeed, all the Chameleons I knew were the same. It was like staring at a group of Hollywood stars every time we met up. In fact, most of the Chameleons I'd met over the last few weeks seemed so perfect, it was almost creepy. I remembered Joshua explaining to me that it was nature's way, survival of the fittest and all that. The good genes guaranteed a mate, and a mate guaranteed procreation. Surprisingly, though, Hollywood had got something right with all those good looking vampires that they put into the movies. I knew how good looking they all were, as I was an avid fan of those movies, and it amused me greatly that I could now be perceived as one myself.

"Right, we have offered to teach you two..." Tara pointedly looked at Peter and I, "...to move fast when needed but also to slow down when near Lights. Any questions before we begin?"

Peter shook his head.

"Nope," I said, knowing that she meant humans when she said Lights, because many older Chameleons used this nickname for humans which I'd heard before. It seemed that Peter understood it too, but then he had been a Trusted Human around Chameleons for all his life.

"Okay then. Firstly, let's see how fast you can move. To tell you how to move fast is tricky because your Chameleon body instinctively does it now. What you have to do is access the 'flight' mode. You know, you've heard of fight or flight, Right?" Tara asked.

Peter and I nodded.

"You kind of have to instinctively let that take over, for some it can be harder to find than for others, but everyone gets there in the end," she said.

"Oh, I don't think that's a problem." Peter said, looking smug.

"I can do speed but have trouble doing slow." I smiled shyly.

"Several Chameleons have had the same problem in the beginning. I know I did, it just takes practice, but we shall come to that later," Michael said, and looked at Tara.

"Okay... back to speed. The best thing to do is to think of yourself at the spot you want to be and just let your body do what it does, if that makes any sense. Your newly evolved minds will see your movements slowed down, which allows you to go around obstacles. However, you actually move so fast that you will simply become a blur to any who are watching. We shall test this out by having a race." Tara grinned wickedly, "The first one to reach the tree line above the waterfall wins..."

Before Tara could finish what she was saying, I saw the tree line from my first visit there, almost a month ago with Joshua, and I was moving without even thinking about it again. Trees floated gently past me as I negotiated my way easily around them to the tree line. Peter and I arrived at the same time, but Tara, Michael and Joshua were all already there.

"Hey! How did you do that? How did you get here before us?" I said, as I enjoyed the endorphin rush of moving so fast. I looked around me and appreciated the view. We were standing at the edge of the tree line and below us, in a small valley, was a beautiful waterfall. In the stony pond surrounding it stood a great willow tree. I remembered this place fondly from my last visit here on a date with Joshua. Michael cleared his throat and brought my attention back to the here and now.

Michael smiled knowingly. "It's simple really, we've had much more practice at this than you and we're able to let our old way of thinking about movement go, and not let it restrict us anymore. You will move even faster the more you do it because you will believe you can, and so you will. Do you understand?"

"Yeah, kind of," Peter said.

"Oh, I get it. So the old way of thinking, the human way, is still stopping us, but as we do it more, the old way will vanish and give way to the new..."

"You got it," Joshua said, and looked at Peter to see if he understood the idea.

Peter nodded. "Well, that sort of makes sense to me, and now that I can control my body more, the way I thought of myself as a human isn't correct anymore. It is all kind of awesome and interesting, isn't it?" he said.

"Yes, it is. You will need to practice that quite a lot to really get some speed going. Now for something a bit harder, time to try not blurring when you run," Tara said.

"This time we want you to concentrate on slowing down the pace and controlling it more, so that you move just like a human would if they ran," Michael said.

"How do we do that?" Peter said looking a bit confused.

"Yeah, not sure about this one," I said.

"In a similar way to moving fast. When moving fast, you visualise the end point and focus on getting there quickly, well, now we want you to do that but focus on getting there at the speed you normally would if you were a human, which is roughly about ten to fifteen miles per hour for someone your age and fitness levels," Michael said.

"So we shall have another race, this time back to the house and we'll run alongside you, to help you see the pace you should be going at. Okay?"

Peter and I both nodded.

I felt a little nervous about this challenge, I wasn't sure I could do human speed again.

"Don't worry, you will get it," Joshua said as if he

had heard the fears rolling around in my brain.

"And go!" Tara said, and set off running through the woods at a normal human pace.

Joshua and Michael accompanied her as Peter and I looked at each other, shrugged, and also began to run. It was a very strange sensation. When I was human and I needed to run anywhere, whether it was on the track at school or just down the lane to the shop, I would concentrate on running my fastest but now I had to hold myself back to control the speed. I had to stay level with them all and not be tempted to burst forth and use my new skills. It felt very restrictive and counter-intuitive. In fact, it was almost unpleasant, and took a great deal of effort, more than I would ever have imagined. I was glad when we finally reached the house and stopped. I knew it was necessary to learn it, but it just felt wrong now, to go so slowly. Of course, none of us were out of breath in the slightest.

Michael smiled at us as we arrived back at the house. "Good, you both did well and, with a little practice, that speed will come as naturally to you as the faster one does. You will, in public, have to pretend to be out of breath too, just to sell it completely."

"Well, that was weird," I said.

"Hell, yes, it was. I just wanted to run faster and faster, it was so hard trying to stop myself," Peter said.

"You get used to it, I promise," Joshua said.

"We will leave you three to practice, and when you have done both fast and slow at least twenty times each, your lessons will be over for the day and you can join us back inside the house. Oh, and, Kate, I think Helena wanted to talk to you about Christmas again, so make sure you see her when you are done, please," Tara said.

With that, Tara turned and began walking towards the solarium entrance of the house with Michael at her side. They were both talking avidly about something that appeared important.

I watched them go and tried to hear what it was they were talking about, but Michael must have used his Chameleon ability and put his protection area up around them, so I could not catch a single word of their conversation, even with my new and enhanced Chameleon hearing.

Now, of course, not hearing their words made me begin to worry. What if they were talking about me? What if they thought my control and other abilities were not good enough for the Council and they thought I would fail my testing?

I sighed and stopped watching them.

It served me right for being nosey because all I got for it was more doubts about myself. 'I should learn to mind my own business.' I thought to myself and went back to practising the speed and slow movement training with Peter and Joshua.

WATCHER

The man stood before his now ex-employer, those who were his superiors. That is, until he had accepted this secret and important mission. However, for him to sell his story and be accepted by his target, it meant he had to be disgraced and run out of the beloved society he had served for his entire life, and, as a Chameleon, that was a very long service record.

"From now onward you will communicate through me. You will no longer have any contact with anyone above me, do you understand?" The Asian man said.

"I understand." The man nodded.

The two Chameleons were sitting in the middle of a quiet playground in a small town just off the M1 motorway in England. Since neither of them lived or worked nearby, it was the closest place they could find to which they had no connection.

"We want you to report to us everything you see

and hear but you must not give yourself away. No matter what, your target must not know the truth, and if they suspect you of spying, they will torture you until you talk. It is imperative that you do not reveal anything, even at the expense of your own life, is that understood? This is much bigger than any single one of us."

"I understand and I am pleased to be given such an important task," the man said.

"Go now. I do not expect to hear from you again for some time, but when you do risk contact, make it count, for you may not get another chance."

"Understood. Goodbye, old friend," the man said, and stood up.

"Goodbye," the Asian man said, and remained seated as the other walked away. He knew he would probably never see his friend again, but also that his mission was more important than their friendship. He watched the local dog walkers pet their animals and clean up their messes. He pulled out a phone and dialled a long distance number.

"Yes?" the cultured, rich voice said.

"It's Kenji, Sir. I have done as you wished and our man there knows his target, and what is expected from him."

"Ah... good, you are serving us well in your new position as Head of Security, I am pleased to be able to count on you Kenji, the Council of Nine is most grateful of your service."

"Thank you, Master Ramy, you honour me

greatly."

"Now, it is time to come home and prepare for this year's testing. Your duties as the Guardian of the Newly Evolved are about to begin and you need to come and celebrate with us on your successful location and the monitoring of our target."

"I'll be back by the morning, Sir," Kenji said, and ended the call.

Placing the phone back in his pocket and brushing his long, black hair from his eyes, Kenji was pleased to finally be in a position where he could watch over his enemies and hopefully, this time, defeat them in battle. He left the park and headed directly for the airport and home, with a hopeful smile on his face. He now had a chance to finally put this right and restore the old ways.

***

"Do you think Kenji's man will do all that has been asked of him?" Empusa said as she lounged on the bed next to Lamia and Ramy.

The three olive-skinned, dark-haired Chameleons looked related despite not being so. They shared an uncommon bond in the world of the Chameleons, a bond that had brought all three to power as Councillors and one of them as the Leader of the Council of Nine.

"I think he will serve us well and then our enemy will undoubtedly kill him, and so neatly remove   a loose end for us." Ramy said as he reclined against the cool silk pillows.

"How many of the newly evolved do you think will fail this time?" Lamia said, as she stroked Ramy's braided hair.

"Possibly two, although it always surprises me that there are more that fail than I ever predict," Ramy said. "Perhaps the young ones are becoming too weak to join us."

"Is the traitor still sniffing around for the truth, or is he worrying like a child about other things? Such as hiding for fear of our retribution?" Empusa said as she ran her fingers over the Egyptian cotton sheet beneath her and which the three of them were laid upon.

"I do believe he is in hiding, although Kenji found him easily enough. However, having him roaming free is more dangerous to us now that he has a following. It is time he saw our true power and that we crush him like the insignificant ant he is," Ramy said.

"Oh, how wonderful. Can we feed him to the animals like the rest of the weak ones? I would love for him to get a firsthand experience of that process," Empusa said with an evil smile, as she imagined the horrors that would await her enemy.

Ramy leaned over and kissed her passionately for several minutes. As he finally pulled away he said, "I do adore you when you are feeling cruel; you come up with some excellent ideas, little one."

"I live to please," Empusa said and smiled, while running her hand down his naked thigh.

"Perhaps we can all watch it live when we feed him to them, wouldn't that be a great entertainment?" Lamia said as she caressed Empusa's back.

"Oh, you are both so deliciously evil, if only everyone knew you like I do... but then, no, I do not like to share," he said and buried his head in Empusa's ample chest.

"What would it matter if all knew? There are none on the Council strong enough to deny you anything," Lamia said.

Ramy laid back again. "Very true. Over the years, they have all become weaker, not stronger, as their lofty positions should dictate. If they had remained strong, our enemies would not have attacked us this summer. There is one, however, who could ruin all our plans," Ramy said as he brushed aside Lamia's long silk gown to expose her slim, naked body and began kissing it from her shoulder downwards.

Empusa moved in closer. "I know of whom you speak and he has not been seen for centuries. No one even knows if he is still alive, never mind watching over us all, still. He is just a story to scare children and the newly evolved now. Worry about him not, my lover," Empusa said and reached out for him.

"Perhaps," Ramy said. "But never let your guard

down. You would be very surprised at his reach, despite being so far away and seemingly uninterested about us for so long. We must always keep our plans to ourselves," Ramy said and turned away from them both, no longer enamoured by the pleasures of the body.

OPPORTUNITY

Ally slumped on her sofa and closed her eyes. Generally, she loved school and came home energized, but not today. Today had been hard work. Not only had she been tired all day from lack of sleep but she had discovered she had feelings for a boy who was in a few of her classes, and she'd made a total ass of herself in front of him.

Also, she was really missing Kate, who was still off school ill. She was surprised by how much she wanted to share things with Kate and tell her about everything. Having a best friend was a great feeling, but it was also a bit scary. It was definitely a feeling she wasn't used to. She'd never really had a close friend before. In fact, she usually avoided making friends, preferring to work hard on her education instead.

She sighed deeply and rubbed her face. Her eyes felt gritty and heavy-lidded as she leant back, laid her head on the back of the sofa and closed her eyes again.

"You okay, Ally?" the soft, silky voice said from across the room.

"Yeah, just tired." Ally replied.

"Want a cuppa? Dinner will be ready in about forty minutes."

"Yeah, thanks Gran. Anything you need me to do?" Ally said, as she opened her eyes and looked at her grandma.

The little old lady with curly grey hair smiled. "No love, you just relax, you have a busy day tomorrow," she said, as she went off to fill the kettle.

Ally watched her Gran potter about in the kitchen, it was where she loved to be. She loved cooking and creating unusual dishes, some of them too strange to work but others, well, Ally thought they were just wonderful. Sadly, however, Ally was a terrible cook, so she helped out around the house in other ways. Ally had lived with her grandma since she was three years old. Since her parents were killed in a car accident. Thankfully, Ally and her Gran got on together very well and Gran was convinced that Ally was so good at science that she would indeed be successful at her dream and conquer cancer one day. Ally felt the same and between them they put everything they had into Ally's education and future career as a scientist.

Ally's mind returned to her two present problems, number one: Mat, the boy at school, and, number two: her recent lack of sleep. With regards to the first, she had to work on her concentration and her poker face for the next time she saw Mat. After all, sitting next to him at lunch, because all the other tables were full, and then spilling OJ all over herself and him was not a great start. For the sixth time she wished Kate had been there, she always had a good way of making a bad situation seem funny. Also, and for her second problem, she knew she needed to be more rested for tomorrow, as tomorrow she would start her new part-time job. A ripple of excitement ran through Ally as she thought about it. It will be warm milk before bed tonight and a relaxing bath to optimize her chances of a good night's sleep, she decided.

Gran appeared by her side holding out a cup of tea toward her, "Did you get a lot of homework?" she said.

"Not that much, thank goodness." Ally said, taking the cup. "Thanks."

'You're welcome." Gran smiled as she sat down on the old chair, which was covered in a brightly crocheted cover, just one more of Gran's multitude of hobbies.

"What's for dinner?" Ally said and yawned.

"Lamb with couscous, roasted squash and pineapple gravy."

"Well, that sounds interesting," Ally said. She was not convinced the flavours would work well together, but she knew better than to dismiss it entirely. Some of her Gran's best meals were just as weird.

"I think it will work, we will just have to wait and see," Gran said.

"Right." Ally stretched and stood up. "I'm going to take my tea upstairs and do my homework. Want it done before dinner so I can relax and have an early night and hopefully get some extra sleep."

"Very wise. I'll call you when it's ready," Gran said.

"Thanks." Ally grabbed her school bag and headed upstairs to her bedroom.

Gran watched lovingly as the young woman slowly made her way up the staircase. She then leaned over to pick up a paperback and began reading while dinner finished cooking and filling the house with a wonderful, if a little unusual, aroma.

***

Later, after dinner (which was a complete success after all), Ally sat on her bed and pushed her glasses up her nose for the umpteenth time. She was holding a folded letter in her hands, which she had now read so many times that the paper seemed softer somehow and the edges crumpled from much use. This letter had brought home the truth to Ally, a certain truth that no matter how she looked at it, or how she read it, was a great opportunity for her, and she still couldn't quite believe her luck.

Yet again, she wished she could speak to Kate about it, but she was waiting until Kate was well enough to return to school. Plus, she wanted to know how the holiday with Joshua and his family in Croatia had went; there was just so much to talk about. Their brief chat on the phone the other night wasn't of much help. Kate's mum must have been in the room, Ally thought, as Kate seemed like she wasn't telling her everything that had happened between her and Joshua. Ally couldn't wait for the gossip. She had never had a boyfriend, so she was living vicariously through her friend. She just plain missed her. Kate was the closest thing she had to a best friend or indeed, a friend. Ally now accepted that she had spent her life studying and had never really wanted to open up to anyone before Kate.

She unfolded the letter again, and there under the name Allison McIntyre, was an offer for the position of unpaid intern, starting tomorrow at 4pm, at the research facility NosGene. Otherwise known as Nostrum Genetics, one of the top family genetics research foundations in the country. Ally's pulse raced for the hundredth time as she read the words. She had gone to an interview last week and, thankfully, the foundation's main laboratory was only a twenty minute drive away from Ally's home. At first, she had no clue how they had even heard of her, never mind how they knew she was interested in an internship with them. Finally, she found out at the brief interview that her biology teacher, Mr. Rightman, had put her name forward and given her an excellent reference, completely without her knowledge.

"He was right, it is perfect for me," she said to herself and thought how kind it was of him. She knew she liked him for a reason, and decided she would thank him, yet again, tomorrow at school.

Filled with excitement, Ally tried but could no longer keep it all in, and grabbed her phone to text Kate, asking if she was well enough for a visit yet. Within moments she got a return text from Kate saying that, actually, she was feeling a lot better now, and Ally could come over tonight, if she wanted to.

"Yes!" Ally said, and clenched her fist in the air. Even she was surprised by how happy she was, knowing she could see Kate again soon and share all the news. She decided that perhaps it wouldn't be such an early night after all. Some things were just too important, and it amazed her just how happy she felt about that decision.

Within forty-five minutes, Ally was locking up her bike outside Kate's front door and knocking. Although the evening was getting cold, she was warm from cycling and began to undo her scarf and take off her gloves as she waited. She glanced upwards at the sky, which was beautifully clear in the crisp late November air. The evening was bright, from the light shining down on everything from the almost full moon. Mesmerized by the stars, she didn't hear the door open behind her.

PRECISION

Anna Croft's name flashed up on the security guard's screen as she passed her ID card over the sensor. The middle-aged guard looked up at her, nodded and smiled, indicating she could proceed. The security was intense throughout the ultra-modern building, even if you wanted to move from floor to floor.

With a smile of thanks, Anna walked past the guards' desk and continued along the corridor to the lifts at the end. Arriving on the ground floor, she walked through the foyer to the scanning area near the external doors where she queued up with the other members of staff who were also leaving at the end of their shift. She waited to be cleared so she could leave the restrictive building and finally go home. Usually, the wait didn't bother her, but today it was different, and she really needed to get out quickly. She tapped her fingers on her folded arms until, at last, she was asked to place her bag in the black plastic tray provided and walk through the full body scanner.

A small sigh of relief escaped her lips when no alarms went off, which meant she was not taking out anything that she wasn't cleared for, and she was now able to proceed though the checkpoint without being detained further. Anna picked up her bag on the other side of the scanning machine and, throwing it over her shoulder, headed for the exit, while resisting the urge to run the last few metres to freedom.

The sunlight blasted her eyes and she blinked until her vision returned to normal. She always hated leaving the building because all the windows had a bullet resistant and reflective film on them, making the contrast in the brightness a shock to the system. She felt like a mole coming out into the sunlight every day. Thankful that her overnight shift was at last finished, she rushed to her car in the car park, which was just out front of the building, past the small, neat gardens. Reaching her vehicle, she climbed in and drove off without a backward glance, knowing she could now enjoy the beautiful day. Some days she felt like a released convict who was escaping back into the world.

Anna drove along the back roads home. She could have used the highway to get there quicker but she always found it to be more stressful. She drove past one of her favourite houses on the way. She loved it and looked forward to seeing it every day. It was a two storey house with wooden siding and a lovely wrap-around porch. The house was surrounded by a fair bit of land with many trees, and stood by the side of a small river. Anna sighed as she went past. One day soon it would come up for sale and she would buy it. She just had to wait long enough and remain patient. She finally headed back towards the city and got on the highway for the last few minutes of her journey and, as usual, she disliked heading back into the concrete jungle. She would much prefer to live in the countryside. However, her detour home from work always helped her to de-stress.

By the time she had reached her apartment building, Anna had listened to soothing piano music for an entire hour and was feeling much more relaxed. She had found that since her recent promotion, her work had become more difficult to bear. It was a lot more stressful and there was an increase in pressure to get results. Her new section boss, Dr. Ryan Schneider, was the only compensation she could think of at present, apart from the healthy salary increase.

Anna unlocked and entered her new apartment. She had moved into it the first month of her promotion and she loved the place. Now, in the bright November sunshine she admired it all over again: it was modern in style and two of the four exterior walls were completely made of glass, giving a magnificent view of the outskirts of Toronto.

Anna hung her coat by the door and was enthusiastically greeted by Gatsby, her brown and white cocker spaniel. His little nails made a light tapping noise on her immaculate hardwood floors.

"Hello handsome, have you been a good boy?" she said and stroked his head. "Do you want to go outside?"

Her dog sniffed her and trotted off to stand by his food bowl which had very little left in it.

"Ah... now I know why you love me," she said and kicked off her shoes, headed into the open-plan kitchen full of stainless steel appliances to fill his bowl and refresh his water.

***

The doorbell rang, just as Anna was putting the last touches to the table for her lunch date. She checked herself in the mirror by the door, straightened her necklace and peeked through the view hole in the apartment door. She smiled to herself knowingly and opened the door.

A tall, handsome, dark haired man stood on the doorstep almost filling the doorway, with an expensive-looking bottle of wine.

"Hello, beautiful," he said in his deeply sexy, Canadian accent.

It was one of the many things she loved about Canada, since moving there from the UK only a year ago. It was their accents which were rather sexy, particularly their lilting 'r's' and elongated vowels, in her opinion anyway and the Canadians seemed to think the same of her English one. It made her smile every time someone mentioned it, and they mentioned it a lot. She had even caught strangers listening in on her conversations when she was out in public as soon as they heard her accent. She didn't mind though; it made her feel somewhat important and interesting.

"Ryan, you are just in time," she said with a smile, and stood aside allowing him enough room to enter.

"I wasn't sure if I'd given you enough time to get home and sort lunch, I just couldn't wait to see you outside of the office."

"You did wait for a while before leaving, after I left, didn't you?" she said, closing the door behind him.

"Oh, yes. I made sure that I talked to a few people too, so people wouldn't suspect us. I know you want to keep our relationship quiet," he said, as he placed the wine on the kitchen counter, turned back around and stepped closer and placed his arms around her. "I doubt if anyone would suspect us though; I may be your boss, but we do work on different floors."

Anna let him hold her closely. She loved the smell of him. "I know, I just like to be careful, but thank you. There's no need for everyone to know I'm dating the boss. No, that would bring us too much trouble," she said as she kissed him passionately, making them both increasingly ardent with lust.

Anna broke away from his embrace. "Shall we eat?" she said, as she moved to the oven, put on the oven gloves and took out the cooked salmon fillets and small baked potatoes. Taking them across the apartment she placed them on her dining table right by a glass wall and the wonderful view. She put vinaigrette on the side salad and began to dish some out for the both of them. "Can you open the wine, please?" she said over her shoulder.

"Sure," Ryan said as he brought it to the table and began to remove the cork.

All through the meal, it was obvious by his hints that Ryan wanted to do other things rather than eat but Anna fended off his suggestive words and watched him, mentally smiling to herself knowingly. She had him hooked now, and she was going to take this slowly and carefully. She was definitely the one calling the shots in the relationship.

After lunch, they loaded the dishwasher together and sat on the sofa looking out on the view, sipping the last of the wine.

"I can't believe how lucky you were to get this place, so few come on the market. Every time I see that view I get jealous," Ryan said as he stood and wandered over to the glass wall.

"Yes, I was lucky in many ways that month."

"Your promotion wasn't luck, it was hard work, if that's what you are talking about." Ryan turned and looked earnestly at her.

"Actually, no. I was talking about us." She stood, placed her almost empty glass on the coffee table in front of her and approached him.

"Oh, you were, were you?" he said.

"Yes, let me show just how lucky I got," she said and held out her hand, and, taking his in hers she led him to her bedroom and pushed him down on the bed.

"Like that is it?" he said, an excited look of surprise on his face.

"Oh yes." she said, as she very slowly unbuttoned her blouse and removed her skirt until she stood before him in her lacy underwear.

Ryan gulped with apprehension and excitement. It was the first time they had gone this far and he was more than ready for it.

"Bring it on," he said with a cheeky, cocky smile.

Anna was more than willing to do as she was asked. It was time for it, and they had waited long enough.

As the two bodies combined and became one in passion, they became enthralled in each other until they were almost spent. Then, at the last moment, when all becomes one in delicious pleasure, one of them noticed a strange red mist floating before their eyes and it seemed to hover around both of their bodies. Finally, as one of them began to fade away into the deep, dark depths of unconsciousness, the other took the red mist into themselves and became stronger and stronger.

Just before the mind's unconsciousness was overwhelmed, they saw a hand fly through the air with such speed and strength that when it was thrust through their skin and rib cage, the victim didn't know what was happening until the damage was done. They began to scream in sheer agony as another hand was quickly and firmly held against their mouth, muffling the agonised sounds. The hand inside the body then forced its way deeper inside, and it grabbed at the wildly pulsating heart within. Then it stayed completely still, cradling the heart, feeling the beat of it get weaker and weaker as the life energy was drained fully away until it could beat no more. The entire energy of the human was absorbed by the Chameleon.

ADRIFT

W hat are you looking at?" I said as I stood in the doorway and I stepped out to look up at the sky.

"Huh? Oh, just the beautiful stars, aren't they lovely? Anyway, how are you?" Ally said as she looked at me, concerned. "Honestly, you have never looked healthier, are you sure you were really ill?" she said jokingly.

"I'm good thanks, much better actually. Come in before you freeze," I said suddenly alarmed, wondering if she knew I was lying about the illness, and I quickly walked back inside. I pretended I was cold, but, in actuality, I had instinctively adjusted my body temperature the second I opened the door. The small changes were now becoming habitual and I barely had to think about them anymore, my body just did them for me.

Ally followed me inside and closed the door behind her and began taking her coat off. "I'm quite warm actually: the ride here warmed me up. It's just such a lovely night. So when are you coming back to school?" Ally said as she pulled off her multi-coloured, crocheted hat, stuffed it in her coat pocket and then ruffled her blond, curly hair and pushed her loose glasses back up her nose.

As ever, the straightforward, practical Ally amused me, and with a grin I said, "Soon. My doctor wants to see me again, to check my lungs are clear, and then I can. I'll let you know when I know." I hated lying to her, but the cover story that we had planned for my absence was that I had caught a particularly virulent strain of flu, which had developed into a nasty case of bronchitis. The story covered why I was away so long and, more importantly, why I had to keep away from everyone. It worked, but I would've loved to tell Ally I was in absolutely excellent health as I was now a Chameleon, and all that truly entailed. I knew, deep down, that that could never happen and so what choice did I have? I had to lie.

"Hello, Ally, how are you? How's your grandmother?" My mum asked as she made her way to the kitchen from the lounge, passing us in the hallway.

"Good, thanks, Mrs. H," Ally said.

"Glad to hear it. You girls want a hot chocolate? I'm making myself one, so say so if you do," mum said and looked directly at me. She seemed a little tense and looked worried, as if she shouldn't have asked.

"Oh, yes please," Ally said.

She hung her coat up on the hook by the door, and thankfully, didn't notice the look from my mum.

"I'd love one, please mum," I said, and smiled sweetly at her.

Mum's face relaxed as she nodded approvingly and she turned to put the kettle on. "I'll bring them up when they're ready," she said over her shoulder.

"Thanks, Mum," I said as Ally and I headed upstairs towards my bedroom.

As we sat in my room, Ally on the sofa bed and me on the bed, I looked around my old room and really noticed it for the first time in ages. Although, I now looked at it with my Chameleon eyes. I realised that it looked like any other teenager's room, with posters of singers and groups, promotional movie posters and images of handsome celebrities covering the walls, but now it felt as if it no longer related to me in any true or deep way. I glanced at the dresser. The mirror was covered in necklaces, and the dresser itself had a fake Oscar sitting on it, several entertainment magazines and makeup strewn everywhere. Everything in the room related to my dream of being a famous actress one day, and none of it seemed to have a connection to me now. It was all from my previous life as a human and not my present life now as a Chameleon. This thought made a strange sadness creep across my chest and I felt a kind of grief for the life I could no longer live. Forcing myself to pull out of my own melancholy, I remembered I was not alone, and I knew I had to keep up appearances no matter what, so I switched my attention back to my visitor.

"You're sure you are well enough for a visit?" Ally said, mistaking the look of sadness on my face as a wave of illness.

"Oh yeah, sorry. I am fine, I promise. So tell me everything, what's this exciting news you have?" I said as I shuffled backwards against the wall and stretched my legs out on the bed, crossing them at the ankles.

"Oh, no way... you are not getting off that easy. Tell me all about Croatia and your holiday with Joshua and his parents. What was it like? What are his parents like? What did you and Joshua get up to?" Ally said, raised her eyebrows and wiggled them suggestively.

I laughed, "Well, I guess you want to know everything then."

"Absolutely. Spill," Ally said as she folded her feet up under her and got comfortable and settled in, ready for the whole story no matter how long it took.

I told her as much of the truth as I could, leaving out all the parts about Joshua being buried alive, people from ancient times still being alive, me being taken prisoner and evolving right in the middle of a judgement that could have sentenced Joshua to death but resulted in an attempted, and failed, coup of the ruling Council. Yeah, I had no choice, I just told her the romantic stuff about me and Joshua, Wil and Tara and what the place, the villa and the island in Croatia was like. It was all the stuff a normal teenage girl would have said, the only problem now was the fact that I was no longer one and all these things seem so trivial and childish compared to the reality of my new way of life and what I had actually seen and experienced in the past few weeks.

Ally absorbed all the information easily. She nodded and squealed at some of the romantic stuff, her face lit up with excitement as she enjoyed my synopsis of the good bits. She seemed so excited and pleased to hear all the news.

"So that's everything, it's your turn now," I said, relieved that the pressure was off of me at last.

"Okay, okay. Well, a couple of days after you left, I got a phone call," she said and smiled proudly.

"Oh? Who from?"

"It was an Invitation to an interview for an internship, so I went and checked it out."

"Wow and? Where was it for?" I said and leant forward with enthusiasm and excitement for my friend.

"And then I got a letter. I brought it for you to have a read," Ally said and grabbed her bag; she began rummaging through it.

"Oh, come on, tell me more," I said, wanting to know all the details.

"You will see, I want to see your face when you read it. Ah... here it is." She grinned and extracted a slightly battered letter and passed it over.

"Thanks." I said as I took the letter and looked at it without opening it. "How many times have you read this?"

"Maybe a hundred. Read it!"

"All right, all right." I opened the letter and began to read. At first I frowned, not really knowing anything about NosGene, but, as I read on, my frown turned into a huge smile. "Wow! That's awesome."

"I know, right?" Ally grinned at me like an excited child at Christmas.

"Yeah. What a great opportunity for you. I can see why you are so excited. Wow, you start tomorrow?"

"I know, I can hardly wait." Ally looked like she was about to burst.

"Wow. That's really amazing, I didn't know you'd applied for it, you never mentioned anything about it before now," I said.

"That's because I didn't, Mr. Rightman put my name in for it."

"You're serious? Our biology teacher? Oh, that was nice of him."

"Yeah, I know. Going to thank him yet again

tomorrow, I think he might be getting sick of my thanking him though. Anyway, he said he heard of the position and the first student he thought of was me. So, as the deadline was close, he talked to them straight away. He said they were very impressed by my test scores so far, and that they would invite me for an interview on his recommendation."

"Nice, but how will it fit in with school?"

"Well, they said at the interview they will work around school but I won't know the details until we sort it all out tomorrow and I get my work schedule. I hope I do well because they only choose two, out of all their interns, to sponsor for University, and Gran could really do with some help on the university fees," she said, looking nervous and worried.

"I'm sure you will do just fine. Your exam results are really excellent, like Mr. Rightman said, and you're awesome, why wouldn't you do great?" I said, truly pleased and excited for my friend.

"Well, we'll soon see. I just hope I'll get some sleep tonight, because worrying about it all kept me awake a lot last night."

"I'm sure everything will be okay. So now, tell me what's been happening at school, I need to know everything I missed," I said, giving Ally another subject to think about so she wouldn't worry about tomorrow more than she was already. I was truly pleased for her. It was going to be such an excellent opportunity, and if she did do well, it could be the start of her whole career as well as being a wonderful experience for her.

Ally told me, while looking thoroughly embarrassed the whole time, all about her accident during her lunch with Mat, and although it surprised me that she liked him, I wasn't surprised by her clumsiness. She really needed to find some confidence when it came to dating or even the possible chances of it. As I continued to listen to all the school gossip about the latest fights, love match ups and tests I'd missed, my mind began to wander again. I truly no longer had any interest in such things, why would I now? Finally, I managed to stop my mind from wandering off again and tuned back into what Ally was saying about the school stuff. It was sad to realise that I found it all rather boring now. It felt really childish to me, but I had missed her and tried to enjoy her company.

By the time Ally and I had finished swapping stories of what had happened since we last saw each other, the evening had worn on and Ally had to leave, due to her having such a big day tomorrow. As I watched her cycle away, I truly wished I could talk to her about how I was feeling. I needed a close friend to talk to about everything and it made me sad that I couldn't. Although I had my Chameleon friends and my mum, it wasn't the same as a good friend, because I was beginning to feel lonely in my new world.

I sat in my room and thought about my life. I

guessed that this is what it must be like for actors, when a film or series comes to an end. When they had a certain life before, their character's, and now that it had completely vanished, they would never be that person again. How did they overcome the separation from one part of their lives? How did they build another life, another character for the next project? For me, it would be another life so completely different to the last that I was beginning to have real trouble relating to my old world now. I could feel a kind of dissatisfaction growing within me; I was now feeling that the girl, the wannabe actress that I once was, had started to fade away, forever.

The new me didn't know what she wanted, nor how she was going to survive during her now very long life. The only thing I did know for sure was that I wanted it to mean something, to do something of importance with it, to really contribute and make my world, this world... the world of Humans and Chameleons, a better place for all. I guessed it sounded like a lofty idea, but what was the point of immortality if you didn't try to make things better for everyone and not just squander it for your own selfish gains. That, to me, was a great crime. I had been given a gift, and I chose then and there to do good with it, no matter what.

REGROUP

The bloody hand withdrew from the chest cavity and dripped the rapidly cooling blood onto the bed sheet. However, preparation was the name of the game, and there was a thin plastic sheet spread under the bedding for just this reason.

Anna stretched and climbed off the still body of Ryan and she licked the blood off her fingers as she stared at him dispassionately. Despite enjoying the taste, she was deeply repulsed by her own actions. Sometimes it just had to be done; she wasn't strong enough to go against her own nature.

She sighed. "The things I have to do for this job. But, from what I've been told about you Ryan, it's better than you deserve, you cheating bastard," she said to the corpse, as her tongue slid up her index finger, catching the last of the fleshy matter still clinging to it. Swallowing the ghastly but tasty morsel, she walked calmly over to her bathroom and thoroughly showered, washing the remains of him off of her completely. She calmly dried herself with a big green fluffy towel, brushed her long hair and pulled it up into a ponytail. When satisfied with her looks, she put on her bathrobe and walked back to the bedroom. She walked around the bed and over to his clothing where he had let them fall on the floor. She searched through Ryan's pockets one by one, carefully collecting his belongings. She found his phone, his keys and wallet and, finally, in his shirt breast pocket, she found the very thing she was after all along: his work pass. She took his items with her as she left the bedroom and walked through her apartment to the hallway and kitchen. She placed the pass on the kitchen counter along with his phone and retrieved her own phone from her leather briefcase by the apartment door. She switched her phone on and dialled a number, then, waited briefly for a reply, and then said to the person who answered, "I have it and I'll be there in forty-five minutes."

Returning to her bedroom, Anna changed into jeans and a t-shirt and put on socks and trainers. She then grabbed a pre-packed backpack from the back of her closet. Placing the backpack by her apartment door, she returned to the kitchen to pick up her phone, and placed it in her front pocket. She then picked up Ryan's, which she placed in her back pocket. Then, she took a small plastic tub out of the kitchen cupboard and searched for its lid.

Having found the counterpart, she filled the tub almost to the brim with ice, leaving a small space in the centre, and collected a small Ziploc bag and a teaspoon from the cutlery drawer.

Anna then returned to the bedroom.

Gatsby trotted along beside her as if everything was normal, and perhaps it was in his world.

Approaching the cooling corpse, she put the items she was holding on the bedside table and wrapped the body in the bed sheet and the plastic cover, but left his head exposed. She then grabbed the spoon and straddled him. She sat looking down at her victim for a moment.

"I always thought you had lovely eyes, Ryan. I think I'll take one with me," she said with a malicious grin, as she held his eyelid open wide and plunged the spoon in, popping the eye out of its socket like a scoop of ice cream from a pot. The eye lay on his cheek until she grabbed the slippery globe and yanked it so hard that the connecting tissue fell away like broken silk.

Gatsby sniffed around the edge of the bed and near the corpse, but soon lost interest and trotted away to find his food bowl.

Anna placed the eye in the plastic bag and then into the container of ice and put the lid on it. She then finished wrapping the body in the sheet and the plastic, and easily carried it down to the basement to dispose of it in the building's old furnace.

The furnace was one of the reasons why she had chosen this building to have her new apartment in. For a start, there was easy and private access to the basement, without any security cameras. Most importantly, there was an old fashioned, if restored, furnace with a big enough access panel to feed a body into the flames. It was a perfect and an amazing find. Not many buildings had a furnace like this anymore, and it was the only reason that she owned the entire building, although, of course, her ownership was hidden behind many layers of shelf businesses and fake names. She had become adept over the years at creating 'shelf' businesses, which were real businesses with employees and actual products, but were constructed for her own financial freedom and laundering purposes, as opposed to 'shell' businesses that could easily be exposed as fakes.

Anna deposited Gatsby with a neighbour, Mrs. Cynthia Brewitt, a lovely old lady who loved Gatsby almost as much as Anna did and was always happy to look after him. She told her that she was going away on holiday for a couple of weeks. Anna then returned home and checked the apartment for any incriminating evidence, and after satisfying herself that she had thoroughly cleaned everything and removed all trace of Ryan, she safely locked up her new apartment behind her as she headed out to meet her contact in a gratified mood of a job well done.

***

Anna sat in her hybrid car just up the street from the small bar where she and her contact were supposed to meet. She sat and watched the people enter and leave for a good ten minutes before she decided to go in. She always liked to get the lay of the land, as it were, before committing herself. The bar was a seedy one, in the forgotten end of the city, where the customers were mostly drunks, hookers and junkies all trying to score something. It was not the sort of place she would usually go to, but needs must, and today her needs must meet with her contact, and this was where he'd said she must go, so here she was. Any other woman would have been worried for their own safety going into such a place as this, but Anna knew better. Let's face it, she was the dangerous one here, and all these fragile humans around her were potential victims, even if they didn't know it yet.

Anna thought through her plan once more, making sure every detail and every angle was considered in their entirety, and every possible outcome was covered with a story that had a background to hold it up. Not just any story: it had to be just right, down to the smallest detail. She had been preparing for this encounter for the last eight months and finally, she was about to put all the planning and plotting into action. She breathed in deeply and let the air slowly and steadily out of her lungs.

This will work, she thought to herself, and climbed out of her car, locked the door and walked determinedly towards the seedy bar.

The inside was dark, the subdued lighting enhanced by years of dust that had collected on the fake Art Deco light shades hanging from the ceiling. The air was filled with the smell of beer, sweaty bodies and greasy food. There was a TV hanging high up behind the bar, blaring out the latest ice hockey game, and a few dirty, scruffy-looking men sitting at the bar, on stools, cheering as someone on the TV scored a goal.

Anna looked around and walked over to the bar.

"Ello dahlin', what can I getcha?" the male bartender said in a cheery voice.

Anna looked at the barman and his bright rainbow aura. She was not surprised by the fact that he was a real-live cockney Chameleon serving in a Canadian bar, but by how good looking he was and still working in this dump.

I'm sure with his Chameleon abilities he could do something better than this, she thought to herself.

A cheer went up from the men at the bar as another goal was attempted, but it was followed by swear words as the team on TV failed to make it.

Anna waited for the noise to calm down.

"Ronny Teson?" she said to the bartender in a wary tone.

The barman heard her accent and looked her up and down, surprised. He picked up a cloth and began to wipe the counter and then nodded towards the back of the bar room.

Anna said thanks and began to walk slowly towards the empty pool table and the darker deeps of the building. She passed a few more of the bar's untrustworthy looking inhabitants, including a few Chameleons. Seeing them told her she was in the right place. None of them even gave her a second glance. Perhaps they were used to people like her coming in and scoring weed, stronger things, or even hookers. As she walked past the pool table, she noticed that the green cloth that lined it was stained with dark patches in several places. She didn't even want to imagine what the stains were and how they'd gotten there.

At the very back, only two empty tables away from the washrooms sat a man at a small, round table with a half-empty bottle of scotch on it. There were two glasses, one was already filled and was near his hand as if he had just put it down, the other was some distance away and it was empty.

"Ronny Teson?" she said, standing before his table, noticing his Chameleon colours as they floated just above his skin.

"Sit." he said from the shadows.

"If you're not him, stop jerking my chain and tell me so," she said.

"You have balls. Sit or die, it's your choice," he

said but didn't move.

Anna sat, she instinctively knew he meant it. "I have what I was asked to get."

"Then you shall live a little longer," he said.

"I want to meet him, I can help him," Anna said.

"Nobody meets him."

"I will," she said confidently with a smug smile on her face, as she leant back in the chair.

"What makes you think that?" he said, the surprise unmistakable in his voice.

"Because I have an extra item, which he'll need very shortly."

"And you think I can't take whatever it is from you? I can, oh so easily, and still you won't meet him."

"Bullshit. If you wanted to do that, I would be dead already. Now when can I meet him?"

The man laughed loudly.

It was a deeply sexy laugh full of heat and chocolate to Anna's ears.

He leaned forward bringing his face into the dim light. "Now."

Anna gasped as she recognised the man before her. "Ronny Teson, my ass," she said and lowered her voice considerably, "You're... him, you're Jonas Alexander, the leader of the rebel Chameleons... aren't you?"

"Yes, I know who I am, thanks. However, you don't have to lower your voice, we're all friends here," he said, and a smile wrinkled his handsome face. He looked away from her and raised his hand to the barman.

Anna thought he was ordering another bottle but the entire pub fell quiet as everyone stopped what they were doing and turned to look at Jonas and Anna. The barman walked to the front door, locked it and turned over the sign to 'Closed', he then turned the TV off and plunged the entire place into silence.

"I wasn't expecting to see you so soon," Anna said, and she looked directly at Jonas as she began to feel somewhat nervous now that she knew who she was dealing with.

"Clearly," he said, poured her a glass of scotch and pushed it across the table toward her.

Anna took the glass and downed the amber liquid in one gulp. She allowed herself to feel the delicious burn in her throat before placing the glass back on the table and looking him in the eye.

He watched her for a moment and enjoyed the view. She had piqued his interest and nobody had done that for a long time.

"They say you went deep into hiding since Croatia. You, Marcus and Grigori."

"So we did, for a while anyway, but that is exactly what they expected of us, so now we do the opposite and they are further from catching us than they have ever been. They are such imbeciles."

"Smart move," she said.

Jonas lifted his glass in acknowledgement of the

compliment and drank down the fiery liquid in one shot. "So, what do you have for me, Miss Croft?" he said, and sat back in the shadows again.

Anna pulled out the electronic work pass with the name Ryan Schneider printed on it next to a photo of the man she had just killed. She also placed Ryan's phone on the table. "I thought someone could send a text from the other side of the country for you, so they would believe he is away, perhaps on a family emergency or something of that matter? That is... after you have done... whatever it is you need that pass for, of course."

"Good idea. I like a person who thinks several moves ahead," he said and smiled at her. Then, with an angry and firm voice, he said to the rest of the bar, "More of you idiots should be like Miss Croft and use your brains at least once in a millennia."

Anna looked around the bar, at the Chameleons and the, now obviously, Trusted Humans who sat around. She was wondering what they had done to deserve that outburst. Her thoughts returned to the job at hand. Now that she had met Jonas would he have her killed or could she persuade him to let her join him?

Jonas' attention snapped back to her and he poured himself another shot.

"I want to join you. I want to help more," she said, coming straight out with her deepest desire. No point in tiptoeing around with this man.

He would sooner kill you than make small talk, she thought to herself.

"Oh, you do, do you? And how do I know I can trust you? What if you are a spy for the Council?" he said, the smile never leaving his face. The only sign he was utterly serious was the cold, hard look in his eyes, and the fact that the smile didn't reach them, not even one little bit.

"I could be," Anna said nonchalantly.

The Chameleons in the bar took her words as truth and were next to her in a micro second, hauling her out of her chair and gripping her firmly between them. The humans were slower to react but they crowded around her too.

Jonas didn't move from his seat but held his hand up and the Chameleons instantly let go of her and the humans backed off a step or two.

"Now that wasn't smart," Jonas said.

"Look, whether I say I am or I'm not working for the Council, you will not trust me until I prove myself, right?" she said as she sat back down and helped herself to another glass of his scotch, drinking it straight down once again to calm her nerves.

Jonas leant forward onto the table, yet again intrigued by her and by her attitude. It was entirely refreshing, when most of the time he was surrounded by sycophantic sheep all agreeing with everything he said, and none of them having ideas of their own.

"I can help you get into and out of the building, I know where the offices are, even the most secret ones, and I have the one thing you didn't know you would need... and that's because I only just found out about it today, myself."

"Oh and pray tell, what is that?" Jonas said, as he raised his eyebrows and leant back in his seat waiting to be impressed.

Anna reached into her bag, and the other Chameleons were instantly by her side again. She slowly withdrew her hand and placed something on the table between Jonas and herself.

It was the clear plastic tub full of ice and the single, fresh eyeball.

Jonas looked at her and a deeply amused smile spread over his face, this one lighting up his eyes, too.

She smiled back at him.

Oh yes, she thought, she definitely had his full attention now.

ACCLIMATION

I watched the morning sun rise over the trees at the end of our garden. The beauty of this event still mesmerized me as much as it had in Croatia, when I saw my first sunrise as a Chameleon. The superior eyesight had given me a new understanding and, I had to admit, a new found awe for the beauty all around me in every second of the day. Everything had changed with my new eyes: I could see the small details, the depths of colours that the human race just couldn't see or had names for. This, however, was my favourite thing to look at, the blaze and range of colours from the dawn that made me gasp every time and humbled me by its incredible radiance.

As I watched, the colours slowly changed from dark to light and at last burst forth as the sun topped the horizon, and I soaked in the brilliance of the new day. But even now, my mind became distracted and I had begun to feel nervous about the day ahead. Today was the day I had been dreading for several reasons. The main one being: would I murder anyone?

"Alright, that was a little overly dramatic, Kate. Get a grip," I said to myself out loud as I pulled my eyes away from the stunning colours of the recent dawn, towards the item that lay in my hands.

It was my simple rucksack, the kind that nearly every student owned. I had already packed it with my books and a lunch, for appearances sake, but it was not so much the bag that had me worried. No, it was what it represented. The fact that it was in my hands at all, was the scary part, because it meant I had been cleared to go back to school. After only a couple of weeks of practice with speed, slowness, feeding and pretending to be human again, I had finally been assessed by Daniel and Helena, and they had agreed that not only had I mastered my control at an astonishing rate, they had also said it was astounding how fast I was able to do it all and, at last, I was deemed safe enough to return to school.

I'd go back to the Marston School of Performing Arts and Sciences, a place filled with hundreds of young men and women, all human. Except for Joshua, his brother Wil and I, all of the other students would exude drainable energy, right there in front of me. It was going to be like sitting in front of a buffet when you were starving. How was I going to be able to resist draining their energy, even though I now belonged to the group of Chameleons known as Hippies and only fed on trees and plants? How would I be able to resist all that energy around me? Thankfully, Joshua would be beside me for most of my classes, but still, I was scared. What if I lost control? What if I revealed to the humans what we were? Both scenarios would be punishable by death by the Council of Nine and I would not be able to escape this fate, as their rule was absolute.

I heard Joshua's car pull up at the curb outside, and I grabbed my bag and left the house, locking the front door behind me as Mum had already left for work. She had also wished me luck as she had rushed out. Luck? I was beginning to think I would need a miracle to get me through this day.

The days were feeling colder now that we were into December. The sky today, however, was clear and the air crisp. I could feel the light from the sun faintly warming my face. I could easily control my body temperature now with just a thought, but I liked to feel the cold air of winter and the weak warmth of the sun upon my skin, and I decided to keep my body at a normal human temperature to enjoy it to the fullest.

"Hey," Joshua said as he stood by the open passenger door. "You ready for this?"

"Yeah, I guess," I said, feeling a little moody. "What if..."

"No, no what if's. You can do this. You're ready. You know you are," he said with a smile.

I looked at him directly. That smile made me think of doing lots of things, but none of them were suitable for school. "Do we have to go?" I said, the look on my face showing my desire for him.

"Sadly, yes. You need to get this first day over with. You'll feel much better when you have. I know what it's like, remember?"

"I know, I know," I said, as I climbed into the car, fastened my seat belt and sat with my arms folded.

I might have to do this but I didn't have to like it, I thought to myself, grumpily.

The journey to school was a short, quiet one. I didn't feel like making conversation, and Joshua didn't push it. The car slowed as it went up the gravel drive of the Marston School. The magnificent reception building was all that could be seen of the school from the driveway. It was an impressive Gothic building, full of leaded light windows and ornate brickwork. The school was surrounded by several hundred acres of parkland and forest, which housed The Marston Theatre, The Mathers Danforth Science Building and The Marston Family Library. Each building was gorgeous in its own right, but compared to the reception building, they definitely took second place. We pulled slowly past the massive wooden doors of the reception building, above which sat the school crest carved in stone with the motto 'Semper Vivendus' beneath it. I glanced up at the crest as we went by, I now knew the true meaning of the school's motto, which was: "Always Living".

Originally, the once private school had been built for the son of a peer of the realm, who was also a Chameleon. That son had been Mathers Danforth Marston III, who was also known as Lord Daniel Marston, Joshua's father.

It was built for him to learn how to act like a human and to look into the science behind the evolution of the Chameleons by the greatest teachers and minds of his species and time. Although nothing of note was found by the science department, the acting lessons had served him well. Over the years, the school had been opened up to young Human men and women who had an aptitude for the arts or the sciences. Hence why I was originally attending, as I wanted to be an Oscar winning actress. Strangely though, I was no longer sure that's what I wanted from my life anymore, now that it could last hundreds, if not thousands, of years. It all seemed so limited as a life plan now.

After parking the car, we walked through the main doors and past the massive reception desk, which I had always thought looked like it had come from an old hotel in the movies. We were now utterly surrounded by humans. Young men and women, students, all of whom were filing past me and Joshua, heading to their form rooms. The colours of their auras whizzed by me and I could tell by the colours what mood they were all in. It was dizzying and confusing as they rushed by, like a crazy kaleidoscope turned by the gods.

"Breathe," Joshua whispered in my ear.

I released a breath I hadn't realised I'd been holding and breathed in deeply.

"That's better. Now slow the images down in your mind so you're not overwhelmed by the colours."

I did as I was bid and mentally slowed the rushing students down to a slower, more comfortable pace as I watched them all go past, almost in slow motion. It was easier to watch, and I began to realise that I had no overwhelming urge to reach out and drain any of the colours, or indeed the attached humans, before me. The auras were hypnotic, yes, but I had no inclination to feed on any of them. A huge surge of relief flowed through me as I finally understood, I truly was a Hippie and no human, no matter their aura would ever be food for me. I suddenly felt calmer than I had in days. I slowly allowed the images to return to their normal speed and I simply watched the humans and their beautiful light float by on their way to their destinations, completely oblivious that we were in their midst.

"Better?" Joshua said, as his hand slipped comfortably into mine.

"Much. Thank you so much for that, I was

beginning to lose focus there," I said.

"How does your control feel?" He looked at me intensely, as if searching my face for signs of weakening control.

"Good, very good actually. I have absolutely no desire to feed," I said, proud of myself.

"Oh, that is great news," Joshua said and hugged me.

"What's good news?" A familiar voice said behind us.

I spun round, letting go of Joshua, not sure what to expect.

"Sorry, didn't mean to make you jump, Kate," Ally said, startled by how fast I'd turned round.

"Yeah, erm... what did you say?" I realised I had moved just a little too quickly, and it threw me for a moment. I just hoped it wasn't inhumanly fast.

"What's good news? Joshua said something was good news," Ally said, pushed up her ever loose glasses and looked from me to Joshua.

Utterly relieved that she hadn't seemed to notice my fast movement, my mind went blank for an answer.

"I was saying it's good news that Kate is back at school, isn't it?"

"Oh, yes, it is. I'm so glad you've finally got the all-clear from the doctor, and with term ending next Wednesday, you won't have many classes before we go on Christmas break, so at least you will be eased back in."

"Yeah, now that is good news," I said and grinned; it really, really was good news.

We three followed the crowd of noisy students up the grand oak staircase to our usual form room. The form room looked more like a lounge than a classroom, except for the desk, where our form tutor sat. The room had several comfy sofas, and there were a few tables with chairs scattered around. Form was a fifteen minute prep class where our form tutor took the register each morning and afternoon. It was also where everyone had a chance to finish last minute homework, cram for exams or chat with friends before the lessons started. This room was also the place where we were allowed to come during class breaks and at lunchtimes, if we weren't in the dining hall or outside.

Joshua could see how much more comfortable I now was and sat with his friend Mat on the next couch to us and, because Mat was so close, Ally became flustered and dropped her bag and its contents twice in the fifteen minutes of Form. By the time the classes started, I felt utterly relaxed and in control of myself, my abilities and my hunger. It was a massive relief, and I tried to get back into the flow of everyday life at school.

Ally and I sat at our usual table in Biology, while Mat and Joshua sat on the other side of the room.

"Glad you're back, it's been quiet here without you," Ally said.

"Thanks, I think," I said, and laughed. "Hey, I

bet you haven't talked to other people and gotten to know them while I was away have you? I can't believe you would just sit on your own. How about Mat, didn't you two talk much?"

"God no. Look what happened 'that' lunchtime. Too embarrassing. I can never think of anything to say anyway," she said, as she glanced across the room at Mat, only to find him looking at her, which made her dip her head behind a book and blush furiously.

"Remember when I first saw Joshua and you thought it was funny, and said how much fun it would be to watch me make a fool of myself because of a boy?"

"Yeah," she said, without raising her head from the book.

"Well, now I see how much fun it is," I said, and grinned at her sweetly.

"Shut up," she said, not amused at all.

The morning passed in a blur and before I realised it, it was lunchtime and the four of us met up in the lunchroom. After a bit of a search, we were able to find space for us all on a table near a window, looking out over the ornate gardens and the woods beyond. I looked up at the sky as we sat down, and saw that the day had clouded over and become grey, with a mushroom coloured sky, it looked like it was going to be a cold, wet afternoon. I much preferred the bright and sunny winter days.

We all sat and ate our packed lunches and Ally

remained shy and quiet throughout. She managed successfully not to spill anything on anyone this time, not even herself, but she still seemed overly nervous around Mat.

"Hey, how's your job?" I said, trying to get her to talk and relax.

"Good. Great, actually. I love it and I'm learning so much," she said, happy for a conversation topic.

"Doesn't it interfere with your school work?" Mat asked her.

She was too shy to look up at him. "Nope, not really." Ally nervously poked her apple core and kept her eyes downward.

"No clue how you find the time to do it with all the homework we're getting at the moment," Mat said, and sat back in his chair, drinking from a can of pop.

"I only work six hours a week and that's on a Saturday, so I get plenty of time to do all the homework during the week," she said, her eyes still focused on the corpse of her apple.

"What do you do, cut up frogs all day?" Mat asked and laughed.

She looked up, directly in his eyes. "Actually, we're looking at genes and their individual arrangement of the mitochondria, which seems to be randomly scattered in the cytoplasm of the cell outside of the nucleus," she said.

Everyone looked at her.

No one said a word.

"What?" Ally said and looked at each of us individually. "What did I say?"

"I love girls with good looks and brains, they're so cool," Mat said and smiled broadly at Ally, just as the afternoon bell went, making us all jump.

I watched Ally spend the entire afternoon with a smile on her face. Mat's compliment seemed to have given Ally a huge boost and all the confidence she needed. I could see her blossoming right in front of me because of it.

If only my life was as simple as that: to only be worried about homework, grades and boys. However, the more I thought about it, the more I knew how fleeting these things truly were, and how there was so much more to life now, especially mine.

I looked at my friends as we left school at the end of the day and felt oddly disconnected from them all, even Joshua, and I was beginning to worry if I would ever really fit in anywhere.

FALLEN

I arrived home, at the end of the last day of term before Christmas, a little later than usual. I'd taken the bus home with Ally, as I would not be seeing much of her over the holiday. I had managed to persuade Mum to let us go with the Marston's to their cottage in Canada for the entirety of the Christmas holidays. Actually, it had been easier than I'd expected. I think Mum had been dreading the holidays, as it was the first anniversary of when she kicked my father out of the house for having an affair with his boss's daughter. I think the last thing mum wanted to do was to spend the first Christmas without him sitting around remembering what happened, and that was really why she had agreed after only two conversations about it.

We were leaving the next morning, after breakfast, and Mum was busily packing our suitcases on the living room sofa when I walked in.

She had left work early so that she could pack in plenty of time and be completely organized.

"How's school?" she said as I walked through the door.

"Okay. Big news of the day is that Ally and Mat are dating now," I said as I hung up my coat by the door and slumped into the chair near the fireplace, watching the flames of the fake fire.

"Really?" Mum turned to look at me with a surprised look on her face, still holding the shirt she was in the middle of folding. "When did that happen? How did that happen? I thought she was too nervous to talk to him."

"Today, and she was, but then he told her he liked brainy girls and they've not stopped talking since, and now, a week later, they are officially dating."

"I guess she just needed a boost in her confidence. Good for her."

"Yeah, it's nice to see them together," I said as I watched mum go back to her packing. "Are you nearly done or do you need help?"

"Nope, that's it, apart from toiletries, which we can pack after our showers in the morning," she said, zipped both cases shut and began trying to lift them off the sofa.

"Let me do that," I said and tried to lift them both, one in each hand. They were heavy, but I concentrated on making my body accept the weight as if it was nothing, and I moved them to the floor in front of the fireplace.

"Thanks. You make that look so easy," Mum said.

"That's because it is," I said and grinned at her.

"For you maybe. For this human weakling, not so much." She laughed. "I know you don't have to eat, but do you fancy a Chinese dinner tonight? I've been craving one all day."

"Actually, yes, that would be yummy. Sometimes I really fancy a certain flavour, even if I don't have to eat to survive. I still crave certain things. It's all very strange, I know."

"Strange but not impossible to get used to. You know I'm very proud of how you're handling it all. It doesn't seem to have phased you one bit," she said.

"Oh, it has, but then I've had longer than you to get used to it all," I said. I didn't want to tell her how I really felt about my lack of 'humanness' and how I no longer felt connected to that life like I once did. If I told her all this, she would just worry, and she had enough to worry about with the coming holiday. After all, she would be the only human there as all of Joshua's family and their friends were Chameleons and now me, of course.

'She must be nervous, deep down.' I thought, as I watched her call the restaurant for their delivery service. I decided we would have a relaxing night together and that we would watch one of her favourite movies with our dinner.

By 8:oo the next morning, we were sitting in a chauffeured car on the way to a private airport, the very same airport I had been to with Tara when we flew out to Croatia, and I was delighted to see that Mum's reactions to the first class treatment were the same as mine. She looked around her, amazed by the luxury of the airport lounge. Everything looked shiny, clean and crisp. We breezed through to a private lounge, where a uniformed woman took our passports and went to complete our boarding passes. Within moments she returned and handed them over, which appeared to be the extent of the passport control and ticket assignment. The lounge had big soft chairs and there were vases of fresh flowers everywhere, even now in the middle of December. There was also a bar that shone brightly with stainless steel fittings and bright lights at the end of the room. Mum glanced out the window and realised she was looking at private jets, and I wondered if my face had looked so surprised when I first came here and saw them.

"Time to board everyone,"(there needs to be an introduction of the other characters here, or a few lines previous to properly set the scene) Daniel said, and followed a Steward named David, out onto the tarmac. Helena followed him, then Wil and Joshua, they were so used to this life that it was nothing out of the ordinary to them, and they were talking about the trail they were going to use the skidoos on this year. Mum and I made up the rear, and I stayed with her as a bit of moral support, because she looked a little like she was on an alien planet.

"You okay?" I said.

"Oh, yes. Isn't this all lovely? How nice it is to be treated like this." She grinned at me like a child in a sweets store.

I laughed, knowing exactly what she was feeling.

We walked out towards the private jet and the small staircase leading into it. I let mum go first, and she was so excited, she turned round to me, grinned and winked. I loved seeing her like this.

I had to laugh as I followed her up the steps into what was now my third flight in a first class private jet. The interior was very similar to the last one I was in; it was approximately eight-feet wide by maybe twenty feet long and filled with big, cream coloured leather chairs with dark, wooden-looking tables and two long leather sofas. It had a beautiful stainless steel kitchen area towards the front of the plane, and I noticed a restroom sign towards the back. Through the open doorway, I could also see comfortable-looking sleeping compartments. Within the cabin, there were enough seats for ten passengers, but we only filled six of them.

Mum was speechless as she looked around her, not sure where to sit.

Helena spotted my mum's dilemma and offered her the seat next to her. Mum accepted and the two women sat chatting. I could see mum beginning to relax and enjoy it all. I really hoped she would have an enjoyable holiday; she deserved it after what she had been through in the past year.

A man's voice came over the intercom, "Good morning and welcome to Aurora Airlines Private Charter. I'm Christopher, your Captain for today. You are travelling this morning in the newest member of our fleet - the Gulfstream G650 - with a typical cruising speed of 0.85 Mach. We will be landing in approximately six hours and fourteen minutes at Muskoka Airport. Your Steward, David, tells me we are just waiting for our remaining guests and he will instruct you on in-flight protocols when they arrive."

I sat down next to Joshua, and opposite Wil, at one of the tables with four seats. "I didn't realise there were more people coming with us."

"Oh yeah, I forgot to tell you. Moira, Tara and Michael are coming out earlier than expected and are joining us on this flight. It will be great, won't it?" Joshua said and kissed me on the lips.

"Oh, yeah... but..." I began to say, not sure if I should continue with my words.

"What?" he said, looking concerned.

"Well, it's just that..." I leant into Joshua a little more. "Well, I've been thinking... won't it be difficult, seeing as Michael is Tara's ex-hubby and she's with Wil now?"

"Nah, we're all friends," Wil said.

I was embarrassed. I'd forgotten about Chameleon hearing and how sharp it was. "Sorry, Wil, I just wondered."

"No worries," he said and smiled.

I was struck again about how handsome he was, but in such a different way to his brother. His features were more angular than Joshua's. A sudden thought entered my mind, and I turned back to Joshua.

"What about mum?" I said, as the inner thought developed and panic began to rise in me.

"What about her?" Joshua said, obviously not making the connection I was.

"Michael's a Feeder and my mum will be the only human there," I said, my heart beating rapidly now. "I know he said he would behave, but still... it's my mum."

"It will be fine, he's not going to feed on your mum. Breathe and calm down, I can hear your heart rate from here," Joshua said, seeming to not take my concern seriously.

I concentrated on my breathing and my heartbeat and felt them both slow, just as Michael appeared in the doorway of the plane. He stepped in looking amazing, I had to admit. I had never seen him look so casual before in jeans and a leather jacket, with his long pale hair tied back. His dark jacket accentuated his strong, fair, Nordic looks.

He was followed by Tara and Moira, two

stunning redheads who were happily chatting away with each other. As everyone said hello and got seated, the captain's voice could be heard again.

"Now that we are all on board, I would ask you to please fasten your seatbelts for take-off. The weather is bright and clear, providing for a smooth flight today, and it is -26 in Muskoka and a beautiful winter's day. Thank you for flying Aurora Airlines and I hope you have a pleasant flight."

We duly fastened our seatbelts and the plane glided along the tarmac to prepare for take-off. We were quickly in the air, a process that was a lot less noisy than Mum and I were used to. Shortly, we levelled out and Tara undid her belt and came to sit next to Wil. I glanced over to where Michael was sitting, to discover him looking at my mum. He must have felt me watching as his eyes soon turned towards me, and then he guiltily looked away.

I knew it, this was going to be a problem and I was going to have to say something to Daniel or Helena. I thought about it for a moment, but what proof did I have that he wanted to drain my mum? So he looked at her, was that a crime? Annoyed with myself, I put on my iPod and closed my eyes. I tried not to think about a Feeder near my mum, but the thought just kept prickling my consciousness and my inner voice just wouldn't shut up about it.

The hours flew by as we all sat and chatted, watched movies and a few of us ate a superb meal with my mum. I didn't want her to eat alone and neither did Helena and Moira. Mum seemed to be enjoying herself during the flight and I kept half an eye on Michael, but I was convinced he would do nothing while everyone was around and so I relaxed a little too. Seeing and knowing how fragile my mum was now that I was no longer human made me feel very protective towards her. I now understood a little how she, as a parent, felt about me.

The flight was a smooth one, and we landed on time. Two limousines picked us all up from the airport and whisked us off into the bright, cold day. Thankfully, Michael wasn't in our car. I was with my mum, Joshua and Moira. Mum and Moira seemed to have struck up a friendship and they were happily looking out the window as Moira told her all about her first visit to Canada. It was in 1886 for the founding of the city of Vancouver, and how she had previously known George Vancouver, the English explorer it was named after, and how she had also been mourning his death with his family in 1798. I briefly wondered how old Moira actually was, and watched Mum as Moira went into her history and she seemed to be enthralled by it all.

"Everything okay?" Joshua said and put his hand on my leg.

"Yeah, Mum is enjoying herself," I said.

"That was the whole idea. You still worried about..." Joshua glanced over at Moira who would be able to hear their conversation.

I understood what he was wanting to say and pre-empted him. "Yes, but I don't think he will do anything with everyone around, so I'll just stay close by her."

"I don't think he'll do anything at all," Joshua said with a steel tone in his voice.

"Maybe so, but I'm not willing to take the risk and I'm gonna speak to him when I get a chance," I said.

"Okay, your choice, but I think you are making a huge mistake," Joshua said in an irritated tone, removing his hand from my leg and visibly closing into himself, allowing no further conversation on the subject.

We spent the rest of the journey in stony silence and I turned to watch the snowy, beautiful landscape whizzing past the window. I tried to ignore my growing annoyance with Joshua as he brushed off my worries too quickly yet again.

At last, we pulled into a recently cleared driveway, which took us off the main road and down a long drive protected by huge evergreen trees coated in a thick layer of snow. The banks of snow at the side of the ploughed road were huge; I had never seen so much of it in my life. As we came around a corner to the left, we finally saw our destination, and it was probably the most beautiful building I had ever seen.

The timber framed 'cottage' was enormous. It

had two storeys, with the second storey windows looking out of the wooden shingled roof like eyes. The first storey was built, partially, upon flat timber logs and stone walls. As the car pulled closer I could see the house was 'L' shaped, and had many wooden windows that looked out at the woodlands that surrounded the place and the lake that sat beside it.

"Wow!" Mum said, as she gaped at our destination.

"Yeah," I said, as my face was a mirror image of hers.

"It's lovely, isn't it? I just love coming to Canada at this time of year. The snow just makes Christmas for me," Moira said as she smiled at us both.

"What do you think?" Joshua said, his past sulk seemingly forgotten.

"I... it's massive," I said.

"Well, not massive, but it has nine bedrooms and ten bathrooms, so it's big enough for all of us," he said.

"Nice." I nodded in appreciation.

The car pulled to a crunchy-sounding stop outside the main entrance, which consisted of two large tree trunks that held up the porch roof over the two big wooden doors with decorative iron work on them. We climbed out of the car and I was struck by how cold the air was despite the bright sunshine. I didn't raise my body temperature, as I again wanted to enjoy the whole experience for what it truly was. I looked over at my mum who was standing next to me, and saw that she too was cold as she pulled her coat closer around herself and stuffed her hands into her pockets.

The others joined us at the front of the cottage while the drivers began to take our luggage from the vehicles.

"Do come on in and make yourselves at home. Our house keepers, Celeste and Don, were told of our arrival and they should have the place ready for us," Daniel said as he took his wife's hand and le d the way inside.

We all followed through the lovely doorway and into the reception area where we hung up our coats and took off our shoes. Every surface was wooden, a deep, warm colour that made everything seem cosy. The reception area led into the main lounge, with its enormous stone fireplace, which already had a fire roaring away in it. Around the room there were various comfy-looking chairs and tables. There were two large, chocolate coloured sofas directly in front of the fire and both of them had colourful, highly patterned blankets laid over the back of them. Antlers hung up on the wall over the fireplace, as well as framed paintings around the room on the log walls.

"As those of you who have spent Christmas with us here before will already know, it is a very special time for us, and we enjoy it fully. This is the one time of the year when we will do many of the things that Humans like to do, such as decorating a tree, drinking eggnog and eating a vast array of wonderful holiday foods for which we all will chip in and cook for ourselves. We also give gifts from us to each of you in celebration of our friendship," Helena said as she stood in front of the fireplace. "In particular, I want to welcome Kate and Caroline, and I hope you will feel at home and enjoy the holidays with us," she said and came over to hug us both in welcome.

"It is very generous of you, thank you for welcoming us into your beautiful home and holiday celebrations," Mum said.

"You are most welcome, Caroline. You are not only a Trusted Human now, but family. I hope you understand why I thought you would enjoy your visit with us, I didn't want you to think we don't do any of the fun things at Christmas just because we are Chameleons," Helena said.

"Well... I... actually, I wasn't sure what to expect," Mum said.

"I thought so," Helena said and smiled. "Ah... here's the luggage."

The two drivers placed all the luggage at the end of the reception hall near the lounge entrance, turned round without speaking and left the building, driving back to wherever they had come from.

"Seeing as the others know where their rooms are, shall Joshua and I show you to yours?" Daniel said as he came over to us.

"That would be lovely," Mum said.

Daniel and Joshua picked up our luggage and headed off down a wooden-clad corridor, which led off the lounge into the depths of the cottage. We passed several rooms until we came to the end of the corridor.

"Caroline, this is your room on the left, and Kate, that's yours on the right. We thought you would like to be close to each other."

"Thank you Daniel, that was very thoughtful," Mum said and followed him into her room.

I followed Joshua into mine and was delighted to see it also had a lit stone fireplace. The bed was huge, with carved head and foot boards comprised of scenes of deer on mountain sides. The bed covers were similar to the brightly coloured blankets in the lounge, and the whole thing looked very inviting. I made a promise to myself then and there to try to sleep in it at least once during this trip, even though I knew I didn't need to sleep very often anymore. I decided I would make an exception for that bed. The rest of the room was filled with elegant and beautiful wooden furniture, and through a doorway on the left of the fireplace was my en suite bathroom. Yes, I had a bathroom all to myself for the entire holiday.

"Now, that's a luxury," I said out loud.

"Do you like it?" Joshua asked as he put my suitcase on the bed.

"Oh, it's wonderful; the whole place is wonderful," I said and smiled from ear to ear.

"Wait 'til you see the rest of it. I'll show you around more tomorrow, but tonight we have a tradition to uphold," he said and stepped closer, stroked some hair away from my face and kissed me.

The touch of his lips on mine sent shivers down my spine, and the familiar soft buzz of his energy, which I always felt when we touched, made my flesh develop goosebumps in excitement. We parted feeling more than a little lustful and just looked at each other. We both knew that we were at a crossroads in our relationship, even if we hadn't spoken about it. The physical need was beginning to get too strong to ignore, and now that we were of the same species, the whole idea seemed easier somehow.

"We'd better get your mum and find the others: don't want to be late," Joshua said and frowned as he stepped away from me, almost as if he was relieved to be out of the embrace.

His parting reaction confused me and I watched him walk out of my room and go across the hall to knock on my mum's open door. There was definitely something on his mind. I could feel it.

"You can unpack later. You have to come and see this," he said.

Mum looked up from her case and stopped removing her clothes from it.

"Oh, okay." She spotted me as we came out of our rooms together. "How's your room?" she said.

"Oh, very nice. Yours?" I said. And looked past her into hers.

"Quite lovely. What a beautiful cottage," she said and smiled.

"Yes, it is." I was pleased that Mum had relaxed and that, as a Human, she would be included in the festivities, at least that's what I understood from what Helena had said.

We all walked back into the lounge to see that they were waiting on us.

"Please feel at home here and take a seat," Helena said to my mum.

"Thank you," Mum said as she sat on one of the sofas in front of the fire, next to Moira.

I sat on an oversized chair that could probably seat two people easily. Everyone else stood or sat and waited for Helena to continue.

"Now as some of you know, every year we go out and select our own tree from an area of our property where we have our evergreen woodland. To manage the woodland properly, the trees have to be thinned out and we will be taking one of the trees that need to be removed as our Yule tree. We will all head out there before it gets dark to collect it, so if you would like to all get prepared, we will leave in five minutes. "Oh and Caroline? I took the liberty of finding you some winter boots and jacket that will withstand the dropping temperatures out there."

"Oh, right... thank you," Mum said, looking a little embarrassed that she had arrived a little under-prepared for such intense cold.

"Actually, do you have any more? I want to experience everything, including the cold," I said.

Helena looked delighted. "Of course, what a lovely idea. I think I will join you. It's been a long time since I had cold fingers and a tingly nose."

Daniel smiled at his wife. "I think it's an excellent idea too, why don't we all do it? Then we can enjoy the true benefit of a hot chocolate upon our return," he said.

With overwhelming assent, everyone dressed as humans would for -12 degrees Celsius, which is what the thermometer by the door said it was outside. As we tramped along the dugout pathway to the woods, on the east side of the property, it began to snow. The big, fat flakes fluttered down as we walked along. The scenery was breathtaking and the walk was wonderful after being stuck in a plane for over six hours. The short walk brought us to the edge of the woods where we began to tramp through virgin snow, following literally in Daniel's footsteps. I stayed by Mum's side as she scrambled her way over the uneven pathway through the trees until we came to a spot where a small tree of about nine feet was being crowded out by much larger trees on each side, both of them well over twelve feet. The small tree had a yellow cross on the trunk marking it for removal.

"Here we are, these trees are white spruces and can grow up to twenty-five to thirty feet high, except this one is being overgrown by its neighbours and needs to be removed," Daniel said.

We all stood by the smaller tree, which had been sheltered from most of the snow by the others around it. I looked at it with my now much improved Chameleon vision. I could see the needles up close, and they were approximately two centimetres long and of a wonderful blue-green colour. As I looked closer I could see the whitish powder layer that covered the needles and was surprised to see that it wasn't snow but its own natural covering. I could also tell the tree was becoming weak from lack of room and sunlight, its branches starting to droop.

"Now before we cut this tree down, would any of you like to taste its energy? I know some of us do not normally feed on trees and plants, but as a mark of respect to the dying tree we owe it to at least pass some of its life on to us," Helena said.

"What's going on?" Mum whispered in my ear.

"This is how I feed, I take the energy from plants and trees. So does Helena, and she is offering the others a taste of that energy before the tree is taken down," I said, hoping not to freak mum out.

"Oh, I see," she said and watched Helena avidly.

Everyone except mum moved over to the tree and placed a single hand on it and absorbed some of its energy. To me it was unlike anything I had tasted before. I loved the taste of a tree's energy, but this one, because it was getting sickly, felt and tasted more watery than other trees I'd taken energy from. It was almost as if it was diluted somehow. We all stepped back and Daniel began to use the axe he'd brought with him to cut down the tree.

"Joshua?" I said.

"Yup?" He turned away from the tree and looked at me.

"When you saved my mum and I from death, you gave us your energy, right?"

"Yes," he said and frowned, not knowing where the conversation was leading.

"Do you think you would be able to give Mum some of the tree's energy?" I said.

"I... I don't know," he said, frowning.

Daniel stopped cutting the tree. "What an intriguing idea, Kate. Perhaps, Caroline, you would like to try?"

Everyone looked at mum.

"Sure, why not?" she said bravely.

"Excellent. We had better try this quickly though, I have already cut into it a fair bit and there will not be much energy left."

Joshua and mum moved closer to the tree.

"I will drain some of the tree's energy and try to feed it to you, okay?" he said and held out his hand to her.

Taking a deep breath, Mum took his hand and watched him move his own hand nearer the tree. Her face showed a grim determination that I had seen many times, whenever she knew something was difficult but she would do it anyway. I called it her courage face.

Joshua gingerly placed his hand on the tree and closed his eyes.

We all stood still, watching and waiting for a reaction from either of them.

Nothing happened at all for a couple of minutes.

"Perhaps I have done too much damage..." Daniel said to Helena.

"Oh my God!" Mum said all of a sudden.

I was by her side without realising I had moved. "Mum? Are you okay?"

Mum's legs gave away under her and she landed hard on her bottom in the soft, wet snow breaking the link between her, Joshua and the tree.

SPREE

The distant light of the moon shone through the windows as the security guard looked up from his desk and was surprised to see a man with long hair and beard, walking towards the locked main door. Presuming, at this time of night, that the man had lost his way or that his car had broken down nearby, the guard walked over to the door but didn't unlock it.

"Sorry, sir, the building is on a lock-down timer and only opens at the start and end of each shift. Do you want me to call for assistance for you?" he said loudly so that the man could hear him through the bulletproof glass.

The man stood at the doorway and smiled. It was not a kind smile, but the type you saw in the movies when the bad guy was about to do something really, really bad.

The guard instinctively took a step back, grabbed his radio from his shoulder and spoke into it.

"Dean, I think we have a problem, some crazy guy is at the front entrance." He let go of the button and waited for a reply, all the while closely watching the man through the glass door as a nervous sweat broke out on his brow and the back of his neck prickled with a fear he couldn't explain.

"Just ignore him, Derek, he'll go away. I know you're new and all, but we get them sometimes. It's just another crazy trying to get attention. Just go back to your desk and ignore him, he'll move on." Dean said back at him from the radio, his voice betraying his boredom at his job simply by its tone.

"Will do," Derek said and sighed. They had never told him about the crazies when he got the job. He looked back at the man at the door and felt strangely fascinated by him all of a sudden. All his fear had left him now, and he felt strangely calm.

The man outside nodded and smiled again as Derek jerkily stepped forward and tapped in the emergency override code into the door's alarm pad, then entered the unlock code. Finally, he pulled open   the door to the dangerous-looking stranger as if he was doing it in a dream.

"Thank you, Derek," the man said in a strange accent as he stepped inside the opening. "I'll just hold the door open for my friends who will be along in a moment. You can go back to your desk now."

Without a comment, the guard nodded and

returned to his seated position as if nothing unusual was happening. He watched as fifteen people, both men and women, filed into the foyer and stood before him. Each one looking as dangerous as the first man.

"Please lock the front door again now, Derek, and then you can return to your post. You will not leave it for any reason, and you will not open the main door for anyone but me. Is that understood?" the long-haired man said.

Derek nodded again and went to re-lock the door. He turned and walked back to his desk and continued to monitor the screens before him, completely ignoring the people around him.

Jonas stepped forward from the crowd. "Excellent work, Grigori."

"Thank you," Grigori Yefimovich Rasputin said. He was pleased to yet again be of service to his friend and leader.

Anna stepped closer to Jonas. "How did he do that? How did he persuade the guard to let us in? He didn't even touch him."

"Ah, Anna, there is much you don't yet know about my friends," Jonas said cryptically and marched over to the elevators, stood in front of them and turned to address the crowd. "My friends, today you will feast. The laboratories and offices housed within this building are full of humans waiting to be our meals, so please feel free to indulge your every whim. But remember, the seventh floor is mine, and you will not go there. Am I understood?" He glared at each one of them menacingly as his eyes found all of theirs. With an absolute assent from them, he pushed the buttons on the four elevators and said, "Enjoy, my friends, for today we show the world how superior we truly are."

A cheer went up from the mob as they rushed into three of the lifts and were carried upwards toward the unsuspecting and locked in workers. Two men stayed behind with Jonas, as did Anna.

"Grigori, Marcus, let us now see how useful Anna will be shall we?" he said, and gestured with his open hand for Anna to walk into the remaining open lift before him.

Anna nervously smiled and walked into the lift, followed by the three most dangerous Chameleons on the planet. The seventh floor arrived all too quickly and Anna, having worked there undercover for the last three months, knew where to go once the lift doors opened. However, she also knew there would be four guards at two separate areas on the floor, so she stood back while Grigori and Marcus moved to the front, near the doors of the elevator, and watched as they waited to spring on the unsuspecting guards once they had opened.

Anna observed the next few fractions of a second in slow motion: the guards turned towards the elevator as the doors opened and, in a blur of speed, Grigori and Marcus sped out of the lift and across the room, breaking both of the guards necks before either one of them could raise the alarm. The guards had no chance against the speed and strength of one Chameleon, let alone two, and their fates were sealed in the blink of an eye.

Before them now lay an empty corridor with two doors a good twenty feet apart, both displaying the sign 'Level Seven ~ Authorized Admittance ONLY', and next to each door was a key pad and scanner. Anna stepped forward and swiped Ryan's card in the left-hand door's scanner and then she punched in his security number. The scanner opened and flashed a green light, informing her it was ready for the retinal scan. Digging the small plastic box out of her pocket, she opened it and firmly gripped the slippery globe as she held it close to the scanner and waited. A second ticked by but to Anna it seemed like an hour. There was a beep, and the door automatically unlocked.

Anna breathed a sigh of relief.

Grigori and Marcus rushed past her and into the ante room of the secret laboratories, where they mercilessly dispatched the two remaining guards.

Anna placed the cold eye in its box and put it safely back in her jacket pocket. She wasn't sure if she would need it again as she hadn't been this far into level seven before. The only time she had been up here was to deliver a box of files to Ryan, who had been the director of the seventh floor, but he had met her by this door, and did not take her any further in. Thankfully, Ryan worked the same shift as her, and came down to the cafeteria every day at 7pm for his dinner, or she would never have been able to seduce him and get what she needed from him.

Jonas walked into the now secure anteroom and Anna followed. She had to admit that she was intrigued about what was behind all the security and what had made Jonas interested in the first place.

The room was about twenty feet in length and ten feet wide, sparsely furnished with a few chairs. One wall was completely made of glass, and through it they could all see a large, very well designed and equipped laboratory with several people working in it.

"Why don't they know we are here? Surely they can see and hear us," Anna said, surprised no one had looked at them as they stood in front of the glass wall.

"They cannot," Jonas said. "The glass is one-way viewing only, and the room is sound proof," he said as he stepped closer to the glass.

"How do you know that?" Anna said as she followed him and peered at the scientists. "I didn't even know that."

"You are not our only insider," Jonas said but revealed no more.

The silence was broken by agonising screams coming from the rest of the building.

Anna tried really hard not to listen to them.

Chameleon hearing is not pleasant sometimes. Anna thought to herself as she remained still, controlling her breathing and heart rate so that she appeared undisturbed by the revolting sounds of humans being ripped apart. She was able to keep her poker face intact as Jonas turned to watch her reaction, as if testing her. Yes, she had done to Ryan what she'd had to. She couldn't, after all, help what she was, but it didn't mean she had truly enjoyed it, as Jonas and his friends most definitely did.

Thankfully, for all, the screaming soon stopped.

"Let us continue," Jonas said, as if he was on some kind of wonderful adventure. and not leading a slaughter of innocent lives.

Next to the glass door was yet another security door and access pad, but this one only required a swipe of a pass card. Anna stepped forward and swiped Ryan's card again and, with a satisfying click, the door unlocked.

Yet again, Grigori and Marcus rushed inside, but this time they used their speed to gather up the eight scientists against a wall, where they forced them to sit on the pristine floor. The scientists were not fighters, and none of them really made any kind of struggle against the massive strength of the two Chameleons. They did, however, ask many questions and demanded to know what was happening and what the intruders wanted, but all of their comments were ignored.

Jonas wandered around the lab picking up paperwork, reading it and discarding it, he appeared to be looking for something specific.

"What do you want? Where are the guards? This is a private facility, you should not be here," the middle-aged, balding man said with authority as if he was the most senior member of the staff present.

In a blur of movement, Jonas rushed up towards the man, grabbed his head and twisted his neck until it broke. He then let him fall to the floor like a rag doll.

"Now, you all understand who is in charge here, perhaps you can tell me where I could find the information on the Iridescent Project," he said calmly to the terrified men and women on the verge of hysterics, who only by the primal force of shock held it back, for now.

Several of the scientists began whimpering incoherently and one man was sobbing into his hands. A woman with a terrified look on her face timidly raised her hand.

"Yes?" Jonas said and moved closer to her.

The woman shied away and pointed to her dead colleague.

"Speak," Jonas said.

"He... he... Allan, he could have told you about it," she said and lowered her arm.

"Well, Allan can no longer tell anyone anything

now, can he? So how about you tell me what you know, okay?" he said in a deceivingly calm voice, and knelt down beside her.

The woman nodded. "I don't know much about... it... but... I can show... you where the... files are," she said and looked at him, desperately hoping that what she knew would save her life.

"Good," Jonas said, and looked at her name badge. "Time to show us, Dr. Klienfeld." He grabbed her arm and roughly pulled her to her feet, and, without letting her go, Jonas spread out his hand before them, indicating that she was to proceed, as if using a gentleman's gesture was going to be helpful.

The woman took Jonas back towards the anteroom and away from the laboratory.

"Grigori, Anna comes with us. Marcus, deal with them and then follow us, we'll leave the door ajar for you." Jonas nodded towards the scientists.

Marcus didn't need telling twice, as he waded into the huddled group, ripping and tearing them apart as he went.

Anna refused to look back. She ensured she kept her breathing and heart rate steady yet again as Jonas would be able to hear the slightest change. She would do whatever she had to. She wouldn't allow herself a single lapse and give herself away as not being a bloodthirsty Bleeder and certainly not a follower of his deluded cause.

Back in the hallway, Dr. Klienfeld pointed to the

other doorway, and Anna moved ahead and repeated the same security measures to gain access.

As soon as the door unlocked, Grigori rushed in, but was soon back again at the doorway. "There's nobody in here, it's just an office," he said.

Jonas, still holding the woman by the arm, dragged her through the doorway and into the office beyond. Anna followed, and Grigori propped open the door for Marcus with a metal waste basket.

The office was a large one, with a reception desk and a partially opaque glass wall separating the inner executive office. Both desks were empty and tidy, as if no one had been working there recently.

As they got closer to the executive's desk, Anna spotted the name plate, and in bold lettering it simply said 'Dr. Ryan Schneider - Director'. Next to it was a framed picture of what Anna assumed to be his wife and two small daughters. She looked away, not wanting to think about the pain she had caused them all today, but she knew they would eventually be better off without a cheating husband and father.

"Problem?" Jonas said to Anna.

"No, not at all," she said, wondering if he had heard her heart rate change. "Just a surprise: I hadn't realised this was his desk," she said, and walked towards the locked filing cabinet. Yanking on the drawer with her enhanced strength, she soon broke the lock and had it open. She started checking through the files, not really knowing what she was looking for except the name of the project.

"The information you want is not in there," the frightened woman said, "It's over there." She pointed to a wall where a small drinks cabinet stood. "Put your hand on the Glenfiddich bottle."

Anna looked at Jonas and he nodded, so she walked over to the cabinet and gingerly reached out for the bottle. The hologram image wavered and vanished, and the cabinet panel slid back, revealing another security scanner with a keypad.

"Now isn't that interesting," Jonas said, and turned to the woman. "Thank you, Dr. Klienfeld."

"That's all I know. Whenever Ryan, I mean, Dr. Schneider, said he was not to be disturbed because he was working on the project, that's what he did, but I was asked to leave this room before he went any further," she said, speaking quickly in her fear.

"I see," Jonas said, realising, just as she did, that she was no longer needed.

The woman saw this on Jonas' face.

"Please let me go. Please. I helped you, didn't I?" she said, her voice sounding thin and reedy with fear as she tried to struggle out of his iron grasp.

"I will let you go, fear not human," he said with a smile.

The woman frowned at his turn of phrase, her eyes looking into his, and she knew deep in her soul she was doomed.

Jonas' hand rushed out with inhuman speed and

punctured her chest cavity. It forced its way into her body and grabbed her heart, draining it of all of her life energy in mere seconds. She fell away from him, hit the ground hard and lay facing upward, exposing the open chest wound and the startled look on her face. Jonas didn't even look at her again as he licked the blood off his fingers indulgently, as if his ice cream had just melted and run down his fingers and hand.

Anna turned from him. She knew that she liked to do the exact same thing when the warm blood touched her skin, but she hated herself for it. Once again, she locked down her emotions and proceeded to swipe Ryan's card one more time. She punched in his security number and used his eyeball again. This time, however, there was a fourth, extra security measure, and a small glass medical slide slid quietly out as the screen beeped, and the words "Enter DNA" came up. She looked at Jonas.

"I didn't know about this part."

"Why, Anna, are you saying you are not as useful as you said you are?" Jonas said, and looked directly at her with a smug expression on his face.

Anna saw his expression had changed and knew that her life hung in the balance. Grigori stared at her, like a hound waiting for instructions from its master to pounce on his prey and devour it.

An idea surfaced into her mind.

"Let me try something," she said, as she thrust

her finger in the back of the eye and pulled it out covered in a sticky film, she then swiped her finger onto the glass slide and prayed that there wasn't too much water from the ice, or that cold DNA made any difference. The slide withdrew itself and a 'Processing DNA' message appeared on the screen.

Seconds ticked by as they all stood and waited without making a sound.

Finally, the word appeared on the screen. "DNA Accepted - Welcome, Dr. Schneider," and a hidden doorway in the wall next to it slid open.

Anna let go of a breath she didn't know she had been holding. "I guess DNA is DNA, and it didn't require more of a fresh sample," Anna said with relief.

"A close call, wouldn't you say, Miss Croft?" Jonas said and smiled at her as if he'd never dreamed of killing her, not even just a second ago.

Grigori led the way with Jonas following and Anna at the rear, just as Marcus appeared by them. Most of him was covered in blood except for his hands, which looked much cleaner, and Anna knew exactly how he had cleaned them.

The four of them entered a corridor with white painted walls, lined with several doors, and as they passed each of the small rooms, they could see medical equipment inside. The rooms looked more like small surgical theatres than anything else. Each one was empty, and at the end of the corridor they found an office filled with computers and monitoring screens showing all of the empty medical rooms, which were all brightly lit. But there was one screen on which there was nothing but darkness.

Intrigued, Jonas sat down at the desk and began to type in instructions on the keyboard, his fingers working quickly, and he was able to manipulate the surveillance software until he found what he was looking for. The dark screen burst into life as the lights turned on in the once darkened room. It looked to be a large cement bunker with no windows, bare walls and without any furniture in it. In fact, the only things that were in the room were eight bodies, dressed in hospital robes, lying huddled on the floor in the middle of the room.

Anna stared at the screen, wondering if they were all dead.

A few seconds after the room light came on, some of the bodies twitched. Others didn't move at all, but one person stood and walked over, with some difficulty, to look up at the camera, which must have been high up in a corner of the room. The woman's face peered into the camera as Jonas stared back at her.

Anna looked at the woman's pale Chameleon aura, which meant she was very weak and had not fed in a long time. She noticed a steel collar around their necks, which had a red flashing light which had begun to make a loud beeping sound. the room must have had a microphone in it, as the noise leapt out of the desk speakers. The woman prisoner covered her ears in distress and stepped away from the camera, she staggered back into the middle of the room and laid down on the floor with the rest of the room's occupants, as if it was something she was trained to do, like an animal. The beeping stopped and the red light on her collar switched off.

The woman stayed where she was and tried to hide herself in the group of bodies. They all huddled together, trying to hide, but there was just no way to do it. They were utterly terrified and showed signs of having lived through a terrible ordeal.

Anna felt righteous anger flow through her body as she looked at her kind in such a distressing situation. She had no clue who or what she was looking at. She turned to Jonas whose face showed pure shock, as if he also knew no more than she did at that moment.

"Why are our kind being held captive here? Who would do such a thing? They look like beaten, scared animals," Anna said, whilst not truly understanding what she was seeing, her brain horrified by the sight.

"It's an untold secret," he said. His voice sounded like it was being squeezed by his throat and that was all he managed to say as he just sat and stared at the monitor.

Anna looked at Jonas and was very disturbed by what she saw in his face.

It was now his turn to look truly horrified.

DISCOVERY

I cried out in horror, "Mum! Mum? Are you okay?" I rushed by her side as she sat there in the snow, looking dazed and confused since her experiment with Joshua and the evergreen tree.

"Caroline, how do you feel?" Daniel said as he knelt in the snow next to her.

"God, I'm sorry Mum. I never thought it could hurt you. Of course it could! What was I thinking?" I glanced at Joshua who was still standing, touching the tree. His face showed such horror that you would think he had just accidentally killed his own mother. I looked away, angry at him for listening to me. "Mum, say something."

Mum blinked and seemed to slowly come back to herself. "I'm okay, I think, give me a minute," she said and closed her eyes. I sat down next to her and took her gloved hand in mine.

"Let's all give Caroline a minute, and in the

meantime, we should finish getting this tree down," Helena said, taking the focus off of us on purpose.

"Well, that... was... different," Mum said, after a couple of minutes, and seemed to be feeling more like herself.

"I'm sorry I hurt you," Joshua said. He had moved away from the tree and stood apart from everyone else.

Although the others watched as Daniel finished chopping the tree down, I knew they were all listening for what my mum would say next.

"I'm not hurt, Joshua," she said.

"But are you okay, Mum," I said.

"Yes, yes, I'm fine, don't worry. It was just a bit of a shock, and I need to process it all," she said, and shakily climbed to her feet, still holding my hand.

"Why don't we all head back in and have a nice mug of hot chocolate to warm us up, and when Caroline feels like talking about it, she can," Helena said.

Michael and Daniel carried the tree and everyone began walking past us, back towards the cottage.

"Thank you," Mum said to Helena as she passed by.

Helena nodded and smiled reassuringly.

We began to slowly walk behind the main group and I could feel Mum was still feeling a bit wobbly. "Do you want me to carry you? I can easily, you know?"

"Don't be silly, I'm fine. I'm just reeling a bit... that was quite something," she said as we walked along.

She remained more quiet than usual and I stayed by her side. I wanted for her to know that she was safe and that I was there for her. We let the rest of the group who walked faster than us go on ahead as mum seemed to want some alone time.

By the time we had arrived back at the cottage, everyone else was settled in the lounge with hot drinks in front of them, and the tree was in a large terracotta pot next to the fireplace, surrounded by several cardboard boxes.

"We saved a spot for you both on the sofa and there's a mug of hot chocy waiting for each of you." Moira said as we took our boots and coats off.

"Thank you," I said as we walked over to the sofa and sat down.

"Thanks," Mum said.

"How are you feeling, Caroline?" Michael asked, his face showing concern.

"I'm fine. Honestly everyone, I'm good," she said, and began sipping her hot chocolate.

"May I ask, what you felt?" Daniel said.

"Well... it's hard to describe. Um... there was a rush, like when you've had too much sugar or caffeine, and then a sort of tingling and a goosebumps sensation all over, and then a strange taste, sort of like when you accidentally get soil in your mouth, kind of mixed with the smell of green if that makes sense," she said, and took another sip of the chocolate as if to take the taste away. "But then... then... it really hit me and it was like running into a brick wall, but instead of hurting, it made my mind incredibly clear, and yet it felt like it processed a million thoughts at once. I can now remember where I lost a ring of Kate's Grandma's, and I remember my old bank account numbers and the name of my dog when I was two, and... and... so many things, more than I can say. It was a wonderful feeling, if a little scary at first, but wonderful in a strangely euphoric, energetic and overwhelming way. Sorry, did I just ramble on?" she said and looked around embarrassed.

"No, no, it's fine, my dear," Daniel said.

"You just experienced a small amount of what we feel every time we feed," Michael said and sat, looking at her.

I saw his eyes on my mum, and I didn't like it, not one bit.

"Is that what it feels like when you feed on a tree, Kate?" Mum said.

Her words pulled me away from looking at Michael. "Yes, only it is more uplifting and happy, but for the rest yes, yes it is," I said.

"Wow, really? That's pretty amazing," Mum said, and sat further back into the sofa with her mug in hand.

"Yup, now you know," I said, and sat back next

to her. It was nice to be able to show Mum what it was like for me, even in this small way.

"How utterly extraordinary, I do believe you are the first human to experience a feeding from our point of view," Daniel said to Caroline and then looked at Joshua. "You, my son, have a very impressive gift."

"It doesn't feel impressive. I could have hurt her," he said, and slumped into an empty chair with the expression of a moody child on his face.

"Well, you didn't hurt me, so don't worry about it," Mum said firmly.

Joshua didn't reply, and didn't look convinced.

"All right then, I think it's time," Helena said. "In these boxes are our holiday decorations for the tree, the fireplace, the two staircases and doors, and, of course, this room. Who wants to do the staircases?"

Helena smiled as she handed out the decorating assignments and everyone pitched in. As the honoured guests this year, mum and I got to do the tree. I was really pleased we got the tree, as I'd always loved decorating ours at home with Mum. We set about it with enthusiasm. Some of their ornaments were seriously old, and we were very careful. Others looked brand new, and as we wrapped the tree in lights, tinsel and baubles, we listened to the music of Bing Crosby. The worries of the outside world just faded away, and by the time we had finished the tree, the entire house was decorated in an enchanting and elegant manner. Looking around, it gave me a wonderful feeling of happiness to be here and sharing this with my friends and my mum. Even Joshua had regained his usual happy attitude and was fooling around with his brother.

The next few glorious days were spent playing games, drinking and eating traditional Yuletide foods, as well as going for walks around the property in the wonderfully crunchy and brilliant white snow. I had never experienced so much snow, and I was like a child again playing in it. At one point we all joined in a massive snowball fight, which ended with us all wet and laughing.

As we ate our way through the usual holiday fare, I felt it was strange to be eating and drinking again, as if I were a human, but as we were all doing it, it was kind of nice to enjoy the full party atmosphere, something I'd thought I'd lost with my new life. How wrong I was.

By Christmas Eve, the group had become a close-knit family, full of cheeky banter and laughter. On this day, the lake was frozen enough for us all to skate on, and although Mum and I had never done it, there was lots of help and advice called out to us as we wobbled and slipped our way along. For some reason, skating made me squeal, and I laughed with delight. I loved it, and being surrounded by woodland, the lake and the cold crisp air with the beautiful cloudless blue sky just made the experience all the more wonderful for me. I was completely enchanted with Canada. However, in all this happiness, my only concern was that Michael continued to watch my mum, like an animal stalking its prey, and it unnerved me to the point that I barely left her side.

When we eventually came back inside from skating for most of the afternoon on the lake, Mum offered to make a warm drink, and everyone settled in the lounge in front of the fire as she headed toward the kitchen.

"I'm enjoying the feeling of the cold on my skin and wrapping up warm, it reminds me of the winters back home." Michael said as he used the fire to warm his hands.

"Yes, I'm glad we all agreed to it, it makes it all the more special somehow, doesn't it?" Moira said as she rubbed her hands together too.

I went over and sat with Joshua and snuggled up next to him.

"You did pretty well out there, considering you've never skated before," he said.

"Thanks," I said as he wrapped his arm around me. I looked across the room to where Tara and Wil were doing the same thing in an over-sized chair. They looked happy together and I was glad to see it, considering Joshua and I helped them to finally admit their feelings for each other, and, by extension, helped them get together.

I bet it still makes Michael uncomfortable

though. I thought to myself and looked around at him to see if he was watching them again, but his seat was empty and he was nowhere to be seen.

"Shit! Mum!" I leapt up, raced out of the room and flew into the kitchen, convinced I would find him feeding on her, and I was right. There he was holding her against the counter, draining her energy as he held her. I blurred across the room, grabbed him and, with all my new strength, pulled him off her and threw him against the wall of ceramic plates and bowls. With a huge crash he landed on them and the shelves collapsed off the wall. I stood in front of my mum ready for his return attack.

"What the hell?" Mum said as she began to move away.

"Stay there, he was feeding on you... he's a Feeder, he feeds on humans," I said through gritted teeth, so angry was I that my teeth squeaked as I forced them together. My focus was so intense that I could only glare at him as he scrambled to his feet and began to speak. My rage deafened me and I rushed at him, throwing him against the wall once again.

"Stop! Please stop, Kate." Mum was shouting.

I could hear her, but the words didn't seem to register as I grabbed for Michael's throat to squeeze the life out of him. He grabbed my arms and pinned them to my sides, his strength far greater than mine, and I was held fast. The blood rushed in my ears as rage took complete control of me.

"Kate. KATE!" he said to my face.

At long last, my eyes looked at his mouth and I could focus on his words.

"Breathe, slow your heart rate. Calm down," he said.

"You were feeding on my mother, you bastard. You promised she would be safe. I knew this would happen, I knew it!" I roared at him.

"Kate, stop," Mum said as she stood beside me and placed a hand on my shoulder. "It's all right."

"How can it be alright, he was going to kill you."

"No, I wasn't. I don't kill humans," Michael said indignantly.

"Yes, you were: I saw you draining her," I said, and struggled in his grasp.

"Kate, I think you have this all wrong," Helena said from somewhere near me.

I hadn't even seen her arrive in the kitchen but it made no difference.

"No, I haven't got it wrong. You weren't here, you didn't see him," I said to her.

"Yes, you have, Kate. Michael wasn't draining me... he was kissing me," she said.

"What?" I looked at her utterly astonished.

"We were kissing," Mum said.

The fight suddenly went out of me as if I were deflating like a balloon.

"Michael, you can let go of her now," Mum said, placing a gentle hand on his arm.

Michael looked at her and did as he was bid, stepping back a little to put distance between us.

"You were... kissing... I... oh." I looked from my mum to Michael and back again. "I didn't know you two were..."

"Neither did we, until just then," Mum said, and blushed.

"Oh God, I'm sorry. I just presumed... I... wait, so that's why you kept looking at her?" I said, realising the depth of my mistake.

"You were looking at me?" Mum said to him with an excited, shy smile on her face.

"Yes, I find you most beautiful and profoundly interesting," Michael said unflinchingly, in his usual forthright manner, as if he hadn't just been thrown across the room.

"Oh, thank you." Mum blushed again.

"Well, that was one hell of a first kiss," Wil said from the doorway.

"Indeed," Michael said. "I'm sorry I worried you, but I did give you my word she was safe, and my word is my bond. It would be a dishonour to break my bond."

I was embarrassed by my overreaction and outburst. I looked away from him and noticed the chaos I'd caused in the kitchen; there were broken shelves and shattered serving plates and bowls everywhere.

"Oh, Helena, I'm so sorry about your kitchen. I will clean it up and pay for the damages," I said, hoping it wouldn't cost more than my meagre bank account could afford. Even if it didn't, I would get a job to pay for it somehow.

"Don't be ridiculous, Kate. It's just a few plates and bowls, which are easily replaced and a couple of shelves. Nothing, in the grand scheme of things. Remember, I have two teenage boys and they make far bigger messes. Don't worry about it at all, we'll soon have this cleaned up." She smiled reassuringly.

"That's kind of you to say, but I still feel bad."

I spent the next ten minutes hiding my embarrassment by sweeping up the broken pieces, while Daniel took the broken shelves outside. Soon the kitchen was relatively tidy again, but I still felt guilty. Not only for the damage but also towards Michael. I had seriously done him a disservice, and I knew I had hurt our friendship. The problem was, I didn't know how to mend it and make everything right again. Adding to that the complication that my mum seemed to be dating him now. I sighed, wishing I could take it all back. Despite being of a supposed "superior race", I still made stupid blunders.

It took a while, but eventually everyone got back into the Christmas spirit, including Mum, Michael and I. Although, conversations between Michael and I were a little strained.

"How are you doing?" Joshua said as he sat by me on the floor in front of the fire, where I was setting up a game of chess.

"Okay, I guess. Feel like a fool though. How could I not see he was interested in her but not in her energy?" I sighed again as I placed the white pieces on the board.

"Don't worry about it, no one was hurt, and I did tell you he wouldn't do it," he said as he set up the black pieces.

I ignored his annoying, "I told you so" comment and concentrated on the pieces in my hand.

"Michael seems hurt by it though. He's mad with me, and that's sad because we always got on well together before this."

"He's not mad, it's just that honour to a Viking is a very important thing."

"He's a Viking? I thought he was Irish, with a name like Michael Conway," I said, amazed.

"Oh, yeah. His real name is Mikkel Sigtryggsson I think I pronounced that right, and he is from Denmark. Apparently he started using the Conway alias a couple of hundred years ago. At least that's what my mother says. Not sure why he changed his name though."

"Oh, how old is he, do you know?" I said, as I looked across the room at him. He was sitting on one end of a sofa, reading.

"I think Tara said he evolved in the 9th century, but I'm not sure."

"Wow, is he the oldest Chameleon here?"

"Yup, and I know he likes playing chess. Perhaps

you should ask him to play with you?" Joshua said, and stood back up.

"Perhaps," I said, and watched Joshua walk away.

I took a deep breath and decided to take his advice. "Michael? Fancy a game of chess with me?" I called across the room.

He lowered his book and looked at me as if making his mind up.

Finally, closing it, he placed it on the side table quietly and said, "Sure, I would love one." His face broke into a smile that lit up his eyes.

As we sat by the fire playing the game, we made small talk, and the conversation between us became much easier.

"How is school?" he said, as he took one of my knights.

"School is school," I said, as I took another pawn of his.

"Sounds like it's not much fun," he said, as he moved his rook.

"Things are different now," I said, and moved my last remaining knight away from his rook.

He paused with his hand over the board.

"How so?"

"Well, I don't really feel like I connect with humans anymore. Yes, with my mum and my best friend Ally, I do, but the rest, not so much."

"Try to explain it more, maybe I can help you," he said, as he moved his rook dangerously close to my king.

"Check," he said.

I was forced to move my king away to safety. "I'm not sure I can. It just seems that everything I wanted before I evolved and that I thought was so important, is no longer relevant or important to me anymore."

"Ah, I see," he said, as he considered his next move.

"You do?" I was a little surprised, I wasn't sure if he had understood what I was feeling and he was the first person I'd mentioned it to. I had no clue if other Chameleons had ever experienced that feeling too.

Michael stopped playing for a moment and looked directly at me.

"You are different now, and life is much more than you ever dreamt it would be. You will now live for hundreds, if not thousands of years and, unfortunately, humans and all human things are nothing but wisps of mist on an early morn, soon gone when the day wears on."

"Yes, exactly." I looked at him with new eyes. He understood as if he had been there, but then I thought of my very human mum and the thought made me sad as I realised our time together would be way too short.

"You need to make a decision," he said as he moved a Bishop to block mine.

"Oh? I do?" I said, my mind coming back to our

conversation, and I looked at the board, thinking that he was talking about the game.

"You must decide if being in school, learning human things, is what you wish for now. You may wish to travel, learning about other cultures, since you can always return to school in ten years or a hundred. Many more opportunities are open to you now," he said and moved his rook into place. "Checkmate."

"Oh, damn it. I thought I had you then."

"Perhaps another?" he said and smiled.

It was a smile that lit up his face and made me feel forgiven.

"Not now, thanks, but perhaps later? I know I have a lot to think about."

"All right, thank you for the game," he said, and returned to the sofa and his book.

I sat and looked down at the board, not really seeing it, and realised I had worried so much about going back to school as a Chameleon, I had never thought about not actually going back at all. The more I thought about it, and whatever else I could now be doing with my life, the more I realised what I really wanted, and I made a decision. I was not going to go back to school after the holidays. There was just too much other stuff to see and do in the world, now that I had so much more time to do it all.

A great peace washed over me as I was finally able to accept my new truth, and to let go of that part of my old human life. I hadn't realised it had been bothering me so much, and for the first time since I'd become a Chameleon, I was truly and deeply happy.

EMISSARY

As I'd promised myself that I would try to sleep in the wonderful bed in my room, Christmas Eve night seemed an appropriate time to do it. I closed the door and climbed in, and I was brutally reminded of how cold sheets really were in winter, when you first climb into a bed. I had not slept a full night since I'd become a Chameleon over a month ago, and wondered if I could still actually do it. As I lay there, enjoying the sublime softness and thickness of the covers while waiting for the bed to warm up, my mind wandered back to the conversation I'd had with my mum just before I came to bed.

She had certainly been surprised that I no longer wanted to be in school, as when I was human it had been all I'd cared about. She soon came to understand that now, with my life being so much longer, I could go in a hundred years and still appear the same age as any of the other students.

For now though, I wanted to discover the world. She had initially liked that idea, until we talked about finances and I told her I would have to work my way around the world, at least until I could make a proper income. Then, she became a bit worried about my safety as I travelled around, but soon realised that my Chameleon abilities would keep me much safer than any other teenage girl travelling with friends.

We had also, if briefly, talked about the incident with Michael. Thankfully, she had forgiven my outburst and completely understood. I was so happy I could talk to her about such things and that she could now know everything. I also truly think she was proud of me defending her. Anyway, this conversation led onto the subject of her and Michael dating, and she told me it was just very new, and although they were greatly attracted to each other, they were so different that she didn't really know what would come of it, if anything. She said she was just happy to take it one day at a time.

I laid there in my extremely comfy bed with my brain whizzing on a hundred different things, and I knew I would never fall asleep like this, even if I had still been human. I concentrated on clearing my mind, and a quiet peace settled over me. I relaxed into it, intent on enjoying every single moment. I then thought about sleep, about letting go and slipping into that wonderful, dream-filled unconscious state.

I was standing in a hot land, the ground completely dry beneath my bare feet, and it was all cracked, as if it hadn't rained in months. I looked around me and saw that I was standing on an arid flatland, which stretched for miles in every direction, occasionally there were bushes and wiry looking acacia trees, but it was mostly dry grassland or bare earth.

It was very early in the morning. The glorious sun had just risen above the horizon, but it was already hot, and the even hotter wind brushed against my skin and began to make me sweat. I remembered that I had been in bed and must have fallen asleep. I guessed I was dreaming, but it felt nothing like any dream I'd had before. For a start, even though I knew it was a dream, it also felt real, as if I'd been transported to this odd land by some strange magic.

"Ello," A soft voice said from behind me.

I spun round to find a pretty black girl looking at me. She looked about my age and was wearing a lovely flowery sundress and had a white flower in her wonderfully curly hair. She stood only ten feet away from me and she was clasping her hands in front of her as she waited for my reply.

"Hi," I said. "Who are you? Where am I?"

"I am Ramla, I been waitin' on you," she said in a deeply accented voice.

"You have?" I said, but deep down I realised I knew that she had been. It was a very odd feeling to *know something you didn't realise you knew.*

"Come, sit under boom. Drink, you is hot," she said as she spread her hand out towards a tree where there was an old log and bottle of water.

"Boom?" I said, looking from her to the tree.

"'Tis what we call this," she said, and pointed at the tree. Slowly she walked over to the log and sat down on one end of it, leaving enough room for me.

The breeze stirred the dry earth between me and the tree and made it move about in dust devils, little tornadoes that swirled past my bare feet, leaving them slightly coloured by the fine dust. I looked down at myself and I was standing only in the long t-shirt that I'd used to sleep in.

My skin was beginning to prickle, and I felt sweat trickle down my spine from the growing heat. I knew I really needed to get in the shade and drink some of that water, but what did this girl want? Why was she in my dream? If it was a dream, somehow it didn't feel like one, but I couldn't work out why it didn't. I tried not to think too much about it as I began to get a headache. At last, I decided to find out more from her and I followed her over to the tree and sat in the wonderful cool shade of the Acacia.

"Ah...that's much better, that sun is so hot and that hot wind, I feel like I'm cooking," I said and looked at her. "So 'boom' is a tree?"

"Ja," she said and nodded. "Tree." She picked up the bottle of water and held it out to me.

I reached my hand out and took the bottle she

offered. Opening it, I drank greedily. The water was cool and refreshing. It seemed to put out the imaginary fire that was burning my skin. Having had my fill, I put the bottle down on the parched earth at my feet. I noticed, however, that it was still full, even though I had drunk so deeply from it.

How odd. I thought to myself.

"Better now?" Ramla said.

"Much, thank you. Where are we?"

"Somewhere and nowhere," she said.

"Oh." I looked out and the sun seemed to be rising faster than it should have been. "Why are we here?"

"I need speak. You must find me, help me die," she said simply, as if her words were nothing more than idle conversation.

"What?" I said as I turned to look at her, startled by her words.

"Come to me and free me," she said.

Her lovely brown eyes looked directly in mine, and I could see a reflection of me in them. As I peered deeper, the image became clearer and expanded, until there was no more savanna, or a pretty girl in the shade under a tree, just a white hospital room with her lying there, connected to machines, looking like she was asleep. I stared down at her small, frail body, lost in the big hospital bed, and I had an overwhelming feeling that something evil and deadly was creeping up on me. I spun round, but there was nothing behind me. Still the fear built and it felt like something from another dimension was trying to reach through and grab me so it could rip me apart slowly until I died of agony.

I sat bolt upright in bed, sweating and panting, as if something fearful was actually chasing me.

"Holy crap!" I said out loud as air rushed into my lungs. "What the hell was that?

There came a great noise, and my bedroom door burst open and banged against the wall as Joshua rushed in.

"Are you okay?" he said, and looked around the room, panicked.

He was quickly followed by Daniel, Michael and Wil. Helena, Moira and my mum rushed in behind them, and Mum pushed her way to the front.

"Is everything alright, Kate?" Mum looked as bewildered as I felt.

"Erm... yes. Why are you all in here?" I said, feeling very confused.

"You were screaming. I thought someone had got in and they were trying to kill you," Joshua said as he sat on the bed next to me, relieved.

"Seriously?" I looked at him.

"You were screaming a lot, my dear," Daniel said.

"I had a bad dream, that's all. No need to worry," I said, feeling a bit guilty that they had all run to my aid just for a nightmare.

"Have you had them before?" Helena asked.

"No. Actually, this is the first time I've slept

since I evolved. I couldn't resist this comfy bed," I said shyly.

"Well, if you are sure you are okay, then we will all leave you be," Helena said, the atmosphere of the room beginning to change, as everyone relaxed.

Most of them filed out of my room, except for Mum and Joshua, who lingered for a while.

"Are you sure you're alright, love?" Mum said, looking worried.

"I'm fine, I promise. Go back to sleep, Mum."

"Okay, if you're sure," she said, and headed back to her room, too.

"What were you dreaming about that was so bad?" Joshua said as he got comfy. It seemed he was not leaving any time soon.

"It was so weird. It felt so real... and yet, it couldn't have been. I'm not sure if I'll ever dare to sleep again," I said, propping myself up on my pillows.

"Tell me all about it, maybe it will help to make it go away," he said hopefully.

As I sat and told him everything about the dream, I watched his face react to the various details. He too was intrigued, and thought it very odd.

"I remember when I used to dream when I was little, I always dreamt something dark and nasty was coming for me, but they were just dreams and nothing to worry about," he said.

"Have you had dreams since you evolved? I

mean, do you sleep and have dreams now?" I said.

"I rarely sleep, but when I do, I don't dream. I just kind of shut down."

"Oh," I said and cuddled into him.

We sat and cuddled for a while, and I knew I didn't want to return to sleep. I had a fearful dread that the thing, man or whatever it was that was trying to get me would come back the moment I closed my eyes. My sleep experiment had not gone well, and I was in no mood to try it again.

"Everyone's in the lounge, except for your mum, of course, why don't we go and see what they're doing?" he said, as if he knew I was not going back to sleep tonight.

"Sure," I said, and began to climb out of bed. "That's a very comfy bed," as I threw the cover back over and sloppily made the bed.

"Yeah, mine is too."

"How do you know if you don't sleep?" I said, raising an eyebrow.

"Well, I used to. Remember it was only last year that I evolved, and I was also just laying on it, reading." He grinned.

His lovely smile made me relax a little as we walked out of my room, headed downstairs to the others, and the dream faded to the back of my mind.

Everyone was sitting around the tree and the roaring fire, talking and laughing. I glanced at the clock on the mantelpiece and saw it read 2:56am.

"Happy Christmas everyone," I said and grinned. They all replied in kind, as Joshua and I shared one of the oversized chairs.

"You all right now?" Moira said.

"Oh, yes... it was just a weird dream," I said.

"That's odd, I don't think I've ever dreamt since I evolved. Have any of you?" She asked and looked around the room.

There was a stunned silence.

"Actually, no. I haven't," Tara said.

"Me neither," Wil said.

I looked at Michael, and he shook his head, then I turned to Helena.

"No, I just sort of turn off."

"Oh," I said, and wondered if Daniel had had any, or if I was the only one here who did. I looked around for him but he wasn't in the room. "Where's your father, maybe he has?" I said to Joshua.

Joshua shrugged.

"I can tell you he doesn't, and he's in his study. He had to take a telephone call. I'm sure he will be back soon," Helena said and frowned. "Perhaps you get the dreams because before you evolved you were getting those visions."

"Visions?" Daniel said as he walked back into the room mid-conversation, and sat down.

"We were talking about Kate's dream. It appears she can still dream since she evolved, and we were speculating that perhaps it was because she had visions before she did." Helena said.

"It turns out that no one else here has had any dreams since evolving," Moira said. "It never occurred to me that we could anymore."

"Perhaps, it is just for those with the special gift of sight," Tara said.

I could feel myself blushing and stopped my body from reacting. For someone who once wanted to be an actress more than anything, it was a shock to realise that I actually hated being the centre of attention.

"How fascinating indeed. Do tell us what you saw, Kate," Daniel said.

I cringed. I didn't fancy the entire room knowing how odd my mind was and how it was able to create such a weird dream.

"There will be plenty of time for that later, husband," Helena said, looking directly at me.

I got the distinct feeling that she knew I wasn't comfortable with sharing it right now.

"Who was on the telephone, Daniel?" she said.

"Oh, yes. It was KC. There is something going on in Toronto, and he wondered if we had heard about it. Apparently, a building on the outskirts of the city had some trouble a couple of nights ago. Some sort of private security company. Anyway many humans are dead from what was described by the local press as vicious animal attacks."

"In Toronto?" Wil said, looking shocked.

"Exactly, the story just doesn't work does it? He will investigate and get back to me, once he knows more of the details."

***

Christmas Day came and went in a flurry of presents, food, games and a good helping of wine and laughter. I'm pleased to say I never once thought about my dad and how bad Christmas was last year. I hoped with all my heart that Mum didn't think of it either. I had been watching her and Michael for most of the day, and they both seemed very happy. He seemed to have the knack of making her laugh to the point of tears and aching ribs, and she was able to make him smile almost the entire day. It was so great to see her enjoying herself and having fun like this.

The day after Boxing Day, Daniel got another call from the same person, this KC, and he gathered us all together in the lounge to tell us the news.

"From what KC said, he has discovered a lot more about those animal attacks. Apparently it was an attack by Chameleons on a human owned and run building. They slaughtered everyone within the building in a most heinous way, hence the description of the animal attacks. It was obviously the work of a group of Bleeders. Although the official line is that of the animal story and that nothing was taken, I understand the truth is that it was a secret laboratory which was broken into, and vital secrets were removed from the premises."

"Oh my God," Tara said.

"Fanden!" Michael said.

I wasn't sure what that meant but it sounded like a Danish swear word to me.

"Dear lord," My mum said, horrified.

She looked shocked and pale. I remembered she had not been exposed to the ugly side of Chameleon society yet and didn't really know how gruesome the details could get.

"There's more."

Daniel and the room became quiet again.

"They wiped all the internal data off the cameras, but KC found one on another building that got a brief glimpse of the perpetrators as they left. That is, before they blurred with speed and disappeared. I'm sorry to tell you all, but it was Jonas, Grigori, Marcus and a whole bunch of other Chameleons."

A huge gasp went round the room and several more swear words uttered.

Then, silence fell.

"Fanden og lort!" Michael said, shaking his head.

"*The* Jonas? The one you told me about? The one who pretended to be Nathan and befriended us just to try to kill my daughter... twice? That Jonas?" Mum said, looking more than a little worried.

"Yes, my dear, I am afraid so," Daniel said.

"I thought he'd gone, he vanished, or something, after his failed attack on the Council in Croatia," Mum said.

"We all hoped that was the case, Caroline," Helena said. "But no one was sure what had happened to him since. I guessed it would just be a matter of time before he raised his ugly head above water again."

"Are we in danger again? Is Kate in danger?" Mum said, her voice rising at the end of the sentence as the fear built within her.

I could hear her heart rate increase, as could everyone else in the room.

"There is no reason to think he's still interested in any of us," Moira said.

"What about revenge?" Wil said.

"Shut the fuck up, Wil!" Joshua said to his brother, his fists clenched in anger.

"Language, Joshua," Daniel said firmly.

"Joshua!" Helena said.

"Sorry, but that was a stupid thing for him to say in front of Kate and her mum."

"Well, it's possible, isn't it? Let's face it, Joshua and Kate are some of the reasons why he failed to take over the Council," Wil said.

"Perhaps, but he has made no move towards them since, and I would know. Anyway, he seems to be over here in Canada now, and not in England," Daniel said.

"What do you mean 'you would know'?" I said.

Everyone looked interested too, as they realised what he had said. Everyone that is, except for Helena, who just looked at her husband with a carefully expressionless face.

"I would know because I've had KC and his employees watching over Joshua, your mum and you, day and night."

Suddenly there was an uproar as everyone spoke at once. I'm not sure who was the angriest between my mum and Joshua, but neither of them appreciated the thought of being watched all the time without knowing it.

Finally, everyone calmed down and an uneasy silence fell over the room.

Personally, I liked knowing the fact that we were watched over; it made me feel much safer than I had in a long time.

"Thank you," I said. "Thank you for keeping us safe, even if it's likely he has moved on from us. I, for one, appreciate it."

Mum and Joshua looked at me as if I'd just sprouted another head.

"You are most welcome, my dear," Daniel said, and looked at least partially relieved.

Joshua and my mum both began to look shamefaced. They might not like being watched, but when they thought about it, they realised it was probably necessary, and it was kind of Daniel to hire a professional to do it.

"Who is this KC? I've never heard of them before," I said, pleased that everyone had calmed down a bit.

"KC, or rather Khalid Cham, is a private

contractor of sorts. He is a Chameleon, one who hires out his services for... a multitude of jobs," Daniel said.

I got the distinct impression that that was a nice way of saying it.

"So a private detective and mercenary all rolled into one then?" I said, thinking I understood the truth behind the careful description.

"Well, that's one way of putting it," Helena said and smirked.

"You are a very astute young lady, you know, Kate," Daniel said and stood, walked over to the fireplace and poked the fire for a few moments before turning back to face us all again. "Whatever KC describes himself as, he and his team are exceptional at what they do, and I have hired two of their more clandestine services. The first is to protect you three at all times, and the other is to investigate and root out the location, and hopefully the plans, of Jonas and his..."

"Band of merry men?" Wil said from across the room without a hint of humour.

"Exactly," Daniel said.

DELIVERANCE

Anna watched Jonas as he grabbed the arm of the dirty, cowering, Chameleon woman in front of him and ordered her to tell him everything. She was the last survivor from the raid on the building. All the others had perished, along with many of his people, as they attempted several different ways to get the collars off the captives. When they had finally managed to remove hers safely, they had left the building, bringing her along with them. The woman whimpered and sobbed, in shock from her ordeal.

"Jonas?" Anna said from across the room, "May I have a word?"

"That will be more than we're getting out of her," he said, as he roughly pushed her away from him onto the old sofa, stormed across the room to stand near Anna and leant against the wall with his arms folded.

They had returned to the bar straight after the

raid and were in the back office and storage room. Anna was the only one who had accompanied him and the hurt woman into the room. Everyone else, including Grigori and Marcus were in the bar celebrating their evening's success and swapping stories of how they killed the entire staff. Anna couldn't bear to hear their stories, and had followed Jonas and the woman into the back.

"What?" Jonas said as he stood just inches away from her.

He was a handsome, powerful Chameleon and Anna had to admit to herself that she was attracted to him, despite the horrors he inflicted on those around him.

"Maybe a softer approach would work better. Why don't you let me talk to her. She is obviously quite traumatised by her ordeal," she said.

Jonas looked back at the woman, whose Chameleon colours were faint from the lack of feeding, and she was so weak, it seemed as if she could no longer calm or heal herself.

"All right, but we need to know everything that she does. The longer that takes, the more the chance of our goal gets moved further from our grasp." Jonas looked at Anna one last time and left the room to join the others in the bar.

Anna breathed out slowly and steadily. She had no idea what Jonas' goal was, but at least she could help this woman. She walked over to the broken woman and sat down beside her. Lifting a bottle of water off the table, Anna passed it to her.

"I'm Anna, what's your name?"

"Nancy. Nancy Collier," she said as she took the water and drank it down greedily, as if someone would steal it from her at any moment.

"Hi, Nancy. Now, take your time and tell me exactly what happened to you."

"I... we were out in a restaurant. Molly had just recently evolved. I was her sponsor, and she wanted to celebrate with human food, kind of a last farewell to it. Anyway, when we left the restaurant, a black van pulled up and... they... the humans...took us to that place," Nancy said, the haunted look of exhaustion showing on her face.

"How many of you were there?"

"Eight."

"How did they manage to overpower and take a large group of Chameleons so easily? You said they were human, right?" Anna said.

"Yes, all humans, but we were weak. I think they had drugged us or something. I couldn't focus enough to rid my body of it and they overwhelmed us."

"Oh, okay... so what happened next?" Anna said, but kept her voice calm despite being alarmed that Humans were now drugging Chameleons and kidnapping them.

"I... we... woke up in that room with the collars on. Some of us began to get our strength back and tried to escape. That was when we lost Marty and

Jake, their collars... went off...."

"I'm sorry."

"You've now seen what they can do. We had no choice but to remain in the designated area." Nancy wiped away the tears that ran down her dirty face. "They treated us like cattle."

"What did they want?"

"I don't remember. They injected us every day and it... the drug... made us weak and clouded our minds. But I know they were experimenting on us, as we were taken away one by one and everyone returned with wounds. After a while, they didn't even bother to dress the incisions they made because they knew we would heal. Even if it was slower than usual, due to the drugs, I guess."

"The ones who cut you, were they human too?"

The woman nodded and drank more water. "Please, can I feed now? It's been so long."

"Soon, you can feed soon. But first, I need a little more from you, and then you can feed as much as you like and clean up, okay?"

She nodded.

"Did you see any other Chameleons there, apart from your friends?" Anna said.

"No, just us."

"Okay, did you ever hear the Iridescent Project mentioned?"

"No. I don't know, it sounds familiar... somehow," Nancy said and rubbed her face with her hands. "I can't remember."

"Perhaps one of your group heard of it?"

"Katherine, yes, I remember now. Katherine told me..." Nancy paused and burst into tears.

"I know this is hard, you are safe now. Take your time."

"Katherine, she is my... was my... wife." Nancy angrily rubbed the tears away again, but she couldn't hold back the grief any longer. She just began to cry, deep, wrenching sobs of agony and sadness that only grief can bring.

"I'm so sorry," Anna said, and reached over to hold the woman in her arms, until the sobbing abated.

Finally, when Nancy was a little more composed, Anna sat back waiting to hear more.

"I'm sorry."

"It's ok, I understand. So tell me, what did Katherine tell you about the project?" Anna said carefully, trying to pry the information out of the woman.

"I remember, she said... she'd heard one of the doctors say that the transportation to Iridescent Project would be here on Wednesday."

"When did she hear it?" Anna could feel her excitement grow.

Was this it? Was this the break we've been looking for? she thought.

Nancy frowned, trying to remember.

"I'm not sure if it was yesterday or the day

before... everything is all muddled up and a blur."

"That's okay, you're doing great. Tell me, did she definitely hear that this week?"

"Yes, but that's all I know. Who were those bastards and what did they want from us?"

"We're not sure, but we intend to find out. Now, there is a small bathroom over there. You get yourself cleaned up and I'll see about finding you something to feed on. What are you?" Anna said as she rose from the sofa.

"A Hippie," Nancy said.

"Hmm... well, I'm sure we can get you a plant to feed on or something," Anna said, heading for the door back into the bar as Nancy slowly made her way to the washroom.

"Well?" Jonas asked, as Anna approached his usual table at the back.

Anna sat down in the chair next to him and recounted the entire conversation.

"Well done," he said to Anna and nodded at one of his followers.

The large man rose off his bar stool and went into the back room and closed the door behind him.

Anna tried really hard to not listen to the sounds of struggle coming from the back room, and then the sound of snapping bones as the man broke Nancy's neck, removing her head.

"Really? One of our own who has suffered greatly in the name of Chameleons everywhere?"

Anna said to Jonas.

"We can have no witnesses or loose ends, at least not yet. You know she was damaged beyond repair and was too weak to be trusted," he said, unfazed that he had just made someone else break the first law of Chameleon society.

Anna regulated her reaction so that it wasn't noticeable and tried hard to concentrate on what Jonas was now saying.

"Hmm... Wednesday. That's tomorrow, huh?" He leant forward and reached for his glass, which was half full of his usual looking amber liquid.

"How do we know if they're still coming? Won't the news have tipped them off that there is no one to collect... because we killed them all?" Anna said.

"We don't, but if these people are who I think they are, then they only use human crews and would never be stupid enough to believe anything the news had to say." Jonas drank down the entire contents of his glass. "We might just have a real chance here." He looked around the bar and motioned for Grigori to come to him.

"Get them ready. We leave in twenty minutes, and I want everyone here with all the equipment. I am not sure what we will be walking into. Tell Marcus to get the helicopter ready."

***

Within the hour, almost every Chameleon from

the bar was brazenly sitting in cars, vans or walking around like members of the general public outside the building they had so recently raided and created a bloodbath in. The building had no police presence nearby, but it did have the "Crime Scene - No Entry" tape across the doors. One of them removed it and went back to his surveillance position. The building looked like it did before the raid, and that was exactly what Jonas wanted.

Anna stood next to Jonas, Grigori and Marcus on the roof of the building opposite, looking down on the street, while behind them, on the roof's helipad, was the helicopter they had just arrived in.

It was a long night as they all remained in their positions, while the snow gently fell around them. Finally, at the break of dawn, an unmarked, dark-coloured van pulled up outside the building, and two humans in workman overalls climbed out.

"Do you want us to take them now?" Marcus said to Jonas.

"No, they're obviously just the transporters. They will know nothing," he said and tilted his head to one side. "Tell the others to go back to the bar; it would be better if we were the only ones following them."

Marcus dismissed everyone else with a few words whispered on the breeze so that only the Chameleons could hear them, and stood beside Jonas waiting for further instructions.

"Start the helicopter, Marcus. Get us ready to

take off at a moment's notice," Jonas said.

Marcus turned and cleared the accumulated snow off the blades and the rest of the helicopter with his bare hands. He climbed in and started the engine.

"When they don't get an answer at the door, they will check in with their boss. Hopefully, they will be told to return to base and then we will follow," Jonas said. "Grigori: watch them. We will await you in the helicopter," Jonas said, and motioned for Anna to walk ahead of him.

Grigori nodded and observed one of the two stocky men who'd climbed out of the van, and tried to get into the building. The man rang the doorbell and stood waiting for a few minutes, then he knocked loudly on the glass doors.

Anna climbed back into the helicopter next to Jonas and prepared for takeoff by fastening her safety belt and putting on her head phones with an attached microphone. "What will this all achieve? If they are only the transporters like you say?" she said.

Jonas climbed in after her, sat beside her and also prepared for take-off. He looked at her and spoke into his microphone.

"We will know several things. Firstly, where they came from. By watching that place, we will see who works there. Then we find their boss, and that person will know where the cargo was to be delivered. Then we will know where to go next. We are playing a game of chess, but at present we are making some small moves, carefully watching our opponents' reactions, waiting for them to give away their strategy."

Anna didn't say anything more, but his callousness never ceased to amaze her. He had actually categorised the massacre at the building as a small move.

What would he do for it to be called a big one? She wondered. Before she could linger any longer on that frightening thought, Grigori rushed back to the helicopter and jumped in, telling Marcus which way the van had driven off.

Soon they were in the air, flying over the city in the early morning light, following the van below. In December, the sun rises late, and rush hour in Toronto is well under way. Roads are busy at sunrise and there was fresh snow everywhere on the ground beneath them. They saw the occasional snowplough working their way around the city streets.

Anna watched as the van, which now looked small enough to be a child's toy, drove along the main roads through Toronto and alongside Lake Ontario. It didn't take long for Anna to realise the vehicle was heading for the Outer Harbour Marina. The harbour water was not fully frozen over, even now in the middle of winter. She knew that Lake Ontario rarely froze due to its depth and location. She noticed that most of the boats had been removed from the water, however, and placed in dry dock for safety against ice damage from the harbour waters.

The transporter's van pulled into the harbour car park. The two men got out and headed towards the end of the harbour to the dry docked boats and some buildings.

"There are virtually no cars down there. Land in the car park, Marcus." Jonas said as he peered out of the window.

"Yes, Boss."

With a flurry of snow, Marcus landed.

"Go back to the bar, Marcus, and watch the others. We need to be a bit more stealthy now, so I'll phone you if I need you." Jonas said, as he climbed out into the almost white-out conditions caused by the rotating blades hurling the snow off the ground.

Anna and Grigori followed him across the car park and they all went after the two men, who were quite some way ahead.

Marcus lifted off and briefly disappeared in the cloud of snow before flying off back into the city.

The two humans didn't head for any of the boats. Instead, they went into what looked like a Port Authority building, which was located at the very far end of the row.

The three Chameleons stealthily got closer to the building and listened to the conversation inside. Jonas found a spot near a window so that he could see what was happening and who was doing the talking, however, his sight was partially obscured by an old shelving rack with boxes on.

"Honest man, there was nobody there, not even the security guards. and it was all locked up. How are we supposed to get paid, when there is nothing for us to transport?" one man said.

"Yeah, Clive's right, Mr. Henry, are we still going to be paid?" the other older and more gruffly spoken man said.

"Yes, yes, gentlemen, you will still be paid for your efforts. Here, take this and be gone until I call upon you for your services once again," a cultured, English accented bald man said, as he passed over an envelope, presumably full of cash.

"Thanks, Mr. Henry. Knew we could count on you," the younger man said, and pocketed it.

The two men left the building and began walking back to their van, apparently satisfied, but completely unaware they were being watched the whole time.

Jonas indicated for everyone to stay where they were. The two men were now irrelevant and were no longer of interest to him. He watched through the grimy window as Mr. Henry pulled out his phone and sent a text, he then pulled his jacket closer around him and headed for the exit closest to the harbour.

"Grigori, I do believe we're going to need that van," Jonas said.

Without a single word, Grigori blurred with speed as he returned to the parking lot to await the arrival of the two men.

Mr. Henry, was a tall, bald figure of a man. He was dressed oddly for a meeting in a harbour warehouse, he was in suit and tie under a thin overcoat and somewhat underdressed for the weather, as if he'd had no time to dress warmly before this meeting. He walked around the building and received a text. He read it and suddenly changed direction and headed towards the parking lot.

Meanwhile, Grigori had overcome the two humans in a fraction of a second and had acquired the use of their van for Jonas' needs.

As Mr. Henry walked over to a silver BMW, Jonas and Anna calmly walked towards the parking lot, as if they were out for an early morning stroll. Once Mr. Henry had begun to drive away, they rushed to the van and climbed in, as Grigori pulled out after him. The three of them were able to sit in the front of the van, thanks to a double passenger seat, but the bodies of the two transporters in the back kept rolling over and banging against the van's sides every time they took a corner. They all knew they would have to get rid of the bodies soon, as it was just too dangerous to be driving around with them, even at this time of day.

Thankfully, Mr. Henry didn't drive that far, and soon they were on the street corner in one of the most exclusive and expensive areas in Toronto: Forest Hill South.

"We won't be able to stay here long, especially during the morning in this area. We stand out too much," Grigori said.

"You're right, of course. Take the van back to the bar and bring back Marcus, Adrian and Ephraim, in one of the cars. Anna and I will be over there in that dog park, looking like normal humans."

"But without a dog." Anna said and raised her eyebrows.

"But without a dog, yes. Don't worry, humans only see what they want to," Jonas said, and seemed completely unfazed by the thought of not having a dog in a dog park.

They walked around the park a little and found a metal bench that almost directly looked towards the house that Mr. Henry had gone into.

"Do you suppose he lives there, or is visiting?" Anna said, feeling a little nervous, sitting alone with Jonas.

"He pulled into the drive rather than parking outside on the road so that suggests a familiarity, but I cannot say for sure."

"Okay," Anna said and nodded, as she desperately searched for another topic of conversation.

Jonas stretched out his legs in front of him and crossed them at the ankles, as if he was getting comfy for a long stay on the bench.

A balding man with ear-buds who was dragging an aged golden retriever along behind him, jogged by but completely ignored them.

"See, Miss Croft, humans don't care about others. They only care about themselves and how they are perceived. They barely see each other, as they rush around in their sad little lives. I told you they would see what they wanted. They are so blind. You are lucky if a human will even glance at a stranger in a park, so sure are they that they will get hurt if they do. It's so ingrained in them not to interact with people they don't know," Jonas said.

"That's not true for all humans. Some are compassionate and care about others," Anna said, feeling he was unjustly making blanket statements.

"Perhaps, but what can they do? Their lives are over so quickly that they don't have time to make any lasting difference in the lives of others, and it's true they are only tolerated by most of us because we feed on them... I see them as the cattle they are," he said.

Anna disagreed but kept that opinion to herself.

"So... why exactly are we doing all this?" Anna said. She decided that she might as well find out as much as she could about his plans, while she had him all to herself.

"Why do we do anything? Because we choose to," he said, cryptically.

"Well, that was helpful," Anna said and laughed despite herself and her job. She was interested in what drove him to do the things he did.

Jonas looked at her as if seeing her for the first time. He was so used to his people following his orders without questioning him that he found her inquisitiveness and humour refreshing. "Have you ever been in love, Miss Croft?" he said.

Anna blinked and stared at him. It was probably the last thing she had ever expected him to say, and it took her a moment to reply.

"Yes, once, a very long time ago."

"What happened? Did the object of your affection break your heart, or did you break theirs?" he said, looking her right in the eyes.

"No, he died," she said unflinchingly, from years of practice.

"Ah, then you understand some of my dilemma."

Anna looked at him, and although she felt no wiser by their conversation, she certainly felt a hell of a lot more intrigued by it.

SIGHT

With the turn of the key, the door unlocked and was pushed open.

The house was cold and felt a bit damp. There was no cheery fireplace with a huge tree next to it. In fact, the sparse decorations made the house seem sad and lifeless.

"I'll put the heating on and the kettle," Mum said as I closed the front door behind us.

Returning to grey, damp England after enjoying the fun and beauty of Canada resonated within me like the difference between a human life and a Chameleon one. The contrast was so stark it was like watching a silent, black and white movie compared to a modern high definition 3D one. I tried not to think about it as I carried the two suitcases upstairs in one go and placed them on our respective beds. Returning downstairs, I found mum leaning against the kitchen counter rubbing her face.

"Do you want me to make the tea? You look tired," I said.

"No, it's okay, I've almost done it now. I'm making you one, I hope that's okay?" Mum said as she stretched her back.

"Yeah, sure. I guess the jet-lag is getting to you, huh?"

"Yeah, a bit. I wish I could be like you and not be bothered by it. It would make travelling so much easier," she said as she poured the boiling water into the teapot.

"It's not that it doesn't make me tired, it's just that I can control my energy better than Lights erm... than Humans... you... and it reduces the tiredness to almost nothing, but it does mean I will need to feed again soon though," I said.

Mum got out two mugs and poured in the black tea. There was no milk, as we had not had the chance to get any on the way home.

"So now you have decided not to go back to school, what are you going to tell Ally? I'm sure she will miss you terribly."

"Yeah, I know. I'm still thinking about what to say to her."

"At least you still have a week until school opens again, that gives you some time to think."

"True," I said, as I took the mug of tea that mum offered me.

"What will you do with yourself now?" she said, as she sat at the kitchen table.

"Not sure. Probably try to get a job so I can save up for a flight, then work through the summer around Europe, maybe."

"Well, that's sensible. At least you will be able to pay your own way."

"Yup."

"I will miss you though," Mum said, blowing on her tea and sipping it carefully.

"I'll miss you too."

A melancholy silence spread between us as we sat drinking our tea, wondering about the future. My phone vibrated in my pocket and I pulled it out to find a text from Joshua.

"Joshua says there has been some news on Jonas and he's coming over to tell us about it."

"Oh, right. I wonder what that could be," Mum said worriedly.

"No clue," I said and looked at her. Whenever she thought about Jonas and how he had tricked her into thinking he was a man called Nathan, befriending her to get close to me, she looked particularly sad. She had really liked him, and he was the first man to notice her since my dad had left.

"When are you seeing Michael again?" I said, hoping the change of subject would cheer her up.

"Saturday. He's coming over to pick me up and we're going somewhere special. He won't tell me where though," she said, and her eyes sparkled with excitement.

"Awesome," I said, just as there was a knock at the door.

Opening it, I was pleased to see Joshua, even though we had only parted an hour ago at the airport.

"Hey you."

"Hey," he said, grinned, and walked in.

"We're in the kitchen," I said and led the way.

Sitting at the table, having turned down a mug of tea, Joshua seemed edgy and nervous.

"What is it? What happened?" I said.

"I don't think anything has happened, it's just that my father heard from KC again."

"Ok," I said.

Mum just looked at Joshua and waited.

"Apparently, they have been able to find out some more of his businesses and they are hoping that one of them will lead them to discovering where he is."

"Still in Canada and far away from us, I hope," Mum said.

"As far as we know, yes..." Joshua shrugged.

"Is that all that you came to tell us?" Mum said.

"Not exactly." He looked at me directly. "Don't freak out because we don't know what it means yet, but he owns NosGene."

"What?" I said, unable to believe my ears.

"He owns NosGene," Joshua repeated.

"Shit. You're kidding me?" I said and was on my feet, pacing, before I even realised it.

"What's Nos Gene?" Mum said, looking from me to Joshua, frowning.

"Nostrum Genetics... that's where Ally works. That's where her internship is."

"No, it's not connected. It must be a coincidence, mustn't it?" she said.

"We have no further information. He may just have shares in it and it's nothing more than that. We simply don't know yet."

I rounded on Joshua. "Really? Do you think it's that easy? This is the devious git who pretended to be Nathan, remember?"

"I know, I know. That's why I came over, I knew you would freak out when you heard," Joshua said.

"I'm not freaking out." I said, irritated that he knew me so well.

"I have to call Ally, see if she's okay," I said, and walked away.

I rushed upstairs, closed the door and threw myself on the bed with my phone. I sat and breathed calmly for a few moments so I would not sound panicked and I dialled her number. I waited, impatiently tapping my hand on my leg.

"Hey stranger, how was Canada?" Ally said.

"Good, great actually," I said, pretending to be my normal self, not that I knew what that was any longer.

"I can't wait to hear all about it."

"That's why I'm calling actually, are you free for me to come over and fill you in?"

"No, I'm at work."

"You're at NosGene? Right now? What are you doing there? I thought you only worked on Saturdays," I said, and tried not to let the growing sense of panic show in my voice, but that was exactly how I felt.

"Normally, I do only work Saturdays, but I'm doing extra hours while we're on Christmas holidays."

"Oh, erm... What time do you finish?"

"Wow, you must have a lot to tell me. Sadly, tonight I finish at 7pm and Gran is coming to pick me up and take me out for dinner afterwards. Can you come over tomorrow?" she said.

"Yeah, I can do that," I said and tried not to sound too disappointed.

"Great, I can hear all about your Canadian adventure then," she said, sounding happy.

We said our goodbyes and hung up. Frustrated, I threw my phone down on the bed and watched it bounce a little before coming to rest on the soft covers.

"She okay?" Joshua said from the doorway.

"Yeah, seems to be, but I know there is more to this. I just know how devious Jonas really is," I said.

"You going over to see her?"

"No, she's working at NosGene right now, but she asked me to come over tomorrow night."

"Okay," he said and sat on the sofa bed and looked at me strangely. "What?"

"What, what?" I said looking at him.

"You have that look on your face."

"What look?" I said, now looking confused.

"The 'I'm about to get in trouble' look. What are you up t   o?"

"What if..."

"Yes?" he said with a raised eyebrow.

"What if we go to NosGene and check it out?" I said.

"Are you serious? It's a private research facility, how the hell do you think we will get in? Never mind that it would be stupid and dangerous."

"No, think about it. We have just found out he owns it, yes?"

Joshua nodded.

"And, we know Jonas is in Canada at present."

"He may still be. What if he has found out that we know he owns it? If you see what I mean."

"Then it's even more reason to go right now and check it out, because if he knows we know then he will get there fast and remove anything he doesn't want us to see," I said.

"That's only if there is anything there and if he has not returned already."

"Worth a try though, and we might never get another chance. We may have him unawares and at a disadvantage for a change."

"Maybe... but we would have to go now," he said.

"Exactly," I said, with hope in my eyes.

"We should get the others," he said.

"We don't know if we will find anything yet. We can call them if we do. I don't fancy looking like an idiot if I'm wrong about this."

"But it could be dangerous," he said.

"C'mon, what's the point of being a Chameleon and having these gifts if we don't use them?"

***

Standing outside of the dark building at midnight, Joshua and I had waited hours for the last person to leave. The only people we thought were left in the building were the four security guards. We quietly walked around the building to the back entrance while carefully avoiding all the security cameras.

"What now?" Joshua said. "How are we going to get in?"

I pointed to the ledge twenty feet above us and grinned at him and said, "Time to fly, Superman."

The building was of a modern design, which would have made it stand out in the area except for the dense woods surrounding it and its distance from the nearest town. The building was mostly made of darkened glass. Every twenty feet or so, the exterior tapered into smaller sections, like tiers of a wedding cake, all the way to the top where the building pointed to the sky.

We got ourselves in position, and with one last

check around us, we ran at the building, leaping into the air and landing deftly on the first ledge. The glass was dark, and we couldn't see what was behind it, but I gently pushed on the frame and was pleased to feel it give on three sides. Except in one spot at the bottom, presumably where the handle and lock were located on the inside. I pushed slowly against the fastening, and with my increased strength, it gave way easily, and the window swung inward with a rush and the barest of sounds.

"You're too good at this," Joshua said.

"Shh," I said and grinned at him.

We climbed through it and into a normal-looking office. We tiptoed across the room and listened by the door, in case we'd aroused the security staff somehow. When there was no visible alarm going off and no sign of guards, we searched through the office, but found nothing relating to Jonas. In fact, we found no mention of him at all.

Deciding we had to try somewhere else, we went back over to the door. It seemed quiet outside of the door, and we gently opened it to reveal a floor full of office cubicles.

"I don't think we will find anything here, he will be hiding his connection to this place, so it's more likely in the higher management offices. I bet they are on the higher floors. We are going to have to go up there," Joshua said.

"What about the cameras?" I said, as I noticed one by the elevators.

"Can you do this?" he said, and shook his head until I couldn't recognise his blurred features.

"Whoa, freaky," I said, and tried.

"That's it. Well, do that every time you are in range of a camera and move fast past them so you are just a blur, okay?"

"Nice," I said. "You're pretty good at this too."

He grinned. "I have to be, if I'm going out with you," he said, and moved off towards the elevator on the right. He moved fast and kept himself a blur the entire time.

I followed his lead and soon we were in the elevator going up to the higher floors to find something, anything relating to Jonas. The lift came to a stop on the twenty-ninth out of thirty floors. The last floor could not be accessed without a pass card of some kind.

"What now?" I said, still keeping my body vibrating because of the camera in the lift.

"We can climb up out of the top of the lift, but we'll have to hurry, I'm pretty sure the guards will know that the lift moved," he said and jumped up, hitting the emergency latch on the trap door in the roof, opening it. He climbed up on top of the lift and waited for me.

I pressed the hold button on the lift panel and jumped up onto the roof of the lift. I was surprised at how dark the lift shaft was.

Didn't they always have lights on in the movies? I wondered to myself. The only light we had was from the opening in the lift below our feet. Approximately twelve feet above us was the doorway to the next floor, and, with the help of another enhanced jump, we were standing on the small ledge at the opening of the thirtieth floor. Joshua easily separated the sliding elevator doors and we stepped through.

We stood looking at the sight before us and then at each other in amazement. The view was certainly not what we had expected. In front of us was a reception desk that looked like it belonged in a hospital, and on each side were corridors full of rooms. It literally looked like a hospital wing, and not at all like an office building.

"Move!" Joshua said and shoved me towards the nearest room.

We sped into the room, which was, luckily for us, empty, as a nurse walked past and went to the desk. Sitting down she opened a file and began writing.

"What the hell is this place?" I whispered.

"Your guess is as good as mine," Joshua said.

"What do we do now?"

"I guess we wait until she leaves the desk again," he said.

"Yeah, I'd like to see if anyone is in these rooms and why they are here. Honestly, I find this all a bit creepy. I know from the movies that nothing good comes from a hospital floor hidden in a private research facility," I said and imagined all sorts of horrors. I now thought that this idea, coming here with only Joshua, might have been a mistake all along.

"We may be reading more into this than we should be. Perhaps it's a testing floor for new treatments or something."

"Yeah, just what treatments though? I'm not convinced this is a good place, not with Jonas owning it."

"Yeah, you have a point," Joshua said and listened hard. "She's moving again, and it sounds like she's walking away from us. Come on."

Joshua opened the door of the room slowly and rushed out. He moved along the corridor, away from the desk and in the opposite direction than the one the nurse went. I followed closely behind him and peaked into every door we passed. They were all empty, and I began to feel like we would never find out anything of use. Perhaps it had all been a huge waste of effort. I felt that way until we reached the last room on the left. This room had a patient asleep in the bed.

We moved into the room in silence, as the nurse walked back up the corridor. I watched out of the little window in the door to make sure she wasn't heading this way, but thankfully, she turned and sat back at her desk. I breathed out slowly and regulated my heart. This sneaking about was very exciting, but a calm mind and body was more likely to make less mistakes.

"She's asleep," Joshua whispered, his voice so low that only a Chameleon would be able to hear it anyway.

"Good. What are we doing in here?" I said.

"I want to check her medical chart to see why she is here, maybe we can find out what this is all about."

We crossed the room to the bed and, as Joshua looked at the charts at the end of the bed, I looked at the patient and I felt as if I'd been hit with a bolt of lightning. The shock of recognition throbbed through my body, making me shake and gasp.

"What's the matter?" Joshua said, and he stared at me. "You look like you've seen a ghost."

"Holy shit," I said.

"What's wrong?" Joshua looked around us for the approach of danger, expecting to see someone coming towards us, considering my reaction.

"I think I have... seen a ghost," I said, and pointed at the patient. "She is the girl from my dream, in Canada."

"What? She is? Seriously? You are sure it's her?" Joshua looked at the girl who lay asleep, with tubes and wires attached to her in many places and a machine that had a little flashing light.

"Yeah, it's her." I moved forward and looked at her young pretty face. "Definitely."

"No shit. Well, I guess you still have your visions after all then," he said.

"I guess so, but why is she here?" I said, as I

reached out my hand towards her, drawn to touch her for some reason.

"Says here she has been in a coma for the last two years." Joshua said, and put the records back in the slot, just in time to see me touch the girl.

The second my skin touched hers I was back in the savanna.

I was, once again, sitting on the log under the tree with the bottle of water in my hand.

"You came. I knew you would. I'm Ramla, do you 'member me?" she said in her deeply accented voice, and smiled sweetly at me.

"Yes. I... where are we?"

"I told you afore, we is nowhere." The girl tapped her fingers together. "Listen to me, lady, we no have long. He who is Hili wants sight from me, he comes and steals it. You must not let him. You must kill me."

"What? No, I can't do that!" I just stared at her, not believing what she had said.

"I cannot do it. I in coma. You must do it before Hili comes back."

"Who is Hilly?"

"He is evil spirit, can you banish him?" she said.

"Erm... no, I don't think so."

"Then you must kill me."

"Why? Why do you want to die?"

"I not show him what he wants. He hurts me but I am strong and I say no. Every time he hurts me, I am

weaker and soon he will see what he wants," she said.

"See what, what do you mean?" I said, confused by it all.

"I show you a thing, you need see this anyhow." The girl gripped my hand and the warmth of the savanna vanished, and the cool air of winter rushed over me as I stood next to a pool, a waterfall and a large tree. I recognised it straight away; it was where Joshua had taken me on our first proper date. It was his favourite place. The scene shifted, and we were inside the cave behind the waterfall, and, in the warm waters of the spring was Joshua, passionately kissing a blond girl.

I turned away, angry that the scene had produced tears in my eyes. "I don't want to see this." I said to Ramla.

"You need to. He will betray you, and if you don't let him, he will follow you and die."

Again the scene shifted and I saw Joshua's headless body lying on stone steps, his head next to him, and he still held a bloodied sword in his right hand.

"No!" I screamed, but it was too late, he was dead and no amount of Chameleon healing could repair him. He was gone forever. I burst into tears.

"I is sorry, you had to understand. Leave him to save him," Ramla said.

"Isn't there any other way?" I said, as I wiped my tears and tried to calm myself.

"No: live or die, choice is yours alone. Just as you must kill me, to stop worse than what is now coming."

"What is coming?" I said meekly, too shocked by her words and the images.

"He must not see my sight. He must not know. It is the only way to stop thousands of deaths."

"What?"

"Do it now. Guards coming. No time. Do it now!" Ramla said.

I was suddenly back in the hospital room holding her hand, I dropped it instantly and looked around me dazed by the vision.

"Where did you go?"

"No time to explain the guards are coming." I said and ran over to the window, breaking the lock easily, I threw it open and let the cold night air in.

"I can hear them now, but how did you already know?" he said as he rushed over to the window looking concerned and confused.

"Go, I'll explain later." I said and moved to one side as he leapt out of the window and landed safely, thirty floors below.

I could hear the footsteps, they were so near... almost at the door, and in that split second I made a decision I would have to live with for the rest of my life. I took two steps forward, reached out and, with my bare hands, I twisted and broke Ramla's all too human and fragile neck in one swift movement.

Without letting my brain think about the horror of what I'd just done and, in what seemed like a strange automatic pilot, I turned from her body and big brown staring eyes, rushed to the window, and leapt from it into the enveloping safety of the darkness below.

EXPOSE

A nna was now sitting in the rear of a car, around the corner from the house that Mr. Henry had gone into and had not left. Four of Jonas' men had arrived in two cars, and she was sitting in one of them with Jonas and Grigori in the front. Marcus and the other men were parked around the opposite corner, so when Mr. Henry left, no matter what direction he went in, one of them would be able to follow him.

They had all been there for hours and were beginning to attract notice from the neighbours. Already, a security guard of the gated community had come to the car and had asked them questions as to their purpose. He was obviously suspicious that we were there to rob somebody. However, Grigori got out of the car and talked to him face to face, and easily "persuaded" him that we were there waiting for friends to come home, and that we were nothing to worry about. In fact, Grigori told him to spread the news around the community that he had looked into us and everything was all right, and that we were welcome guests.

Grigori's powers of persuasion never failed to impress Anna, but they also frightened her. It was a very strong gift, if that's what it was, and it meant he could go anywhere and do anything that he set his mind to with no way to stop him, that sort of power should not be in his hands nor Jonas' for that matter.

Jonas' cell rang and made everyone jump.

Jonas quickly dug it out of his jeans pocket.

"Yes?" he said, pausing a moment, then barked into it. "What? What happened? Fuck!" He listened and then abruptly hung up, angry at his caller. He swore a few more times and sat staring blankly out of the window towards the house where Mr. Henry still was.

"When we have done this, we have a killer to catch," Jonas said at last to Grigori in a voice that was much too calm after the anger of a few moments before.

Of course, both Grigori and Anna had heard the entire conversation on the phone with their enhanced hearing, so they knew what he was talking about.

Anna realised, however, by listening to their bodies, that both Grigori and Jonas were still absolutely furious about the very important person who had just been murdered. She had no idea who this Ramla was. She had never even heard of the name before, that, she was definitely sure of. She wondered why she had been so important to Jonas and his right hand man. Sadly, she could find no more out without risking her life against that terrible anger, as neither one of them mentioned the incident again.

Subdued by the phone call, they all waited in the car until the afternoon slowly turned into evening, then into night, but still there was no sign of Mr. Henry. It seemed like he was never coming out.

"Time to resolve this," Jonas said, as he climbed out of the vehicle and blurred up the driveway.

Scrambling after him, Anna followed Jonas and moved towards the house with his men following behind her. They all rushed around the property in colourful blurs and disabled the house's security system and cameras. Jonas crept around the building to the back where he peered through the large, stately windows, trying to see if there was anyone else inside.

Anna kept close to Jonas and followed him everywhere. She was not going to let him out of her sights unless she had to. She desperately wanted to know what this was all about. Sticking by him seemed to be the only way, as he had given her absolutely no hint so far.

It appeared that Mr. Henry was alone. However, the house was enormous, and not all the rooms could be checked easily from the outside. It was well appointed with security measures on each entrance, and it was obviously the residence of someone wealthy who needed to protect the contents and occupants. Little use were such measures against one Chameleon, never mind a whole group of them.

Marcus, waiting for the go ahead from Jonas, stood by the door leading from the house to the rear garden. He was almost as tall as the door and as wide, with his huge, muscular frame.

Jonas nodded and everyone sprang into action. They rushed into the building from many different access points and began searching the rooms. Of course, the silent internal alarm was triggered and it flashed red lights at them all, until Ephraim, a tall Arab man, ripped the cover off the alarm box and overrode the system. The lights stopped flashing, but they all knew the security company would be on the way very soon to check on the property and its owner.

Jonas, followed by Grigori, blurred up the main staircase to find the master bedroom. Anna followed, and although she didn't know quite what was going to happen, she had a rough idea.

Mr. Henry, who had been reading in bed, was now lying face down on the floor, unconscious.

Anna doubted he even knew what had hit him. She knew a Chameleon's speed was barely registered by a human's mind, and he would, of course, not have had any chance to react, never mind fight back.

"Put him in the car and let's get back to the bar before the security company arrives," Jonas said as he blurred out of the house, leaving the others to follow in his wake.

Grigori picked up Mr. Henry and blurred out of the house, back to the car, where he dumped him on the rear seat. Anna climbed in the back with him, while Grigori got behind the wheel and drove them off into the night and back to the bar.

On the drive back, Anna looked at the unconscious man. She peered at him closely as he sat slumped against the side door, in what looked like a peaceful sleep. She knew better, though, and did not envy his fate this night. She contemplated her next move. Although she didn't want to be any part of the interrogation that was to follow, she also didn't want Jonas and his men to suspect her of any weakness, and of not being fully committed to Jonas' plans. Her own plan depended on the fact that they did all believe in her, absolutely, 100%. There could be no mistakes or she would pay with her life, and she had decided that was not going to happen, if she had any say about it.

Back at the bar, Mr. Henry was carried in to the back room and tied to a chair in the middle of it. It was the very same room where Anna had, so recently, comforted a broken soul, only to hear her being ruthlessly murdered afterwards. This time though, she did not have access to the back room and what was inevitably going to happen in there. There was a part of her that was grateful for it.

Anna had controlled her body and its responses to everything around her, so as to not reveal her true feelings, and now she sat in the seedy little bar again with a large stiff drink in her hand. She needed to hear what was happening in that back room, but she would have to do it very discreetly, and concentrated her enhanced hearing so that she could. To keep up appearances, she also pretended she was doing something on her phone and had it primed in the middle of a game of backgammon, so at least she appeared not to be listening and had covered herself if anyone came over to talk to her.

***

Jonas' looked at the unconscious human. The man's balding head was dipped low on his chest and his red check pyjamas were all askew from the kidnapping and being carried into the pub. He wondered how much this man truly knew and decided it was time to wake him up.

"Marcus?" he said.

"Yeah, Boss?" Marcus said, as he stood up from the old sofa where he had been sitting next to Grigori, and looked at Jonas.

"Wake him up," Jonas said. "It's time to do some digging. Let's see if we can find out who he works

241

for."

"Yes, Boss," Marcus said, and grabbed a full bottle of water from a crate by the door and threw the contents of it into Mr. Henry's face.

Mr. Henry opened his eyes, gasped, coughed and looked around him with wide eyes.

"What the hell is this?" he said. "How dare you take me from my home? This is outrageous!"

Jonas stepped forward and held up one hand.

"Mr. Henry, let me introduce myself..." he said.

"I know who you are." Mr. Henry said in a firm voice, which was as cold as ice.

"I see my reputation precedes me, so tell me, why is it that you know of me, and yet, I've heard absolutely nothing about you? Why is that?" Jonas said as he leaned in closely and stared at him.

"I am informed, you are not."

"Indeed, so it seems. Do you know that I could rip your heart out right this very moment without even breaking a sweat?" Jonas said with a smug smile, as he stepped back, sat down on an old chair and put his feet up on the nearby table, making the scotch that was already on it slosh around inside its glass bottle.

"I do." Mr. Henry said.

"So then, perhaps you will afford me the courtesy of answering a few questions before I actually do it."

"I will not. I will give you nothing," Mr. Henry said bravely.

"Ah... I thought you might feel that way," Jonas said and nodded to Marcus.

Marcus stepped in front of Mr. Henry and held a phone against his ear.

"Daddy? Are you there?" A weak female voice came from the ear piece.

"Kelly, is that you, my darling? Are you okay?" Mr. Henry said, horrified to hear his daughter's voice.

"I... it hurts, Daddy. Make... him... stop," the young woman said, in pain.

Marcus took the phone away and closed it, ending the call.

"What have you done to her, you bastard!" Mr. Henry said, seething with rage.

"I personally have done nothing to your daughter Kelly-Anne. She should, however, be careful with whom she talks to in the campus bar. You really shouldn't have so many photos of her in your house, especially the ones showing which campus and dorm she is in at present. One never knows who is snooping round your house when you are not looking," Jonas said, as he examined his finger nails, completely unconcerned for the man and the young woman's plight.

"What's happening to her? Please don't hurt her." Mr. Henry said, his voice sounded both pleading and defeated at the same time, as he realised his fate.

"I will not hurt her, of course, but my colleague

who is presently holding her... well, that's another matter entirely. You see, Marvin is a special kind of person, he likes what he does. So much so that it's very difficult to make him stop, unless, of course, you tell me what I want to know."

"I can't." Mr. Henry said and gritted his teeth. "They will kill me."

"Not even for your only child? My, my, what a terrible father you truly are. Oh, well. Marcus, tell Marvin to conclude our business. We shall be dealing with this problem on our end after all."

Marcus pulled out his phone, pressed the speed dial button and waited for it to connect. "Marv, the Boss says have fun."

"No! Wait!" Mr. Henry said. "I'll do whatever you want. Please, please don't hurt her."

"Cancel that order, Marv," Marcus said, hung up and stuffed his phone back in his pocket. He turned away from Mr. Henry and went to stand by the door, near Grigori, who was still sitting on the old sofa, intensely watching the events unfold.

"Now that's far more civilised, isn't it?" Jonas said, and poured himself a shot from the bottle on the table. "Now, where to begin? Ah... yes, who do you work for? Exactly."

"They will kill me," he said, but without any strength behind his words this time.

"We have been through this once, know that I will kill you and your daughter, so choose," Jonas said, beginning to feel bored.

"All right, all right... I work for the Iridescent Project."

"What is that, exactly?"

"It's a team of the best minds and scientists tasked with investigating your species."

"And just how did you know we existed?"

"We have known since the 1920's, and our members have dedicated their lives over the years since to finding out everything we can about you. We have been watching and cataloguing your kind since then."

"How intriguing. So very cloak and dagger, like some dark mystery tale, isn't it? But do tell me, human, when did you start taking my people and torturing them?" Jonas said, all sense of amusement faded from his voice, and his words were threaded with anger and steel. He swiftly took his feet off the table and leant forward to intensify the meaning behind his words.

"Torture? No, no... medical investigation only." Mr. Henry looked surprised and shocked.

"You call keeping my people as prisoners, forcing them to wear collars like animals, drugging them to sap their strength and then cutting into their bodies just to watch them heal over and over, a medical investigation?" Jonas raged and sped across the room. His hand thrust deep into Mr. Henry's chest and held his heart while it pumped erratically.

Mr. Henry cried out in agony, he spluttered as

blood began to dribble down his chin. Gasping for breath, he begged for Jonas to stop.

"Tell me now, and I will end this. Why are you doing this to my people, and who is helping you?"

"To... get a vaccine... to help... us... live... longer, to heal... and." the man said, getting weaker by the second as his life drained away with the blood that ran down his body and pooled on the old ginger carpet.

"And?" Jonas said, his face only an inch away from Mr. Henry's.

"...because... you... throw... your people... away." Mr. Henry's voice was barely a whisper.

Jonas looked extremely shocked and pulled back just a little. He frowned deeply at the man, and carefully held his heart in his hand. He waited for more information. He needed to know more, right now.

"What do you mean? Explain now!" he said.

The man was fading quickly, far too quickly.

"You are... such a... careless breed. You... disinherit and... discard... your... own and we just... make... use..." Mr. Henry said, and exhaled for the final   time.

Jonas exploded with anger at his own impatience; he knew that if only he'd held back a little he might have gotten more out of him. With one last look at Mr. Henry's face, he ripped the dead heart out of the still body and threw it against the far wall in frustration, where it hit with a wet splat and slid down onto the desk below, leaving a bloody trail.

"Fuck!" he said, as he paced around, maddened by the man's words and the lack of leads he now had.

Grigori and Marcus stared at Jonas. They knew better than to talk to him when he was in this kind of mood and waited until he spoke directly to them.

"You two, find out everything about Mr. Henry: all his business dealings, everything. Now," Jonas said, and continued to pace.

"And the girl?" Marcus said.

"Tell Marv to interrogate her on her father's life, business and friends... everything. Once he thinks he has everything he is going to get, tell him to do whatever he likes with her."

"Yes, Boss." Marcus pulled out his phone and tapped the same speed dial button for the third and final time that night.

***

Anna realised she had been clenching the glass hard enough to crack it, and she placed it back on the table. She had heard everything, of course, and she knew there was nothing she could do for the man's daughter without risking her own life: her work was far too important for that. Despite her own feelings about being here right now with the most dangerous Chameleons on the planet, she had to follow through with her promise, and she had to find out what this was all leading up to and what Jonas' master plan was.

She had made an oath and would stick to it, even though the supposed "hell and high water" she knew she would have to go through for that oath had pretty much arrived already. She ensured her poker face was intact and went about her business as one of the faithful followers, just as she was expected to be, but as always, she was gathering information and watching and waiting for her chance.

Yes, she would stay and do her job, but she swore to herself that she would do the right thing when the time came, and by right thing, she meant that she would end the life of Jonas, one way or another. Even if it was the last thing she would ever do and she knew it was very likely to be that: the last thing she did.

DISTRACTION

I looked down at my hands as I lay soaking in the bath. I had been in there so long that my skin had changed on my fingers, and the water was completely cold.

I didn't care, so I didn't alter my body to keep warm.

I had killed someone, taken their chance to live from them forever, and what was worse, it was a human. A weak, sick human.

With my bare hands.

I shuddered and dry-retched again.

All I could hear in my head were her last words as I held her head in my hands.

"Thank you," she had said in my mind, and smiled sweetly at me. Tears streaked down my face and I sobbed, my tears adding to the bath water over and over again.

Thankfully, when I'd arrived home there was a note from Mum saying that she was out with

Michael.

It was a relief to be alone; I couldn't face anyone right now.

When we had run away from the building, I had not told Joshua what I had done, and had barely spoken two words to him when he dropped me off at home. Now, after sitting and staring at the wall for two hours, my mind tried to handle what my body had done. I could calm my body's reaction, the panic and fear of such a terrible act. I could even calm my mind, but the disbelief that I had actually taken a life still remained, and I knew it would stay with me during the entirety of my very long life.

I tried to reason with myself, telling myself it was what she had wanted.

From what Ramla had told me, it was better for the world that I did it, but deep in my soul I knew it was wrong, so wrong I loathed myself for it.

I climbed out of the cold water and let my body ripple with goosebumps. What did I care? I towelled off, put on my bathrobe and went to sit on my bed to think, but all I did was stare at the wall.

Minutes passed into hours and, eventually, my mind began to work again and I made some decisions. There was something I just had to do and I could not put it off any longer. I nodded to myself as if I agreed with me, and looked at my phone on my bedside table. Grabbing it, I rang Joshua.

"Hey." He said in an unsure voice. "You okay, you didn't say much on the way home."

"Yes, I'm okay," I lied. It was just another one to add to the ever growing list.

"Listen, I just told everyone here about what we did," he said.

My heart raced: did he know? Did they all know?

"About NosGene and that weird hospital floor and the coma girl," he said.

I relaxed a little, of course he didn't know: no one did. "What did they say?" I tried to sound interested but honestly, I didn't give a damn what they said, thought or did, not any more.

"Well, at first they were mad that we did it and that we went alone, but in the end they were glad of the tip and my father phoned KC to relay the information. KC is flying out to look into the place himself."

"Okay," I said.

"You sure you're okay? You've been acting weird since we found that girl."

"Yeah. Listen, Joshua, I know this is bad by phone, but I don't think we should see each other anymore."

There was a terrible and heartbreaking moment of silence.

"What?" he said. He couldn't have sounded more shocked if he'd tried.

"I'm not happy and I don't want to see you

anymore," I said. I worked really hard to make my voice sound strong and not emotional.

"But we were fine and in Canada, that was good too. I don't understand."

"I've not felt we are right together for a while and it's over."

"I... wait."

"Sorry, Joshua. Goodbye," I said and hung up. Again the tears coursed their way down my checks but, like Ramla said, there was just no other way. I tried to console myself with this thought. If I stayed with him, he would die, and I'd seen his future with the blond girl. I knew he would live and find love again. I would just have to ignore my heart.

Anyway, I'm a heartless killer of innocents now, who needs a heart, I thought to myself, and lay on my bed, staring up at the ceiling.

I set my phone to "Do Not Disturb" and continued to lay there. However, my phone lit up as a text came in. I looked over towards it but I didn't move. I presumed it was Joshua trying to get me to talk, so I ignored it. Again it received a text and again I ignored it. By the fourth text, I leant over to switch it off and I realised all the texts were from Ally, asking me to call her.

I sat up and pressed the call button, and as I waited to connect with her, I began to worry. Was she working in a lab again? I wanted to know everything was okay with her.

"Hey, tried to text you a few times," Ally said in

an excited voice.

"Yeah, sorry, I thought you were Joshua."

"Oh, nope, I'm not, sorry. Listen, something horrible happened at work," she said.

"Oh? What happened? Are you Okay?" I tried hard not to sound panicked.

"Of course, why wouldn't I be?" she said, confused.

I realised too late I had no reason to be concerned about her. Well, none that she knew or that I could talk about. "Just making sure is all. So what happened?" I said, steering the conversation back to her news.

"We had a break-in and, from what I can work out from the TV, someone destroyed some important research," she said, sounding excited.

"Oh, do they know who it was?" I said, as my heart began to beat rapidly, and I had to concentrate to calm down and sound normal again.

"Nah, my guess is that it's some animal protesters or something. I know they have live chimps up on the eighteenth floor. I bet they were there for that."

"Oh, right, yeah, makes sense," I said, and realised, of course, that the truth wouldn't be revealed to the humans. The "important research", as they called it, which was destroyed, was in fact the murder of Ramla. The death I caused with my own bare hands. Remorse flooded through me and I missed what Ally said next. "Sorry, what did you say?"

"I said, why are you ignoring texts from Joshua? What did he do now?" Ally said.

"Nothing. I... we... broke up," I said, as I struggled with too many strong emotions at once.

"What? Why?" Ally said.

I had no reason I could share with her. "I... it's just not working," I said, hoping it would do as a reason.

"Oh, I am surprised. You sound upset, want me to come over tomorrow morning?"

"I am but, no, thanks. I'm going to town with mum tomorrow," I said and lied, again.

"All right, but ring me if you want to talk, ok?" she said.

"Yeah, thanks."

"Okay, see you at school on Monday then. Bye." Ally said and hung up.

I sat looking at the phone, I hadn't had the chance to tell her about my decision about school yet, I guessed I would have to tell her later when I was thinking a bit more clearly, if that ever happened.

***

I did not return when school started again the following week. Although Ally was shocked by my decision to leave it, and didn't really understand the feeble reason I gave her, (that I no longer wanted the career of an actress) she accepted it and we pledged to remain friends. Worried about her, I took to creeping around at night watching Ally's back when she was at work, just in case Jonas ever showed up there, although he never did.

The weeks of hating myself, and missing Joshua turned to months and, before I'd really taken much notice of the world in general, it was summer, the sun was out and all my indoor skulking-about became outside skulking-about. I was listless, bored and I had retreated into myself. My mum had tried so many things to make me come out of my shell that we argued a lot and things at home were very strained.

At least my Mum was happy dating Michael, whom she said was trying very hard to be a Hippie and not a Feeder for her, even though she had never asked him to change his feeding habits. Tara and Wil were still dating, or at least that's what her emails and copious texts ever talked about, once, that was, after she had stopped asking me if I was okay.

I knew that I would never be okay, and I had accepted that.

That, and what I'd done to Ramla, but it invaded every thought and action I took. Eventually, I conditioned myself not to think about it anymore. It was just too horrible and painful, so I closed down my emotions and just existed. I read many, many books and watched many hundreds of movies to find some sort of distraction. I'd forgotten why the month of August was so important until one Tuesday night when the phone rang.

"Hello?" Mum said as she picked up the phone from the table beside her. "Oh, yes, hi... sure, hang on." She held out the phone across the sofa. "It's for you: it's Helena."

My heart beat rapidly in my chest and I grabbed the phone. "What's happening?" I said, panicked.

"Nothing, Kate. Don't worry. Everything is fine," she said.

"Oh, okay," I said. Although, I doubted anything would be all right ever again.

Mum looked at me, surprised, and I shook my head to tell her there was nothing wrong. She nodded and returned to the book she was reading.

"I just wanted to tell you that we will be picking you up at 8am tomorrow, after we get Peter, so be ready."

"Erm... you will?" I frowned, wondering what was going on.

"Yes, we will. You didn't think that because you and Joshua are no longer together that we would decline to be your sponsors, did you?" Helena said, and her voice sounded like she felt hurt at the thought.

"Oh, no... of course not. 8am, yes, see you then," I said, as a rush of fear spread through my body.

"Great, see you tomorrow," she said.

"Yeah, bye," I said, and hung up.

"8am? What are you doing with Helena tomorrow?" Mum said, and placed her book on her knee.

"I... shit, I can't believe I forgot."

"Forgot what? What's going on, Kate?" Mum said, a look of concern now on her face.

"I have to go to Castrum Lucis tomorrow for my testing and interment," I said, and stared at her, wide-eyed as the panic, fear and terror flowed through my body at an alarming rate.

It was the most alive I'd felt in months.

***

The flight back over to Canada with Helena, Daniel and Peter was a quiet one. My mum had been panicked when I left, but at least I knew Michael was there to comfort her. She wasn't allowed to accompany me. Only the sponsors could do that, and Helena and Daniel were sponsoring both Peter and I. He was quiet too. I guess he was nervous, as he'd never been to one of these before. At least I had some experience of it from when I went to Joshua's.

I explained to Peter that as our sponsors, Daniel and Helena would present us to the Council of Nine, the senior Chameleons who ran the society with an iron fist. The Council would then take us into their care and teach us the history of our race, and then we would face our interment testing.

For most of the journey, I sat and thought about what was to come. I knew that I would be locked in a coffin, probably buried in the grounds of the castle and held there for ten days with no food or water and unable to feed on anything. I would then be released in a public place on unsuspecting humans, and if I didn't feed, I would be considered a Chameleon fit to enter their society as a successful newly evolved and I would be announced at the Evolution Ball. Just like a debutante being admitted into human society via a posh high society ball.

All the way over on their private plane, no one mentioned Joshua, not even once. I presumed they didn't know what to say; I know I didn't. They would think I was mad, if I told them I left him because of Ramla's vision. I didn't even dare to think what they would say if they knew the whole truth about Ramla.

The car from the airport drove into the night until we finally stopped in a small coastal town. The driver transferred our luggage to a small speed-boat and the four of us zoomed off into the night with Daniel driving. If I hadn't been so nervous, I would have been excited by our adventure.

My first sight of Castrum Lucis was the glow of light off in the distance. As we raced along, the lights became bigger, but it wasn't until we were much closer that I finally saw it. Sitting on a private island in the middle of a huge lake was a very old, stone castle, complete with turrets and arrow slits. It stood, majestically, a hundred feet above the water on top of a rugged stone cliff. Surrounding it were many spruce trees, and as we travelled around the island to the small harbour, I realised there was no obvious way up to the castle.

"Look at that," Peter said, his eyebrow raised in surprise.

"Wow," I said as I stared up at the intimidating building. "I didn't know that Canada had castles."

"It doesn't, usually," Helena said.

"The Council brought this 11th century castle over from France. They took it down stone by stone and rebuilt it here, exactly as it had been originally," Daniel said.

"It's a bit scary-looking."

"That's the idea," Daniel said, as he slowed the boat and brought it near the landing stage, where an old man grabbed the rope which Daniel threw, and then tied the boat to the dock.

"Don't worry, Kate. Although I am here just two nights, Daniel is staying to work in the archives for the entire time," Helena said.

"Oh, that's good. I didn't realise the archives were here," I said, looking at Daniel, then turned back to Helena. "Why are you here for only two nights?"

"That's as long as the Council will allow me to

stay apparently," she said, and looked meaningfully at her husband.

"Yes, Ramy himself requested that no one but the newly evolved and his people remain on the island until the Evolution Ball, when you are all allowed to return and celebrate the successful candidates," he said.

"Oh, I didn't know that. At least, I won't feel so alone with you here," I said.

"You aren't alone," Peter said.

"You know what I mean."

Peter nodded; he did indeed.

We climbed out of the boat, lifted out our belongings and began to walk to the end of the quay where there was a wooden boathouse and an office of some sort.

"This way," Daniel said, and led us past the buildings towards the sheer stone cliff that the castle sat on. The lower cliff walls were lit every ten feet or so, and lead to a metal door with a metal panel on the wall next to it, housing a single button.

Daniel pressed the button and looked upwards. "Look up at the camera," he said.

We looked up. A buzzer sounded, and the metal doors slid open to reveal a wood-clad lift, like something out of a five star hotel. We walked into the lift, which had no buttons, nor controls of any kind, and, within moments, the doors closed and we sped upwards. The journey was not a long one and we pulled to a stop. The doors glided open to reveal an opulent room with high stone walls, vaulted ceiling and red velvet curtains hanging at the large windows. There were tapestries and antique furniture everywhere. It seemed that although the exterior of the castle was still 11th century, the interior had been upgraded for comfort and style.

As we walked out of the lift, our footfalls echoed on the stone floor and around the walls, making them seem louder than they really should have been. Before we were more than a few feet into the room, a tall, slender woman with a long blond plait hanging down the back of her dark business suit, appeared as if from nowhere.

"Lord and Lady Marston, welcome back." The woman nodded as if she knew them and turned to Peter and I. "Good evening and welcome to Castrum Lucis, the Council welcomes you to their home. I am Miss Kovacs. Please follow me," she said, and without another word, turned and marched off down the stone corridor at a quick pace.

The four of us followed her: Daniel and Helena in front and Peter and I behind.

"Wow, look at this place," Peter said, as he tried to walk along while his head was turning in all different directions, taking in the rooms we passed and the art on the walls.

"Must be nice having your own castle, huh?" I

said, more than a little impressed myself.

"Yeah, no shit," he said.

"Lord and Lady Marston, your usual room, of course," the woman said as she paused by an arched stone doorway which held a dark oak door covered in iron fittings.

"Thank you, Johanna," Daniel said in a friendly tone and followed his wife towards the room.

Helena gave a brief smile and nod over her shoulder in encouragement before she disappeared through the doorway.

"Miss Henson and Mr. Mathews, your rooms are this way. You, of course, will be staying on the third floor alongside with the other newly evolved," she said, and set off at yet another fast pace.

We went along two more corridors, up a flight of stone stairs, and along a wood-panelled hallway to a corridor full of arched doors.

"Miss Henson, this is your room on the left, and Mr. Mathews, you are directly opposite," she said, and gestured towards an identical door across the hall.

Peter raised his eyebrows, grinned, and crossed the hall towards his room.

"Thank you." I said to Miss Kovacs.

"You're entirely welcome, Miss Henson. Someone will come for you both at dawn," she said ominously and strode away.

I grabbed the wooden, carved handle and turned it. The heavy door opened easily into the room, as if someone was on the other side, pulling it. I stood in the doorway and smiled to myself at the sight before me. My room was enormous. It had three very large objects in it that utterly defined it: a huge, four-poster bed covered in satin pillows and luxurious bedding, a massive stone fireplace with a roaring fire in it, and an enormous window and doorway leading out to a small, stone balcony.

I threw my suitcase on the bed and went to look out of the window. Sadly, I couldn't see the view, as there was nothing but darkness outside, and my face reflected in the glass. I looked away, as I tended to avoid mirrors these days. Well, as much as possible anyway; I didn't want to see myself and be reminded of what I'd become.

I looked around me and noticed the only light in the room was coming from the fire and several lit candles situated on the furniture. The room also had a large, dark, wood wardrobe and matching chest of drawers, and two comfy-looking chairs in front of the fireplace, with a small table between them. I noticed a door to the left of the bed and went to open it, presuming it was the bathroom. I was correct, but it was one the likes of which I had never seen before. The counter looked like rose-coloured marble, as did the bath and sink. The shower was so large that you could get four people in it easily, and it had several shower heads all pointing into the centre of the larger, stone shower cubicle. The enormous mirror above the sink was in a fancy gold-coloured frame. The entire room was fit for royalty, I decided.

I peered closely at the mirror's frame, determinedly not looking at myself in the reflection, "I wonder if that's real gold," I said aloud.

"Probably."

I spun round to find Peter leaning on my bathroom doorway with a huge smile on his face. "I could get used to this," he said.

"You made me jump," I said, and smiled back. "Yeah, me too. What's your room like?"

"Sorry, your door was open. My room is just like this one, only my bed and bathroom are on that wall," he said, indicating the wall opposite my bed.

"Cool," I said as we walked back into my bedroom. "Did you hear what Miss Kovacs said about someone coming for us at dawn?"

"Yeah, sounds a bit scary, doesn't it?" he said, and sat in a chair by the fire.

"Yeah, exactly what I thought," I said, and sat in the other.

We sat and chatted for hours, neither of us wanting to be alone in the hours left between now and the dawn.

CLASS

I'd spent most of the night with Peter as we talked about anything and everything except what was ahead of us here. In fact, we avoided the topic like the plague, as if not discussing it would make it go away somehow.

Finally, as the sky showed the merest hint of changing colour he left my room, returning to his, and heading for a shower. I did the same, and soon felt refreshed and willing to take on the day, no matter what it brought. I knew one thing at least, I would be meeting the other newly evolved today and we would be going through this all together, side by side. Daniel had once said that the ones you go through testing with remain your friends for life, and a kind of bond is formed during it. I wasn't sure if that was true, and seeing as my life was so much longer now, I couldn't conceive of having a friend forever, literally. I wasn't even sure anyone would want to be my friend, or even be in the same room as me, if they knew the truth about me being a murderer of the innocent and helpless. I didn't care that most Chameleons thought that human lives were not important. To me they still were, and always would be.

Needing some fresh air to blow away such horrible thoughts, I stepped out onto the stone balcony of my room as the sun slowly came up behind the castle, and the sky in front of me began to gradually change colour. The early morning twilight always drew me in, no matter where I was. The colours of night changing into day fascinated me, both by their never ending cycle and their beauty. I found the dawn calming for my mind and body, and relished the peace and quiet while I could, as I watched the sky change. Although the sun was still hidden behind the stone walls at my back, I knew I would have an excellent view of the setting sun from my balcony tonight, and I looked forward to watching its splendour reflected on the deep, dark waters of the lake below.

I heard a knock at my door and took a deep breath. I slowly crossed my room and deliberately slowed my heart rate down, as I could feel the fear of what was coming next, building inside me. I opened the door to find Peter and Miss Kovacs standing in the hallway.

"Good morning," I said to them both.

"Hey," Peter said.

I noticed he wasn't smiling today and thought

that perhaps he was as nervous as I felt right at that moment.

"Good morning, Miss Henson," Miss Kovacs said. "I had not been expecting to see you both so soon again, but we all do what we must in these times of crisis," she said, without explaining her meaning. She turned on her heel and, once again, stalked off down the corridor with the presumption that we would follow, almost as if she resented having to fetch us.

Peter and I looked at each other, shrugged, and followed behind. We were led through several corridors and up two flights of stairs to a medium-sized room with the nine thrones of the Council at the far end, and approximately twenty smaller chairs, set out at a distance in front of them. On a few of the seats at the front were piled several robes and, in various stages of putting them on, were what I presumed to be the other newly evolved, some of which looked up when we entered.

"Please dress in the ceremonial robes and stand over by the wall there. Do it quickly." She pointed to the back of the room on the left hand side. "When your name is called, you will walk in front of the Council and stand before its leader, our beloved Ramy, with your backs to the audience and your sponsors. Do you understand?"

We nodded in unison, got dressed in the long, plain black robes and stood where we were told to.

Before we had much chance to think about what was going to happen next, the proceedings began. The sponsors of all the newly evolved filed into the room and took their seats in front of the Council's thrones. They seemed subdued and were quietly talking amongst themselves. I spotted Daniel and Helena, and Helene nodded in our direction. Black-robed guards filed in and placed themselves around the room. The sponsors fell silent, and the next couple of minutes stretched by. Suddenly, the doors were opened at the other end of the room behind the thrones. The Council of Nine walked slowly and imperiously around to the front of the thrones in their long, deep red, hooded robes and stood waiting for Ramy to take his seat. Once he had, they all sat down.

An Asian man walked out in front of us and stood, watching Ramy, and with the briefest of nods from his leader, the man turned to the audience.

"I am Kenji Akiyama. I have been given the honour of being the new Head of Security for Castrum Lucis and the privilege of being the Guardian of the Newly Evolved," he said in his richly accented voice, and bowed deeply to his audience.

There was utter silence. The sponsors didn't know whether to stand and bow or to clap at his promotion. Instead, they sat in silence, pondering the fact that Grigori, the previous Guardian, had been Jonas' right-hand-man.

They also remembered his betrayal and murder of Council members during the failed coup last year.

At last, one person clapped, and the others followed suit.

Kenji bowed again and continued with his duties. One by one, he read out the newly evolved names, and watched as they walked out to be formally presented to the Council of Nine.

So wrapped up in my own worries and fears was I, that I barely noticed what was happening until I heard my name being called.

"Kate Henson," Kenji said.

I took a deep breath, stepped out from the shadows, walked in front of the Council, and stood with my back to the seated audience, facing Ramy as instructed. I swallowed hard, clasped my hands in front of me and tried to focus so that my heart would stop pounding so loudly in my ears.

"Kate's sponsors are Lord Mathers Danforth Marston III and Lady Helena Marston," Kenji announced, as Joshua's parents stood up in the front row.

I heard them being called out as my sponsors, and it was so strange to hear Daniel being called by his birth name and not the name I knew him by. One day, I would ask him why he went by another name rather than the name of Daniel and not Mathers any more, I decided.

"Do you, Mathers and Helena, proclaim that Kate is ready to be tested?" Ramy said from his throne.

I looked directly at Ramy; he looked very handsome with his long, black braided hair and dark eyes rimmed with Kohl. He really did have the face of an Egyptian God, beautiful and terrifying just as you would expect a pharaoh to be. His voice was quiet, yet filled the entire room somehow. I remembered my voice lessons at school and knew that he had the voice projection lesson down perfectly.

"We do," the Marstons said in perfect unison.

Ramy looked directly at me. "Kate Henson, after your instruction on the Chameleon Laws and our history, you will be interred for ten days. Do you understand what is expected from you?"

"I do," my voice rang out and I was surprised; it sounded stronger than I actually felt.

The Councillor nodded, and I returned to my place in the line of the newly evolved.

I glanced along the line and realised that only Peter was left. He looked at me with such a look of terror that I wanted to hug him right there and then.

"Peter Matthews," Kenji said.

I watched as Peter went through the same thing that I did, and the Marston's stood up and proclaimed they were his sponsors too. Peter said his "I do", and returned to the rest of us in the lineup. He looked relieved, and my attention was brought back to Ramy as he gave out his last instructions to us.

"You have a short time left to prepare yourselves and learn what you can from your tutors before you are collected by Kenji for your   interment. If you pass the final test, you will be reunited with your sponsors at the Evolution Ball. If you fail, tonight will be the last time you will see your sponsors and all your loved ones. May you do well," he said.

The audience stood and applauded as the ceremony came to an end, and we were allowed to go to the audience. The sponsors surged forward, surrounding the newly evolved, and proudly embraced them. I couldn't help but feel it was all very strange. How happy these people were to put us, their charges and or loved ones, through such a gruesome and harrowing ordeal.

The Council of Nine walked out of the room, leaving the newly evolved and their sponsors to enjoy their last amount of time together.

However, too soon the sponsors had to leave and goodbyes were said and lingering hugs given. Helena wished us both good luck and hugged us before walking away. I could have sworn she had a tear in her eye as she left.

Having removed our ceremonial robes, we were again escorted by Miss Kovacs through the maze of the castle. This time, we were brought to an incredible room with a vaulted ceiling and walls lined with bookshelves. In the centre of the room were chairs and small tables with reading lamps on them.

"This is the reading room. Please stay here until your mentor arrives," she said curtly, and walked away. We were all still a bit shy of each other and kept to ourselves.

"Wow, someone "got out on the wrong side of the bed" today," Peter said about Miss Kovacs and began looking at the books on a nearby shelf.

"She's a Chameleon, so she probably got out of the wrong side of the bed a hundred years ago," I said, and grinned at him. "Nice library."

"Reading room, Miss Henson," he said, while pretending to have a stern look on his face.

"Smart ass," I said, making us both smile. I saw out of the corner of my eye one of the other newly evolved, a girl, who laughed to herself. I figured she, like all of the others, probably heard our conversation so I smiled at her and she returned the smile happily.

Unfortunately, there was no more time for joking around as we could hear footsteps getting closer from the corridor outside.

"Everyone is here, I see. Good," said a male voice from the doorway.

A short, middle-aged man in a tweed suit came into the room and looked around at us all.

"Welcome, welcome," he said, as he scurried through the doorway and stood near one of the bookshelves in the centre of the room.

He was followed across the room by the other newly evolved, five in total, not counting Peter and I. I watched them nervously move around the room and look at each other. None of us had been given the chance to get to know one another properly yet.

"All right." The small man said, and rubbed his hands together. "I'm Professor Algernon Lovel. I'm a Professor of Anthropology at Oxford University, and I'm here for three days only, I believe. I am here to talk you through some of the history of our wondrous Chameleon society," he said, paused, and smiled at everyone. "Now, do be seated and shortly we will start with a basic explanation of what we will be working on over the next couple of days. Oh, and we will have another newly evolved joining us very shortly. A late arrival I'm afraid," he said, and looked rather disapproving, as if being late was an unforgivable crime in his view.

I watched Professor Lovel, assessing him. He looked very much as I presumed a professor would, unless, of course, that's exactly what he wanted us all to think. He might have altered himself, using his control over his body, to do exactly that. It was easy to see how humans could be entirely deceived by us.

"Firstly, I'd like you to introduce yourself to the rest of the class, I mean newly evolved," he said, smiled shyly, and drew up a chair in front of the bookshelves.

As we went one by one around the room saying our names and where we had come from, I realised that everyone in here, the three girls and four boys, were all about the same age and also equally as nervous as the one sitting next to them. I learnt that the others had come here from all over the world, and that Peter and I were the only ones from England. We had two Americans: one girl and one boy, a girl from Australia, another boy was from Russia and the last boy was from India. I discovered that the girl who had smiled at me earlier was called Bethany and she was from Australia. She seemed nice, and I hoped that I would get a chance to get to know her while we were here.

"All right, we can't wait any longer," he said impatiently. "Let's get started, shall we? Well, welcome to Castrum Lucis, which if you haven't already guessed, means Castle of Light in Latin. It is the name adopted by the Council for their home, considering that humans, or Lights, as we call them because of their glowing auras, are our main source of energy and sustain our life force," the Professor said.

"Not all of us," I said, and everyone turned to look at me.

"No, that's true. Kate, was it?" he said, looking at me intently.

I nodded, but I wasn't sure if I had done wrong

speaking up like that.

"But at the time that the castle was named several hundred years ago, it was more true than it is now," he said.

"Oh, ok. Sorry, I didn't mean to interrupt you," I said, and felt a bit awkward.

The professor seemed completely unfazed by my interruption and continued without even a pause.

"Presently, we find ourselves in the reading room, where you will be doing most of the work with me. You will be given some basic history about our society and way of life. Later, you will be taken to our senior archivist who will show you around the archives, and you will be taught about our collections. He will then give you a research project. So then we shall see if you have been paying attention and listening to our teachings. After that, you will be handed over for typing, that is to say, we shall test what type of a Chameleon you are. Finally, you will be interred in the grounds of the castle for ten days, at which point you will be released into a public space and your control will be measured."

The boy from India raised his hand.

"You do not need to raise your hand, Swaran."

Swaran looked flustered as he lowered his arm. "Sorry, um... I... just wanted to know, what happens if we fail?"

"By fail, I presume you mean lose your control and feed on the unsuspecting humans in the area of your public release?" the Professor said.

Swaran nodded, looking terrified.

"Well, let's just say you won't be presented to our glorious society at the Evolution Ball, your sponsors will be extremely disappointed, and yet another outbreak of humans contracting rabies will be reported in the human world."

Silence sat around us like a cold, wet blanket.

All of us dreaded that moment, the one where we would find out if we were strong enough to resist feeding on the humans in public after ten days of starvation. It was one of the few Chameleon rules that we couldn't break, we could not allow humans, unless they were Trusted Humans, to know of our existence. Those that failed this public test were known to disappear without a trace, and were presumed dead for breaking the rule.

Thinking about it, I realised that the professor had not fully answered the question, but before I could bring it up again, he had already begun talking again.

"Right, let's go a little deeper, shall we?" the professor said and made himself comfortable. "We are not exactly sure when humans began to evolve into Chameleons. Yes, we have some records dating back many, many years, but we have no definitive start date for our species. We do know the amount of the newly evolved is increasing, and we can see a distinct rise in our numbers every hundred years or so. This process, that you are now embarked upon, actually began only five hundred and sixty four years ago. When it was decided, by the then ruling Council, that some measures should be made for a newly evolved to earn the right to enter our society. This happened after several, um... shall we say, extraordinary measures were needed to control a certain group of Chameleons from exposing our society to the humans."

"Were they Bleeders?" Peter said.

Two of the group visibly stiffened at Peter's words, and I wondered briefly if they were Bleeders too, or if they were just scared by the thought of them.

"Actually, no. We did not have such names for ourselves back then. We were not aligned to one group or another. We simply fed on whatever we needed to feed upon whenever we needed to. The separation of Bleeders, Feeders and Hippies is a relatively recent one. I believe it came into being at the beginning of the nineteenth century, although I believe the term Hippy is of later origin."

"Oh, I didn't know that," I said. "I had thought it was much older, for some reason."

"That, young lady, is why we are here," the professor said, and smiled at me. "Many of the older members of our illustrious society come from a time when someone who was different was revered as a God or Goddess, and, if you research any of them you will see this."

"Like Ramy, you mean?" I said.

"Ah, yes, of course, you have previously met our wonderful leader. Yes, like Ramy indeed. For those of you who have not met him beyond your initial introduction today, he is the leader of The Council of Nine and his full name is Ramses II. He was once a pharaoh of Egypt and considered a God because of his long life. Indeed they called him Ramses the Undead because of it."

Professor Lovel paused for dramatic effect and then continued.

"There are many members of the Council who have such a noble standing. For example, there is Macc Oc, who was sadly taken from us in Croatia last year. His full name was Oengus Macc Oc, otherwise known as Aengus, and he was considered an Irish/Celtic God. He was the God of love and youth and he was also known for his physical beauty. His name means 'Son of the Young'."

I began to wonder about Gods and Goddesses and how they could all easily be Chameleons, now that I knew the truth. I was lost in the fantasy of choosing which God and Goddess I thought would be cool if they were real, when I heard footsteps in the corridor approaching the Reading Room. The sound brought me back to the events around me and I looked for the person the sound belonged to.

"Ah, I believe our latecomer has finally arrived, thank goodness," the professor said, and looked towards the door. "Come in and quickly be seated, we have already begun, young man."

Everyone was interested to see who the latecomer was, and they all turned their heads in that direction too, just as a young man appeared in the stone doorway.

Peter made a sharp intake of breath as he saw him. I think he rather liked what he saw.

I, however, watched him enter the room and felt my stomach drop with dismay as I recognised him. He hadn't noticed me at first, but as he came closer and stood near the group, he glanced over and a look of recognition and shock spread across his face.

I was absolutely sure it was the same facial expression I had, except mine also showed hatred and a great deal of it. He may have been tall, dark and handsome, as they say, with his almost gypsy looks, but one look at him made my blood boil.

"You?!" I said in a strangled whisper. I was filled with so much anger, I could barely speak, never mind think straight.

"Me," he said, and glared right back at me before sitting down and pointedly ignoring me.

KNOWLEDGE

As the look of shock faded on both our faces, he sat on a nearby chair almost within touching distance and refused to look at me.

I stared in incomprehension at the dark-haired person before me. He was tall and lean but in a fit, healthy way. He wore light coloured jeans and a dark red shirt, his handsome face and brown eyes were turned away from me but there was no mistaking him, I would know him anywhere.

I couldn't believe my eyes.

What the hell is he doing here? my brain said to itself and immediately answered back, *The same as you.* I looked at his Chameleon colours, that rainbow of floating aura around his body that only we have, and I couldn't deny what he had become. I shook my head in amazement. What were the chances of him... him... evolving within the same time-frame as I and coming to the same testing?

"Do you know him?" Peter said, noticing how

disturbed I was by the newcomer's presence. Although he'd asked quietly, in a room full of Chameleons, nothing was actually quiet anymore and every one of them had heard the question, and a few looked directly at me.

"Yes," I said through clenched teeth. "Tell you later." I turned away from looking at him and endeavoured to ignore his very presence for the rest of the day, despite him only being a few feet from me for the entirety of it.

Professor Lovel introduced Max Vasile to the group and informed us that Max had just come from a private introduction to the Council due to his delay in getting here in time for the group introduction. He then continued as if nothing of import had just happened.

Finally, we were dismissed from our first but rather general and short first lesson in the early afternoon with a warning that our education of all things Chameleon would begin in earnest the next day.

Peter and I had heard from some of the others that there was an excellent swimming pool here and so after stopping at our rooms for our swim-wear and towels, we headed off in search of it. Down more stone corridors and stairs we went, until we came across two huge, dark oak doors, again covered in iron fittings. Pushing one of the doors open we found what we were looking for, and it utterly surprised us both. It was not the typical type of pool either of us had ever seen before.

The walls were carved into the stone, as was the ceiling over the actual pool. In fact, the entire pool room was carved out of the rock that the castle stood on. Around the walls were glowing orange lights in cast iron holders, giving a warm candlelight glow, making the room seem cosy and warm. Even the pool had low lights in it, making for a very enchanting atmosphere. At one end of the room there was a massive dark, oak coloured bar with an impressive array of bottles on the wooden shelves behind it. Also, one entire side of the room was made of glass. We skirted around the pool to look out and we could see down onto the lake surrounding the private island.

"Nice," Peter said, grinning.

"Yeah, what a swimming pool. This place is awesome. Last one in is a..." I said, and, as I was already in my swimming costume, I jumped in the pool leaving Peter gaping at me from the side.

"Cheat," he said, and hurled himself in.

The water was lovely and warm. We splashed around, laughed and swam some lengths, chatting all the while. It was exactly what we both needed to shrug off some of the tension of being there.

"Shall we have a drink?" Peter said.

"Do you think we are allowed?" I said, looking around as I trod water.

"Well, there is no one here to say no. What do

you fancy?" Peter said, made his way to the edge of the pool and climbed out. He grabbed his towel and headed for the bar.

"OJ?" I said from the steps at the side of the pool where I now sat half in the water and half out. I watched Peter move, he was graceful and well built. It was not two traits that normally go together well in a male, but he pulled it off brilliantly.

"We can do better than that. We have a whole bar to ourselves here," he said, as he rummaged around, checking bottle labels and cabinets.

Brushing the wet hair from my face, I watched Peter walk back to the pool with two glasses in his hands. "What's that?"

"This..." He said and held out a glass, "is a 1939 Macallan scotch. It's one of the most expensive bottles in the world and we are going to taste it."

"Seriously? Won't we get in trouble?" I said, and took the glass from him and peered at the contents. I must have looked shocked as Peter burst into laughter.

"Do you really think the Council can't afford it? Let's face it, they have a bottle by the pool so it's not exactly their most treasured item, is it?" he said and sat on the steps next to me with his legs in the water.

"I guess." I sniffed it. It smelt strong and kind of earthy. "How do you know so much about scotch then?"

"My dad loves the stuff. He belongs to an

appreciation society and Daniel buys him a really nice, but different, bottle of scotch for his birthday every year. Dad usually lets me have a taste of each one."

"Oh, well that would explain it. Have you tried this one before?"

"Nope, this is very expensive stuff," he said and smelt it too, before raising the glass to his lips and taking a taste. "Wow, that's nice. Strong though," he said, and took another sip. "Hmm... better on the second taste. Try it."

Gingerly, I took a sip. The fiery liquid burned my tongue and throat as it slid down, but then I got the amazing taste of earthiness and of fruit and toffee. I took a second sip, and although it still burned going down, the aftertaste increased, and it was quite delicious. "Oh, that's lovely. I can feel it burning all the way down into my stomach, but the taste is divine."

"Worth feeling naughty for?" Peter said with a cheeky grin.

"Hell, yes. I like the way you think, Peter Mathews," I said, looking at him appreciatively. "It's good to have you here, Peter."

"Thanks, you too. Talking of being here, I was thinking about that new guy. Max was it? He's worth feeling naughty for," Peter said and waggled his eyebrows suggestively.

"Yeah, Max Vasile. I wouldn't waste your time on him, he is a nasty piece of work," I said, and took another sip of scotch to take the nasty taste away from my mouth, which had now appeared at the mere mention of his name.

"Really? That's a shame. I rather like his dark, Romany gypsy look. How exactly do you know him? C'mon spill the gossip," he said and a look of excited glee on his face.

"Well... last year, my mum and dad split up because my dad was having an affair with his boss's daughter... well... Max is her son," I said, and looked down into the water as I wiggled my toes, trying not to let the emotions overtake me.

"Oh, shit, I'm sorry," Peter said, and placed his hand on my arm in concern. "Look... don't hate me for this, but surely that's not his fault, is it?"

"No, but you don't know everything," I said.

"So tell me."

I took another sip and let the liquid burn its way down before replying. "I... we went to St. James' park in the summer last year, to celebrate Mum's birthday with a picnic, and accidentally bumped into the three of them there. Dad's girlfriend was pregnant too. Everything was weird and mum and dad began to argue and then he... Max... started in on me." Tears began to well in my eyes at the memory and I forced my body to calm itself. "He was really nasty and said some very horrible things, they were so bad that I felt like punching him, but I didn't, and Mum and I packed up our picnic and came home. We were both very upset. It was the last time I saw my dad," I said. Actually saying the words out loud made the entire thing real again and sobs burst out of me without any warning.

"I'm sorry, Kate, I didn't mean to upset you," Peter said, and slid along the step towards me and held me close.

I let myself be hugged. It had been months since I'd gotten a hug from anyone other than my mum and, after all the guilt over what I'd done to Ramla, I'd really needed one for a long time.

***

The next few weeks of study flew by in a blur of books on Chameleon history and the laws, with endless details about the ageless society. Peter and I had become firm friends, and Max was completely ignored. Not that he tried to make contact. Oh no, he avoided us like the plague too. The rest of the group was fun, and as we studied together we became friends, and even joked about this being a modern day quest for immortality.

The professor was actually able to remain at the castle for the entire first two weeks after all, and we learned a great deal from him.

At the end of the second week, we were taken down to the archives. Again, the castle seemed to be much bigger than it had first appeared. I now realised it had several floors below the actual building, which were all cut into the rock, and these floors were where the archives were housed, in the cooler depths of stone.

Daniel met our group at the door, and it was a relief to see him. It was good to see something familiar from home even if we had been, strangely, enjoying ourselves so far.

"Welcome to the Chameleon archives. My name is Daniel Marston and I'm the senior archivist. We have here at Castrum Lucis six miles of archival shelving, housing hundreds of collections of original books, drawings and parchments. We even have a rare collections floor, which houses our papyrus documents, precious artworks and, of course, the Hainslea Stone."

"What's the Hainslea Stone?" Jennifer said.

I looked at her as she rarely spoke up and asked questions. She was a small, dark-haired girl from New England.

"The Hainslea Stone and the rest of the collections will be explained as we take a tour round. Now, if you will follow me, I want to introduce you all to my assistant, Amanda," Daniel said as he led us away from the stairs and through a steel door, after passing a card key over the security pad on the wall. "This way, please," he said, as he held the door open for us all to pass through.

As I walked past, he smiled down at me.

"How is it going, my dear?" he said, as he let the group move away in front of us.

"Good, great actually. I'm learning a lot and it's

been surprisingly fun, not what I thought at all."

"Excellent," he said, strode off again and placed himself in front of the group next to a young blonde woman who was standing next to the documents table.

I instantly recognised her, and, as her eyes roamed the group, she spotted me and smiled. It was so nice to see Amanda Carver again. I hadn't seen her since Croatia, when she had been one of the newly evolved herself, alongside Joshua. The thought of Joshua brought the usual sadness and pain to my chest and I concentrated on making the feeling go away, just as I had hundreds of times since we split. I knew we couldn't be together, but that didn't stop it from hurting.

Perhaps, one day, I won't feel it so often, I hoped. I was brought back to my surroundings by the sudden movement of the group further into the archives.

"Where are we going?" I whispered to Peter, having missed what was said.

"To see the collections..." He frowned at me, "are you okay, because I'm pretty sure you were standing next to me when they said where we were going."

"Oh, yeah. My mind wandered off," I said, and followed him and the rest of the group.

The main room of the archives had a few rooms leading off of it, where document repairs were being worked on, but the main area was full of mobile shelving with hundreds of buff-coloured boxes with white labels on them. The shelving units had big black handles at the ends and, as Amanda now demonstrated, you could move a whole stack of shelving easily with a simple turn of the handles. The shelving slid across the room on a sort of rail system in the floor. As I watched her demonstrate, I also noticed the room was cooler than the rest of the castle, and I could hear some sort of air ventilation system humming in the background as we wandered past the many shelving units and their mysterious boxed contents.

"This is the first of three floors, and this one also houses the conservation rooms, the scanning room and the Council's collection, which consists of records of rule, our laws and where every Chameleon in our society is recorded as they are presented at the Evolution Ball," Daniel said as he stood in the centre of the floor between the towering stacks. "Now, if you will kindly follow me, we will go down into the rare artefacts room where you will be privileged to see some of the rarest items in our collection and indeed the world."

"Why do I get the feeling this is more of a PR stunt than for any teaching purpose?" Max said to Carl, the male American candidate.

"Perhaps they want to impress our sponsors with their treatment of us," Carl said.

"Maybe, but I'm not buying it," Max said and followed the main part of the group towards an elevator doorway.

We all stood inside the rather small metal box as it went down two floors. I had noticed how Max and Carl had bonded during our time together, and although Max had never spoken to me, I had caught him looking at me out of the corner of his eye, just as he was doing right now. I looked away, embarrassed at being caught looking at him, and thankfully, the lift doors opened, and we stepped out into the rare collections room.

The stone room was huge, and had several glass cubicles dotted around it. Presumably they were display cases. There were also pieces of art up on the walls and the odd sculpture stood around, some on pedestals.

"This is the rare artefacts and collections room. In these smaller archival cubicles we are controlling the environment and lighting more precisely so the precious contents don't get damaged or deteriorate. The large glass room at the back holds our papyri collection, we have papyrus documents from Egypt, Nubia, Greece and Rome. We also have examples of ancient scripts, including Hieroglyphs, Hieratic, Demotic, Coptic and Meroitic, amongst many others. Please feel free to walk around and look at the items. You won't be able to enter any of the cubicles or indeed the collection room at the back, but you can wander around freely and take a good look at our collection. We do, of course, have several galleries of paintings and other works of art in places all over the world, but the ones in here are our most precious. Please, do go forth and enjoy, I will be here if you have any questions," Daniel said and smiled as he watched us go off to investigate like eager children.

Peter and I wandered around together, looking at all the examples of Roman pottery, paintings from old masters and more than a few documents in foreign languages. Eventually, we'd seen everything and we'd even peered through the glass of the big collection room at some of the papyrus on show inside and looked at some of the strange ancient writing, including the Hieroglyphs.

"I see no stone," Peter said.

"Oh, yeah. We were supposed to see some kind of special stone, weren't we? What was it called?"

"The Hainslea Stone," the male voice said from directly behind me.

I spun round to find Max standing just a little too close for comfort.

"Kate," he said looking down at me with an utterly serious face, no hint of emotion showing.

"Max," I said, not knowing where to look.

A quiet, furious kind of tension throbbed between us. I believed I could have reached out and touched it, if I'd tried. Neither of us knew what to say or do next and silence descended upon us like a heavy, cold rain cloud.

Finally, the awkward silence was broken by

Daniel as he addressed us all from across the room.

"Ah, yes. As Jennifer here has just pointed out, there is apparently no stone on show, and that is, of course, because it resides in a secure vault over there," Daniel said, and moved across the room to a far wall where there was a steel panel with a card scanner on it. Nothing else was visible to the naked eye.

Thankfully, Daniel's words broke the tension. Max walked away and, with one last look over his shoulder at me, he joined the rest of the group on the other side of the room. At last, I breathed out a breath I had been holding for far too long.

"Oh, he just smoulders, doesn't he?" Peter said as he watched, in an appreciative manner, Max walk away.

"You can have him," I said carelessly.

"Would love to, but he isn't on the same team as me, if you know what I mean. Shame though, but such is life." Peter grinned and winked at me.

I looked over at Max as he stood next to Carl. "I doubt he's on anyone's team but his own," I said moodily and headed off to catch up with the others.

Peter followed me across the room and didn't mention Max again.

Daniel stood next to the wall and waited for us all to arrive. "Good. Gather around, if you will, please. All right, inside this vault is the Hainslea Stone. It is so named after Hainslea Park in

Ontario, Canada where it was found by Dr. Michael Albsom. It is the earliest known image of a Chameleon, and it has been hailed as one of the most important finds in centuries. It is considered to be far older than any other petrograph, and the first estimates date it to the 2nd millennium B.C.E., but it may be even older. The image is of a very unusual construction and is utterly different to all previously found artwork of the time period." Daniel pulled his security card out of his pocket and passed it over a blank metal plate on the wall and stood back.

Part of the wall slid back to show a dark room. The lights automatically switched on to reveal a stone room and within that yet another glass cubicle. This one, however, held a huge chunk of stone with a drawing on it. The stone showed a kind of stick figure man with some kind of protection above him that could possibly be interpreted as his Chameleon aura and an unmistakable red heart or mark of blood in the middle of his chest.

An odd silence worked its way around our group. We stepped forward almost as one entity until we were all standing very close to the glass and all peering at this very basic but utterly fascinating drawing.

The fact that this was the proof that the Chameleons had been around for many thousands of years amazed me, and I found it was more humbling to see than I had imagined when Daniel described it. I felt like it meant something to me personally, and as I stared at it I realised it was my ancestor, the first Chameleon. A strange feeling of recognition and belonging rippled through me and it left me feeling strangely complete and strong.

I contemplated these feelings as we moved away from the exhibits and returned to the first floor of the archives. Our group was quieter than usual, perhaps it was because of the stone and the knowledge that we were all now interconnected and part of its history.

"All right, for the rest of the day you will be tasked with a research problem where you will have to use the archives on this floor to resolve it. Sort of a historical detective game. It's a great way to experience and understand how the archives work, as you never know when you will need to visit them over your very long lifetimes. Amanda will assign you your research projects and, finally, I would like to wish you all strength for your interments," Daniel said.

With his last words, Daniel looked directly at me, smiled, and walked away from the group.

The rest of the day was spent sorting through various documents: from fake wills and inventories to weddings and baptisms for new identities, we followed a Chameleon's human family holdings and descendants too, until we reached the required person to end the game. It was fascinating work and an interesting look at the lives of Chameleons over the years. However, the fun was soon over and, in subdued moods, we left the archives and returned to our rooms for one last night of freedom before our interments at dawn on the next day.

BLACKOUT

I stood in the warm, fresh air outside and looked at the topiary bushes and sculptured water fountains that were all layered on various terraces in the castle's gardens. The well-kept grounds looked out over the waters of the lake surrounding the island, and from the terrace I was standing on, I could see them all below me. Summer flowers bloomed at the base of the fountains, the beds of roses formed a spiral maze on one of the terraces, while on another, the path through the gardens flowed in between beds of colourful blooms and variegated leaved plants. There were wooden carved seats dotted along the paths with arches over them, covered in climbing roses, clematises or passion flowers, all of which grew wildly over the trellis of the arches. They were wonderful little places of peace and quiet, which begged for lovers to be sat in, and I wished I could do that with someone right now instead of the real reason why I was in these lovely gardens.

All of a sudden there was a warm breeze blowing across the garden making the leaves on the trees rustle. I looked up and noticed the day was beginning to cloud over, and I could feel the first indications of a summer storm brewing and heading this way.

Despite being in only my jeans, a t-shirt and bare feet, I wasn't cold. The air was too warm for that, and I had not regulated my body's temperature to suit the warmth of the summer's day. I wanted to enjoy it a little while I still could. However, I was nervous, and no matter how much I tried, I really could not make that go away. I knew I wasn't alone in doing this terrifying thing, but deep down inside I felt it.

Around me stood the other newly evolved, all of which looked as nervous as me, even Max, which surprised me a little.

"Well, I guess this is it," Peter said, and reached out to hold my hand.

"I guess so," I said, and squeezed his hand.

Kenji and two others, a man I didn't know, and Miss Kovacs, stood at the edge of the lawn terrace with us, next to the area where eight freshly dug graves lay open. The soil from each was piled to the left. Inside each hole was a steel lined wooden coffin that would be welded shut once we were inside and the wooden lid nailed down.

I swallowed hard and tried to control my

breathing as one by one we were called forward and sealed into our coffins. Four of the newly evolved were already entombed, which left only Peter, myself and Max standing by our graves. It was an odd feeling to realise that this was probably going to be my one and only grave. That I got to see it and be in it and, most importantly, that I would get out of it. It was not something most people ever got to do, and it felt weirdly creepy and scary at the same time.

"Peter Mathews," Kenji said.

Peter turned to look at me with a look of panic in his eyes.

"Everything will be okay," I said, and tried to give him an encouraging smile.

"Uh-huh," he said and took a deep breath. "See you on the other side."

"You bet," I said.

Peter let go of my hand and stepped round his grave and climbed in. Laying down, he looked around him one last time and closed his eyes as the unknown male Chameleon lowered down the steel lid and welded it into place. Once done, he closed the wooden coffin lid, nailed it in place and began to shovel the soil back into the hole, covering it entirely.

Watching the whole scene and waiting for it to be my turn was excruciating, and I then realised that was probably all part of the testing too. My mouth went dry with fear and expectation and I looked at Kenji, hoping he would call me next so I could get past all the waiting and get on with it.

"Max Vasile," Kenji said.

Max stared at the grave but didn't move.

"Max Vasile, either you get in by yourself or Reece and I will put you in there," Kenji said firmly.

"I can do it," Max said and stepped around to the side of his grave and looked over at me. "Good luck, Kate," he said and jumped down into his coffin.

So stunned was I by the fact that he had actually spoken to me directly, and without any trace of anger or hatred in his voice, that I missed my chance to reply. He was quickly sealed in and buried deep.

"Kate Henson," Kenji said and looked directly at me with a stern expression.

"Yes," I said feeling, just for a fraction of a second, that I was back at school and the teacher was reading out my name for the register. The feeling did not last long, however.

"Please take your place in your coffin," he said and stood there looking at me expectantly.

"Ok," I said and took one last, longing look around me at the beautiful garden. I took in its lovely fragrances, I saw the petals on the flowers, heard the birds in the sky above me and felt the gentle, warm breeze caress my skin. I wanted to hold on to those peaceful images and feelings within my mind as long as I could.

I looked down at my open grave and my heart raced as if it were trying to escape my chest and I had to calm it in order to move. Climbing down into the grave and standing on the edge of my coffin, I remembered that we Chameleons had excellent hearing and I whispered, "You too, Max." We all knew that talking to the other newly evolved was forbidden once in your coffin, but I had managed to sneak that comment in before I was actually in mine, so I knew I would get away with it, thankfully. Finally, I lay down inside the cold, unpadded steel box, all the while biting my lip with nerves.

The now-named other Chameleon, Reece, climbed down into my grave and placed the steel lid over me, and there was an instant darkness with just a sliver of light around the edges of the lid. As he began to weld the lid closed, the brightness of the welding torch blinded me and I raised my hand to my face to block it out. Slowly, as he moved around the lid, the sliver of light began to vanish until I was left in darkness with the glowing red line of the weld, which was slowly fading and leaving me with absolutely no light. The air smelt of hot metal and I began to panic, knowing my air would run out all too soon. I heard the wooden lid being nailed on and then the sound of soil being thrown over my coffin. At first, it sounded like rain, but as more and more was shovelled on, the more distant the dull thuds became. I could, of course, have used my excellent hearing to listen more closely, but I decided I did not want to hear myself being buried alive in that much detail, and I made a concerted effort to shut all the noise out.

My heart was pounding and the fear of a dark, enclosed space with very little air crept up my spine, making me break out into a cold sweat. I concentrated hard and fought off the fear with some success. I managed to reduce my breathing to the barest minimum possible, and I knew if I could stay in this state, I would be able to get through this nightmare. Well, that was the idea, but in reality I was not sure if I had the strength of will to actually do it, and the fear swelled over me again. Carefully, I tried to calm myself without using up much of my precious energy.

Gradually, my mind relaxed and I began to focus on what we had been taught since we arrived, and I spent a long time thinking over every detail. I then moved on to creating a floor plan of the castle in my head, with all the floors and rooms I'd seen, plotting it out like a blueprint in my mind. Eventually, I thought about the people who were important to me, about my mum who would be worried half to death by all this and I was so grateful she had Michael to comfort her. And, since she had become good friends with Moira after spending Christmas with the Marstons, I knew she would also help my mum, as would Helena. Of course, thinking of the Marstons naturally led me to thinking about Joshua and at that point I forced myself not to think at all and decided to try some meditation techniques to distract my mind from where I was and why.

Time seems different when you have nothing to measure it by. There was no way to tell if I'd been in the darkness for an hour or a day. All I knew was that it was completely dark and cold when you were six feet underground. I was beginning to feel the need to feed, and I knew that would be the most difficult part, not the loneliness nor absence of light, but that urge. Unfortunately, I would be rapidly using up my energy to lower my breathing so that the air would not run out and it would bring me to the point of desperation and extreme hunger. How would I cope with that? How would I resist my baser instincts and the natural wildness within. How would I maintain my control and not feed on humans, once I gave in to the wildness? I wondered about all these terrible and frightening things as I lay there unmoving.

I listened to the storm get closer and closer, its thunderous claps and downpour of warm summer rain made the other sounds of the world above me muted and strange. I could hear water running underground somewhere nearby, and I heard the water find its way through the soil to escape into crevices and pools before soaking away and giving life to the plants, flowers and all other life that now lived above me. I was determined not to think about all that was above: the steel lid, the wooden lid and the many shovelfuls of earth placed upon both, weighing it all down. I tried not to think of this small space, of how tiny it was and how I could be crushed. I felt my mind spiralling in my fear of small, dark places and forced all such thinking away from me and from my mind. I concentrated on everything and anything that was not in the six feet radius of my body and my mind began to relax once more.

Random thoughts began tumbling around in my brain. I remembered a quote from my classic studies class: "Endure and persist; this pain will turn to good by and by." I tried to remember who it was that said it, and after struggling for some time, it finally came to me. It was by Ovid, the Roman poet. The words spiralled around my mind and I envisioned a blackboard and I wrote the quote on it with white chalk, then rubbed it off and did it again and again and again. I wrote the quote, carefully drawing each line slowly on an envisioned sky in my mind, I wrote it in blood, in clouds, in grass and in leaves. I took to the earth with a stick and wrote it out, to a desert flying high above it and watching a river appear and spell out all the words before it returned to sand.

I flew away from the desert and over towns in my mind's eye. I saw my birth home of London from the sky and wondered how I knew what it would look like from above. I flew in the radiance of the early morning light over our newest hometown, Shipton-under-Wychwood, a small town by comparison, but a far more beautiful one. I flew over the Marston estate with the big house and the farm, over the field of horses and the woods and onward, racing over the land until day became night and night became day once again. I saw unknown places I had never been to from the air and oceans I had never crossed. My mind swam with the incredible images and soaked it up like a sponge as I soared over continents and around this beautiful globe.

Eventually, I came back to myself and to the reality of now, this darkness, this growing hunger and this feeling of being trapped. I began to feel the urge to feed more keenly as it grew within me, it grew and spread and spread and grew until there was nothing in my mind but desperate thoughts of feeding. At first, I thought of my favourite trees and plants, those I'd been feeding on since I evolved but then I thought of the time I accidentally fed on my mum when I first returned from Croatia and how it made me ill, only now even the thought of that disgusting-tasting energy enthralled me. I began to fantasize about feeding on anything and everything from plants to birds, from pigs to horses, from tigers to humans. Anything that would give me life was welcomed as my brain gave way under the weight that was the hunger, as the pressure built within and battered all my good sense to the back of my mind.

I heard screaming. I presumed it was from one of the other newly evolved that were buried nearby but as we were not allowed to communicate with each other, I could do nothing but listen. Now I realised the need for having a guard posted next to the interments, like I saw on the island in Croatia. It wasn't protection for the newly evolved, no, it was so they would listen to us and inform the Council if we broke the rule of talking to each other. The temptation to try to reach out and comfort another was terrible. It was truly a form of torture I had not imagined when I thought of the horrors of this moment. I had no idea it would be so hard to hear another suffer and not be able to do or say anything to help, I tried to shut out the noise but I was unable as I grew weaker and weaker.

Time moved and I didn't. I lay still for long quiet periods trying to ignore the immense pangs of hunger as they rippled through me, tearing my mind apart. Sometimes, I was more conscious than others. Sometimes, it was my turn to lose control and start kicking and lashing out at my hellish coffin. I became more and more verbal, shouting for someone to let me out, let me feed.

I succumbed to screaming and sobbing myself, as the hunger swept away all self-control and dignity. There were lucid periods where I was still able to calm myself and control my emotions, but they were becoming shorter and less frequent, as I began to drown in my own madness.

I believe I swirled into and out of that madness, I cannot say how long it lasted, as I was barely there myself. It felt like I was living in the back of my mind while a viciously hungry predator was trying to escape its cage and find food. For some short periods of time I was on the surface of all of me. I was rational and logical and could think for a while. In those times I did everything I could to distract my mind from the endless darkness. Other times, when I was cowering at the back of my mind, I tried to ignore that other part of me: that wildness, that caged monster, that hunger.

Sometimes, when I was present and in control, I would listen to the others, my companions in this hell, imprisoned in their own minds, going face to face with their demons, their fears, and their own wildness. I would hear some scream so hard that their voice broke, as others just sobbed and whimpered. One male, I do not know which it was, argued with himself loudly as if he and his inner beast occupied the same coffin and both were trying to overtake the other in a terrible and endless battle of wits. It was horrifying to feel and witness the true nature of our hunger in its rawest form.

I continued to live in my mind more and more. I found that the only way to stop the screaming was to go to places like I had in the beginning. I often found myself on the beach in Croatia when I saw my very first dawn as a Chameleon. I wallowed in the colours and the energy on my skin until I could actually feel the warmth of it caressing my bare arm and cheek, making them tingle with the subtle energy I was drawing from it. It soothed me and gave me something to hang onto as I waited. My mind shifted and I was standing in the forest, in the middle of a clearing, looking at a large, old oak tree. Again, the sun shone down on me and I felt it on my body, felt its delicious warmth soak into me and revive me. I let its energy flow into me and around my body, healing and feeding it as it went, and I slowly and steadily began to regain my strength. I let it flow and cherished every second of it. It felt like it was the most satisfying feed I'd ever had.

My mind sluggishly cleared of its beautiful vision. I realised that I could see the red of my eyelids, and my eyes shot open. The brightness almost blinded me, and I blinked over and over until I could see clearly once again, but what I saw was not the dark inside of my coffin nor any of the other places I'd been in my mind. I found myself looking up at a huge, old stone framed window. The sun was shining down through it onto my arm and upper body.

Hmm... yet another vision. Where was I this time? I reasoned, as I tried to look to my right and away from the light so that my eyes could adjust. There on the floor next to me were the rest of the newly evolved, all filthy and dishevelled from so many days of interment.

At last, the truth dawned on me and left me speechless.

I was actually out of my coffin and out of my grave, but where the hell was I now?

REVOLUTION

Anna waited in the dark. She could feel the warm presence of Jonas' body next to hers, but she could hardly see him, unless she concentrated on him and her Chameleon vision kicked in. She had done that once tonight and regretted it. Jonas' face was full of anger and hate as he glared forward towards their goal.

She was crouching in the bushes with five others: Jonas, Grigori, Marcus and two others from the bar. They were waiting to hear from their "man on the inside" and for him to open the door. He was late, though, and Jonas was getting more and more impatient. Since he had interrogated Mr. Henry, Jonas had changed. He had become a driven machine like nothing Anna had ever seen before. Jonas had called for a lot of meetings with Grigori and Marcus since killing Mr. Henry, all of which she wasn't invited to. She had tried to listen in on them but she believed he was blocking their conversation in some way, although she had no clue how. Perhaps that was another strange Chameleon gift of Grigori's.

At last, the doorway opened and they rushed from the bushes, sped across the gravel yard and into the old building. Once inside, Jonas called a sudden halt by holding his hand up in the air.

"Anna, you, Stefan and Nick stay here to cover our exit. Grigori and Marcus, come with me," he said, and blurred across the warehouse floor and through the far doorway.

Anna hated not knowing what was going on. She didn't even know why they were there, just that they were in the middle of a rundown industrial area, in what looked like an abandoned warehouse. Sounds of a fight and screams came from deeper inside the building, and the three of them looked at each other, Jonas had not left instructions about what to do if there was trouble.

"Stay here." Anna said to the two other Chameleons. Taking the initiative, she rushed across the warehouse floor after Jonas to see what was happening and if he needed help. She would not lose him to some stupid raid until she knew what his final plans were.

Just as Anna reached the far door on the other side of the warehouse, Jonas blurred up the hallway towards her, carrying a body in a blanket, blood pouring from a wound on his head, which was rapidly healing before Anna's eyes. Anna backed out of the way and let him pass.

"Get the van," Jonas shouted as he burst through the doorway.

"Grigori and Marcus?" Anna said to him as she sped alongside him and out into the open night air.

"They are coming. Move!" Jonas said.

Stefan had gone for the van, and it came to a screeching halt next to Jonas. Nick threw the doors open and everyone climbed in, just as Grigori and Marcus rushed out of the building and the entire place exploded behind them.

Fiery pieces of the metal structure flew out in all directions. Smoke and flames billowed into the air and filled it with toxic fumes, as a second explosion went off, destroying the building completely. A single piece of burning metal flew directly towards Marcus as he ran away from the explosion and towards the van. He did not see it coming and could not escape its deadly aim as it hit the back of his head, shearing the top part of his skull and brain right off and his bloody, limp body fell to the ground heavily, never to move again.

Anna screamed in horror as Grigori climbed in the van, glanced in the direction of Marcus and slammed the door closed. "Go!" He shouted urgently to the driver, Stefan.

The van turned around and, with a spray of gravel, raced away from the burning ruins of the building and the inert body of their comrade.

"The whole place was rigged," Grigori said as he

stared at Jonas.

"No shit," Jonas said. "One of them triggered the self-destruct system, bloody idiot humans. They killed many of their own people to hide what they were doing in there."

"Shouldn't we take... the... Marcus' body? So the humans don't get their hands on it?" Anna said, trying to process everything that had happened in such a short time.

"No point: the humans already know all about us." Jonas said and he carefully lay the body, still wrapped in the blanket, down on the floor of the van.

"They do? Since when? How?" Anna said, her mind reeling.

Jonas ignored her questioning and stared down at the body with a haunted look on his face.

Anna watched Jonas as he watched the body. There was just something about his reaction to it that unnerved her.

"They knew we were coming," Grigori said.

"What? How could they?" Anna said, while looking from Grigori to Jonas.

"There is a mole," Grigori said, his face contorted with anger. "I shall root them out and make them pay in pain for many, many years," he said through gritted teeth.

A small groan came from the body under the blanket.

"Who is that?" Anna said, staring at the bundle

on the floor between them.

"That is the reason for this trip, and a weapon for our success," Jonas said, and gently laid a hand on the shoulder of the curled up body whose face was still hidden from view.

***

Since the rescue of the mysterious stranger from the exploding building, Anna had been kept at arm's length from Jonas' inner circle, presumably because they knew they had a mole amongst them and they were right, of course, they did. She was the mole. However, she was not the one who warned the owner of the building about the raid, which meant only one thing... there was another mole in their midst.

As she was not now privy to any of Jonas' plans, Anna had no idea why the entirety of Jonas' followers had been transported across Canada to a small town with a harbour. They were, at present, sitting in an old, rundown farmhouse on the town's outskirts, waiting for even more of his followers to join them.

Anna sat and watched everything around her, taking in the smallest of details to see if she could piece together why they were there, and what they were going to do next. One thing she was sure of, it was going to be a large event, because Jonas was waiting for more of his followers to be flown, driven and boated in from around the world. Something big was definitely going down, but how could she find out what it was, without giving herself away? So she did all she could do, which was to watch and wait.

Anna turned her head and saw Grigori marching across the room directly towards her, and for a brief second she felt butterflies in her stomach. Had she been found out already? She quickly squashed any feeling of fear and maintained a normal heart rate.

"Come with me," he said gruffly, giving no hint to the why or wherefore.

Anna stood and followed behind him, once again feeling distaste for the large, aggressive man whose long hair and beard always looked like it needed washing. Despite his looks, she knew he could be so very persuasive and often wondered if that was a gift of his Chameleon nature or if he was just a very good con man. Indeed, many people, including royalty, had succumbed to his will over the years, and it was impressive no matter how he did it.

Grigori led the way to a small room at the back of the farmhouse, where Jonas had been holding court for the entire night, since their arrival mid-afternoon.

"Ah... Anna, come in... come in," Jonas said and smiled handsomely.

Nothing was more suspicious than when Jonas

was being nice, and Anna could feel her instincts screaming at her to get the hell out of that room, right that second.

"Jonas," she said, sat down in the proffered old chair and faked a warm smile. "How can I help?"

"Firstly, you can tell me how long you have been working for the Council, and then how you thought you would get away with it. Then you can perform one last service for me before you die," he said. The smile remained on his face throughout the words and even deepened when he said the word "die".

Anna blinked, her mouth opened and her face showed utter shock. "I..."

"Don't try to deny it. Marcus had his suspicions about you right from the start. I said we would let it play out as you might be of service in your efforts to please me as one of my followers. You did prove to be useful, I will grant you that. But I understand you were seen listening to my conversation with Mr. Henry before he unfortunately died and I had not authorized it. Did you take what he told me and warn them?"

"I have no clue what you are talking about. I am a loyal follower, of that I think I have proved myself. Who is it that claims I am not?" Anna said and feigned amazement and anger, not just with her voice and face but also the rest of her body, because she knew he would be listening to it.

"You have a right to know your accuser: it was Stefan who said he saw you and he has been watching you for a while. Marcus told him to keep an eye on you."

"Stefan? Seriously? You are taking the word of an ex-feeder and a disgraced bodyguard of Ramy himself, over me?" she said and watched as the news sunk in.

Jonas glared at her and his face, for a brief moment, showed disbelief, which slowly turned to anger and was quickly brought under control again.

"I see you didn't know. I have been watching him myself for some time, as I once saw him talking to Ramy many years ago before he allegedly "escaped" the Council's punishment for some made-up crime and joined you," Anna said confidently. This had always been the plan. She had kept Stefan as a scapegoat from the beginning, just in case this happened. She had used her ability to utterly control her body more than her fellow Chameleons could. She did not give away herself now as a liar and a mole. This was the main reason why she'd been chosen for this job in the first place, her unusual gift would serve her well once again.

Jonas watched her and listened to her body. He had heard Chameleon liars many times before and had heard them struggle with their heart rate and breathing. It usually was only for a brief second, but it was always there. There was nothing with Anna, she was absolutely telling the truth, he knew it.

"Bring Stefan here... now," he said to Grigori.

Grigori silently left and Anna and Jonas watched each other, neither one giving away a hint of what they were truly feeling.

Soon Grigori returned with Stefan, who looked a little worried, but obviously did not truly understand how worried he really should have been.

"Thank you, Anna, that will be all. Please ensure everyone is ready to leave as soon as Jeremiah gets here from the airport."

"Ok, will do," Anna said, and left the room. She was happy to not be in there any longer. She was utterly relieved that he'd believed her, and knew it was going to be very unpleasant for Stefan. She busied herself telling everyone to be ready for... well, she didn't know what, except they would leave when the last of the followers arrived, which no doubt would be shortly.

Anna tried to gather her own thoughts together despite the screams that were coming from the study, she looked around her and noticed that some of the others were trying hard to not hear them too. Thankfully, they soon stopped and Jonas emerged with Grigori. They both had blood on them but it did not concern them in the least.

At last, a group of eight walked into the farmhouse, led by Jeremiah, a stern-looking man who might have been a panhandler in an old western, with his long, forked grey beard. Anna knew the final followers had arrived and things would soon kick off.

Within thirty minutes the entirety of the followers were briefed only on their individual and specific missions. They were told only what they needed to know about the main mission and nothing more. Not one of the assembled crew, apart from Grigori and Jonas knew the full details. Anna had no idea how they had kept the information to themselves, but they had, and she still knew virtually nothing of the full plan.

Anna followed along as everyone dressed in dark colours and congregated in the garden outside. It almost looked like the overgrown garden had decided to grow a bumper crop of ninjas, Anna thought to herself, and tried not to laugh out loud at the silly thought. Before she could think any further on the weird garden, they were all climbing into a large moving truck and off to do God knew what to God knew who. She mentally allowed herself a sigh of relief. She was just grateful she was alive and had not shared Stefan's ghastly fate, whatever that had been.

***

Upon the follower's arrival at the secret location, the fighting had erupted the second they'd arrived, although they had managed to gain entrance rather easily, but the guards were now coming at them from every direction. It was all Anna could do to save herself, never mind trying to warn anyone at their location. That would only have blown her cover anyway. The stone hallways echoed with the sounds of screams and the noise of battle as Chameleon was pitched against Chameleon. Body pieces flew in all directions, as men and women were ripped apart, Chameleons locked in battle blurred past Anna as she fought her way through to Jonas' side. She had to stay with him, to be there, no matter what, because she had to report everything he did even when he and his followers invaded the home of the Council of Nine.

She watched him fight those in front of them as he ploughed forward fearlessly. He preferred the use of a sword when facing such numbers, and his flashed through the air, decapitating as it went. He left blood splashes from each kill stroke in the arch back and downward fall of the blade as the blood flew off his sword, before he aimed it at the next poor soul before him. It was both beautiful and horrific to watch as he was deadly accurate with a sword.

Anna narrowly missed being beheaded herself by a guard in the ubiquitous black robes of the Council guard. Grabbing the chance, she swiftly moved towards the guard as his blow missed her and ripped his head off in one quick movement of her hands, letting the bleeding, still warm head fall from her fingers onto the cold stone floor. She moved closer to Jonas as he and Grigori ploughed their way ever forward, not caring about the carnage they left in their wake.

Still more guards poured out of doors, hallways and stairwells, but Jonas had planned well and had brought enough followers to overpower them. Due to the speed and strength of Chameleons, the battle lasted for only a few moments and Jonas was utterly victorious. He stood smiling at his remaining followers, he was covered in blood, a look of wildness in his eyes.

Anna couldn't manage to stop the shiver of revulsion that slid down her insides and pooled in a cold heap in her stomach as she looked into those blood-crazed eyes.

Jonas spun around, stepped over the bodies in front of him and pushed the huge wooden doors of the great hall open with immense force. He calmly walked into the Council's inner sanctum, fulfilling the prophetic vision that Ramla had given him such a short time ago. The doors banged violently against their frames, and the personal guard of the Council rushed into the chamber and spread themselves round the room, protecting the Council members. Kenji, with his Samurai sword in his belt, stood in front of the Council, his hands defiantly on his hips as he waited eagerly for the chance to kill Jonas.

Ramy, ever the leader of The Council of Nine, stood and commanded silence to silence the chaos around him caused by Jonas' brazen entrance.

Jonas' sword was gruesomely covered in blood and gore, which slowly dripped onto the stone floor like gentle red rain. Jonas now registered that his own right hand, the one he so loved to feel the dying beat of his human victims' hearts with, hung loose and damaged by his side. However, the smile of victory was on his face as he felt it slowly begin to heal and he looked triumphantly upon his prey. He had known this exact moment would come, and it thrilled him to his core.

Kenji and the guards moved forward, as did the Council members. This time, Jonas and his followers who had gathered behind him in the doorway were outnumbered, and for the hundredth time Jonas had wished he'd seen more of this part of the vision from Ramla, for he knew not who would prevail.

Anna watched from the door as Jonas and Kenji moved closer together.

"Let us settle this," Kenji said, drawing Jonas out in a one on one battle.

"I warn you, Kenji, you need not do this. Surrender and I will spare you in honour of your father," Jonas said.

"My father was wrong to teach you our ways, you are gaijin."

"I may have been an outsider once, but your father made me family."

"You will never be my family," Kenji said, and

withdrew his sword.

Anna watched and knew that once a samurai's sword was drawn it could not be returned to its sheath without spilling blood first. It was a matter of great honour to the samurai.

Jonas gripped his sword tightly and in a blink of an eye they went at each other, their rainbow auras blurring with the sheer speed and ferocity of the fight. The swords reflected the light as they flew past and hit each other with resounding clangs that echoed around the stone room. Back and forth, the fighters' movements went, a continuous ballet of light, colour and sound. Round and round they went, moving forward and backwards. It seemed they were evenly matched, as the fight lasted much longer than any other had so far on this day.

Anna had no idea that Kenji and Jonas even had a history together, never mind an acrimonious one at that. She couldn't help but root for Kenji, as it would solve the problem of Jonas once and for all. She tried to watch their movements and slowed down the image as much as she could to see it all more clearly. Still their movements were fast and ferocious as they swirled around each other, each trying hard to get past their opposition's defence and cause a fatal injury.

Jonas was surprised at how much Kenji had improved his skills since they had last met on the battlefield. That time, it had resulted in a tactical retreat for him, but not this time. Oh no, this time all the years of bad blood between them and his need for revenge would be resolved.

Kenji pressed his new advantage of superior skill and thrust his sword through a misstep and a definite error in Jonas' defence. His sword penetrated Jonas' chest just below the diaphragm, narrowly missing the heart.

The colourful dance stopped mid-beat as everyone saw Kenji holding his sword deep in Jonas' chest.

The Council watched the fight, and Ramy stood unconcerned with a knowing, smug look on his face. He was very aware of his new Head of Security's fighting abilities. It was what had got him the job in the first place.

The Council's guards maintained their positions and enthusiastically watched as the Kenji and Jonas fight looked like it had just come to a grisly end.

Anna and the rest of Jonas' followers did the same and held their places, not knowing what to do next if Jonas actually died. The thought of them losing had never crossed their minds before.

The sword was pushed so far into Jonas' chest that the end came out of his back. Kenji knew that it wasn't a fatal wound and would heal, but knowing he would win now, he quickly withdrew the blade and swung it around at lightning speed to remove Jonas' head from his body.

A hush filled the room as Kenji's sword flew through the air.

Jonas turned at the last millisecond and thrust his sword upwards and through the unprotected neck and onward into Kenji's brain. Jonas withdrew his sword and swung around with it so hard that it struck Kenji's head. His head and heart were finally separated forever. It was so fast, and such a powerful strike, that Kenji's head was cleaved from his body entirely, and it flew across the room towards the Council, landing neatly at Ramy's feet.

The Council scrambled backwards in shock, and Ramy growled in anger as he signalled for his guards to attack.

Colours blurred as swords and bodies clashed.

The two opposing tribes of Chameleons set forth into a battle that could change their entire society forever and have serious repercussions on the human world too.

REBIRTH

My eyes blinked open.

"You're awake at last. I was worried," The voice said from my right-hand side.

I turned my head and saw Peter sitting on the floor next to me, his face streaked with dirt and a worried expression crowding out his lovely features. "Where are we?" I said.

"I have absolutely no clue. I woke up just a little while ago. I tried to wake you but you looked like you were dreaming or something," Peter said.

"It was a dream," I said and looked around again, and, as I moved my head, I felt something restricting my movement. My hands shot to my neck and felt a strange metallic collar around it.

"What the hell is this?" I said, as I felt all around my neck in panic; it seemed to have no joint or way to open it and get it off.

"Don't know that either, but we all have one," he said.

I sat up and froze when the collar beeped. I stared wide-eyed with terror at Peter.

"It's okay, they do that when you move. It seems that sitting up gets you two beeps, standing gets three, moving about gets you four," he said.

"What happens at five?"

Peter shrugged and raised his eyebrows.

"What the hell is going on?" I said, and got to my feet, and as predicted, the movement got me three beeps from my collar. The other newly evolved were sitting around me. Some had just awoken, and others looked wide awake. A thought occurred to me: why were we all asleep in the first place? Chameleons don't sleep, unless they want to. "Have you all been asleep?" I said.

I got various nods and assents from everyone. They all looked as confused and lost as I felt.

I frowned, closed my eyes, and thought about the functions of my body, examining each and every one as they came to mind and I realised we had all probably been drugged and indeed still were under the influence of that drug. I rationalized it must have been very strong to last in a Chameleon's body and I tried to remove its hold over me, but nothing worked, not even with my Chameleon control of my body. I wasn't sure which frightened me the most: being drugged and locked up in a room with these odd collars on or the fact that a drug had been developed, by God knows who, that could immobilize and reduce the superior bodily control of Chameleons.

A bird flew into the glass window behind me and made everyone jump, and a few small nervous laughs broke but they were soon quieted. It seemed everyone was more than a little on edge like me.

I wandered aimlessly around the empty room. The movement was slow and sluggish, just like my mind felt. I no longer felt like a Chameleon and it was like being a weak, fragile human again with the awkward movement and the confusing emotions running through my brain at once. I sat back down near Peter feeling exhausted by everything that had been happening to us since we arrived on the island.

"I think we were drugged somehow," I said.

"Drugged?" How? By who?" he said, and looked around at the others for answers.

"We were drugged?" said Bethany, looking appalled.

I looked at the girl who had smiled at me in the Reading Room. "Yeah, I think so. Search your body and you will see what I mean, everything feels off, subdued somehow."

"We can't have been drugged," Carl said and stood up. "We are Chameleons, who would want to drug us?" he said as he began pacing.

"Where's Max?" I said, suddenly realising he wasn't in the room with us.

Carl spun round quickly and looked about the room as if he had only just noticed he was missing too. "I don't know, I've just woken up myself. I thought he was here."

"Perhaps, he didn't make it," Peter said, looking solemn.

"What do you mean?" Carl said as he came closer to Peter.

"Honestly, I have no clue... I have no idea what is going on. They were supposed to unseal us, one by one, and then transport us to the local town for the final testing. I've never heard of them drugging the newly evolved and putting them in a room together before we've finished the testing. Joshua said he only got to see his group after the testing was finished and in the hotel suite where they were all to get ready for the ball." he said.

"I don't like this; it doesn't feel right at all," I said.

"No, you're right it really doesn't," said Bethany.

I stood again and slowly moved over to the window, nervous of the collar, and was rewarded with the sound of four beeps. Looking out I realised we were still on the island and possibly in the castle from the view I had, but I had no idea where. I turned swiftly and took in the room. There was only one door, a thick wooden one, and the wall with the large windows. There was no other item in the room and the walls were simply painted plaster as if it was an unused spare room. I walked towards the door, trying to ignore the four beeps and as I reached out to grab the door handle, to see if it was locked or not, the handle turned on its own. I stepped back and desperately looked around me for a weapon. Of course, there was nothing for me to use.

The door creaked, slowly opened, and there stood Max in the doorway. He had already gotten cleaned up and changed out of his clothes from the interment and, more importantly, he was not wearing a collar like the rest of us.

I stepped in front of him. "You! I should have known. Who are you working for? What is going on?" I said and deliberately got in his face. "I knew you couldn't be trusted, you nasty piece of work."

"Back off," he said and glared at me.

His stare was so intense, so filled with instant rage that I couldn't help but back away.

"Firstly, all of your collars are now live. This means if you deviate from the planned route I'm about to take you on, by even a single step, they will terminate your life faster than you can think of moving, even if you still had your Chameleon abilities. There are sensors within each of them, which will release a razor-sharp and very hot wire that will cut through your neck severing your head from your body, and it will cauterize your neck as it does so. The only warning you will get is five beeps and that's it, you are done. Do you all understand?"

Everyone nodded in silence.

"Good. You are to follow me. The guards will be watching you all very carefully, so don't try anything stupid." Max turned on his heel and marched from the room.

"Wait! What do you mean 'if we still had our Chameleon abilities'? What have you done to us?" I said as I followed him out of the door with the others following behind me.

"I have done nothing to you, but I know you have all been given a new drug that will inhibit your Chameleon side and you are now only as strong and as intelligent as you were when you were human," he said.

"This is crazy, what is going on?" Peter said from behind me as we walked one by one up a flight of stone stairs.

"Just do as you are told and you may live through this." Max said and strode ahead allowing for no further conversation or questions.

We all filed into an orderly line behind him and we were led, with guards on either side of us, along several of the old stone corridors of the castle. We were led to a great antechamber, beautifully decorated with antiques and enormous tapestries.

"You will all wait here," Max said and turned to face me.

He looked me directly in the eyes as if he was going to say more, but I looked away, utterly disgusted by him and uninterested in anything he had to say. We lingered by the doors awaiting our fate. In the centre of the room there was a large table with twelve chairs around it, and at the far end stood a large mahogany cupboard with its doors open, revealing a large flat-screen TV and what looked like a computer hooked up to it.

Perhaps it was the Council's conference room, I pondered as we stood waiting, and I realised I could hear faint voices coming from somewhere close by, but without my enhanced hearing, I could not make out any of the words at all.

The great doors opposite were slowly opened, and we could see into a long room lit by torchlight, but weren't allowed to move forward into it as the guards held us in place. It was a very plainly decorated room full of arches, torch-lit wall-sconces and a massive, vaulted stone ceiling. It reminded me of some dark, dusty crypt-type home that a Vampire would live in, and then it dawned on me: that's exactly what it was. At the very far end of the room were nine large but empty thrones; the seats of the Council. There was a group of people talking near the thrones, some of them with their backs to us. None of which I recognised from this distance. At last, the guards moved out of our way as if by some silent signal, and we were now ushered into the huge room.

It echoed with the four beeps from our multitude of collars as we all walked across it.

At last, all of the group ahead of us turned to watch our approach.

I stopped mid-step, expecting to see the Council members, but instead I could see only one face...

his face. The man who had ordered me killed twice and who had succeeded once. The man who had deceived and killed my mum and, if it hadn't been for Joshua's amazing gift of healing, we would still both be dead. The man was Jonas, the Jonas who had demanded Joshua be put to death for protecting me by killing a Chameleon and who had fought the Council in Croatia, lost the battle and tried to kidnap me for whatever his crazy reasons were.

Yeah, that Jonas.

"Holy shit," I said. He was the last person on the planet I had ever wanted to see again, and now he was in control of the Council's home?

Where are the Council and all their guards? What the hell was going on? I wondered desperately as I looked at his deceptively handsome face.

"You!?" I said, and I stared in disbelief at him from across the remaining distance between us and them.

Jonas Alexander stood proudly at the centre of the group with a huge, smug smile upon his face.

"So, we meet again, Kate," Jonas said in a smooth and calm voice as he sat on the central, larger and more ornate throne. "I would say it's great to see you again, but really, it's not."

The other newly evolved looked between me and Jonas, each of them with the same uncomprehending expression on their face, wondering why and how I knew the most notorious and dangerous Chameleon criminal of our time, and, especially, why we were on first name terms with each other.

If I had stopped to think about it, I think I would have wondered the same thing too, but I was past caring about how I had come to know him. I now wanted to know what was going on here. I looked along the group of Chameleons who had, like Jonas, seated themselves in the Council' chairs as if they were in charge, but there was only one that I recognised and he was unmistakable with his long, lank hair and scraggy beard.

Grigori Yefimovich Rasputin leered at us all with such disdain I could almost taste it.

He was definitely my second least favourite Chameleon and yet another I'd hoped never to see again. He and Jonas had caused so much trouble in the past, that I knew, deep down, I really wanted to be anywhere in the world but here. I desperately didn't want to be involved in whatever they had planned this time.

I stepped forward, distancing myself from the other newly evolved a little. I wanted to hurt Jonas so badly for everything he had done to me and mine that unbidden words just flew out of my mouth without me taking the time to stop and think about the consequences.

"I hear you lost your seer. It must be hard to be you now, especially when you now have to fight without knowing the outcome and cheating," I said boldly, despite a cold sweat running down my back and making my skin prickle.

Jonas blanched, his eyes bulged with rage and he gripped the arms of his chair.

"How did you hear of it?" he demanded.

From the corner of my eye I saw Max flinch at the anger in Jonas' words and I saw his head swivel from Jonas to me and back again.

"I was there... I was the one to whom she begged to do it," I said, as my voice trembled. I wasn't sure in that moment if it was from fear or shame. It was, after all, the first time I had verbally admitted killing her to anyone. The words had dried out my mouth with their true horror and before I could truly contemplate the wisdom of telling Jonas what I had done, he blurred across the room and grasped me by my upper arms.

"It was you?" Jonas looked at me with a look of true anger, which gave way to one of deepest sadness.

It was the last thing I expected.

"Yes." My voice definitely trembled this time as a rush of remorse hit me and tears tumbled down my checks.

He let go and staggered backwards. "Why? Why would you do such a thing? Do you realise what you have done?"

"I... yes, I stopped you from manipulating that poor girl's visions for your own sick needs and released her from the hell you kept her in," I said in a voice that sounded more determined than I felt. I was definitely the centre of attention now, every single pair of eyes looking at me, some with horror, some with anger and even some with pity in them. I didn't dare look at Max. I didn't want to see his anger again... ever.

"You stupid fool! I didn't put her in a coma... I was keeping her and her gift alive. For us all... for Chameleons everywhere," Jonas said, and shaking his head, he slowly turned and walked back towards his throne. He walked even more slowly than a human would walk. He did not say another word until he reached his chair and sat back down.

"What did she show you? She must have shown you something for you to do that. I know you are a Hippie and do not have the bloodlust like we do."

"She showed me a few things, but it was when I was talking to her that she persuaded me. She wanted nothing more..."

"Wait! You spoke to her? How? She did not speak." Jonas perked up suddenly.

I frowned at his reaction. "She showed me visions but most of the time we sat under a tree in Africa, talking. She thought you were an evil spirit called Hilly or something and she didn't want you to see what was coming, at least that's what she told me. She said you hurt her to get the visions."

Jonas nodded and an enlightened look spread over his face. "I now understand why Ramla showed me that you were the key last year and why she showed me taking you from Ramy as my hostage in Croatia. If only she had also shown me you would escape my grasp and still manage to do her bidding after all. Well, you will not escape from me or your fate this time, it seems," Jonas said as he leant back, looked smug and put one leg over the ornately carved wooden arm of his seat obviously feeling full of his own importance.

"What do you want with us? Where is the Council?" Swaran said as he stepped forward from the huddled group of newly evolved.

"Ah... now we get to the point. I was wondering who would have the courage to ask," Jonas said and smiled grimly at his audience. "You are now afforded the opportunity to join me and become one of my followers. You will be taught how to feed properly, none of this Hippie or Feeder nonsense," he said, and waved his hand in the air, dismissing the very ideas as ridiculous.

"And if we don't?" Peter said as he took a few steps forward and stood next to me.

"If you don't, you will die," Jonas said.

There was a collective sharp intake of breath from all the newly evolved.

"You can't do that. We've done nothing to you," Peter said.

"Many of you haven't and that is why you get a choice. However, Kate, here, does not get a choice. She will be put to death with the other traitors from our society," Jonas said, and nodded at Max.

Max grabbed me by the arm and pulled me to one side. It was all I could do to stagger the few steps and stand up. My legs had turned to jelly and my heart raced utterly out of control. Oh, how I missed everything that was Chameleon in that moment.

Panic spread throughout the little group of newly evolved and two of them, the girl, Jennifer, from America and the boy, Evgeny, from Russia made a run for the door. Their collars beeped and they instantly stopped moving forward. They turned back to face the hall with terrified looks on their faces. Their collars made five beeps each and within a fraction of a second their eyes opened wide in horror as their heads were instantly severed from their bodies. As they crumpled to the ground, the smell of burning flesh filled the room from their seared necks, which gave forth no blood. The heads, still with the look of horror on their faces, hit the floor, rolled a little and came to a gruesome stop with their dead eyes gazing out at the remaining newly evolved.

The hall was absolutely silent. No one even breathed for a moment.

"Well, that was entertaining," Jonas said, and grinned.

Several of his followers laughed in sycophantic unison at his callous remark, giving me shivers. The remaining newly evolved huddled ever closer to each other.

"Bastard!" I shouted, and struggled against Max, his strength overpowering mine easily as I was still weakened by the drug.

"Such a drama queen. What's the problem? We just have two less to convert now, rather than two more who don't realise how superior we all are, in every way. Saves us time in the long run." Jonas shrugged and leant over to say something to Grigori, who stood up and indicated to the guards to take the prisoners back to the holding room where they had just come from.

Max began to move in the same direction, his hand still clamped on my arm, dragging me with him.

"Not her, Max," Jonas said.

Max stopped, turned us around and awaited instructions   .

"Put her with the other traitors. I think she needs some alone time," Jonas said and laughed to himself.

"Yes, Sir," Max said.

I looked at Max. "I'm not a bloody traitor: you are. Let me go," I said, and again tried to struggle against his grasp.

"It will do you no good trying to get away, you have nowhere to escape to," he said and began to move across the hall.

"I hate you," I said through gritted teeth.

"I know," he said in an oddly neutral voice.

Max turned and dragged me towards a doorway

off to the other side of the hall. The guard, who was stationed at the doorway, moved aside to let us through, and I gave one last glance back over my shoulder into the hall.

The last thing I saw was Jonas watching my every move like a bird of prey watches the rodent that's about to become its lunch.

REVELATION

I turned my head, "Get your fucking hand off me," I said, as Max dragged me down one old stone corridor after another.

"That's not gonna help, you have to be smarter than that," he said, but didn't look at me. Instead, he just kept staring straight ahead in the direction he was going.

I yanked at him to a stop but failed.

"What do you mean?" I said, frowning in confusion.

"Did you really kill his seer?" he said, as he looked at me directly.

My eyes dropped and I looked at my hands in shame.

"Yes," I said. It was such a small word but the meaning was so huge. Once again, I could barely comprehend what I'd done.

"Why?" he said.

"Because she begged me to and because she

knew... not believed but knew... that Jonas mustn't see what was coming next. She said that by killing her I would possibly save thousands of lives."

"Now that's some heavy shit."

"Yeah." I looked back up at him. He wasn't acting like I'd expected him to. "Why are you being like this? Why are you working for Jonas?"

"I do what I need to do, to survive. I think that's something you may have learnt recently, too."

"So you're not with him?" I said, shocked.

Max shook his head and pointed to his ear. I understood what he meant, he was being careful in case anyone was near at that moment and could hear our conversation.

I raised an eyebrow at him and he smiled. It was the first time I'd seen him look anything other than angry, and what a difference it was. I was stunned for a moment. He looked like a completely different person, but before I could comment he continued to pull me forward and down the flight of stone steps.

I found myself in the depths of the castle and walking along a dark, cold corridor with steel doors on either side. The only other modern things in the entire corridor were the keypads outside each door and the lights overhead. Max stopped in front of one door, put in a number in the keypad and I heard a click as the door swung open. Inside, the cell was dank and dark, and there was a subdued light high up on one wall with a metal cage around it and no window. Max pushed me into the cell and let go of my arm.

"Don't try to escape. You see that?" He pointed upward to a sensor way above the door.

"Yeah?" I said looking back at him.

"That's for your collar. If you even try to get near it, it will send the signal to cut your head off. If you try to leave this cell it will do the same. Do you understand?"

I nodded and rubbed my arms as my body temperature was beginning to drop from the cold air of the room. I tried to raise my temperature but I couldn't, no matter how hard I tried.

"The drugs they gave you will reduce all your abilities, so you will get cold and feel hungry. I will bring you food and a blanket when I can," Max said.

"Why are you helping me... really?"

"We can talk later. Just stay as warm as you can until I can come back, ok?"

I nodded again and watched as he closed the door and shut out most of the light. I glanced up at the light on the wall but it only gave out the barest of illumination. I could just see there was a modern army cot against one wall and a bucket in the far corner, but these were the entire contents of the cell. I moved across the room and sat down on the cot, pulling my legs up under me. I tried to make myself as small as possible to keep in what little heat I had. I began to shiver as the deep cold from the ground underneath the castle seeped through the stone walls and into me. For the first time since I'd become a Chameleon, I was scared, and felt more human than I cared to admit, even to myself. I was cold, vulnerable and had no idea what was going to happen next. I hated feeling this way and would have done anything in that moment to get my abilities back. How quickly I had gotten used to them.

***

My eyes burst open as the door swung inward letting in the light and I realised I must have dozed off, the deep cold making me sleepy, and I shivered uncontrollably.

Max walked in and passed me a blanket, a bottle of water and a plate of cheese and bread. "Here this will help, the drugs will be administered again tonight, so you will need these because Jonas doesn't want any of you to die before he can kill you." Max made a half-laugh and looked embarrassed.

I looked directly at him for a moment. "Erm... okay, thanks," I said, and took the items he offered. I immediately put the blanket around me, shivering the whole time.

Max turned to go back out into the hallway.

"Wait..." I said.

"Yeah?" He turned back and looked at me,

waiting for me to speak.

No words came out as I looked at him. I had never seen him this calm before, I wasn't sure what to think about him. "When did you evolve?" I asked.

He had the grace to look ashamed.

"It was last summer, wasn't it? When mum and I were in the park on her birthday and we bumped into you with my dad and your mum." Suddenly everything seemed clear to me.

"Yes, that very day. I did not mean half of the horrible things I said to you. I had no idea what was happening to me. I felt so angry. I shouldn't have taken it out on you though, but I couldn't control it."

"Well, that makes sense now. So that was the typical rage that accompanies the evolution into a Chameleon then. I couldn't understand what I'd done to you. I thought you were just some nasty rich brat whose mum had stolen my dad," I said, and half laughed, but suddenly stopped as I realised what I had said.

"Yeah, well, you were probably right about all that anyway," he said, and grinned.

I noticed his eyes then. There was a warmth and honesty in their brown depths that I had not seen before, as if he had been hiding himself.

"What's going to happen?" I said, a cold shiver running over my body, reminding me of my present predicament. "To me, I mean?"

"You are to stay in here for the week, until they have gathered up all the traitors for execution," he said.

His face clouded over with a strong emotion, but it was hidden before I could see what it was.

"Why a week, and not now? Not that I'm in a hurry... I mean, why not now? What is Jonas waiting for?" I said and frowned at him.

"I guess you don't know what day it is, then? The Evolution Ball is a week today. Jonas wants everyone to see the executions, and see that he's now in control of Chameleon society."

"Oh shit! Everyone will be here."

"Exactly," he said, closed the door, and left.

***

It was hard to tell what time it was, as I had no window. When a young Asian woman came into my cell and overpowered me so that she could inject a brown liquid into my veins, I knew it was night-time, but apart from that, I had no knowledge of the hour.

I must have snoozed for a while on the cot, snuggled in my blanket, as I suddenly realised I was hearing a struggle and shouting coming from somewhere nearby. I listened carefully with my now feeble human hearing, and I thought I recognised one of the voices, but the argument ended, and there was utter silence once again.

I heard my door unlock and swing open. The bright light from the hall blinded me, and I squinted to see who was there. I saw three figures: one being dragged along by another, and the third standing by, having probably just opened the door. All I could make out was their silhouettes as they threw the limp body into my cell and slammed the door, plunging me back into semi-darkness. I closed my eyes and counted to five, then, opened them, relieved that my eyesight had now readjusted to the degree of light available. I looked down to the floor where the body lay on its side, its face turned away from me.

At first, I was nervous to go near whomever it was, but a voice in my head reasoned that this person was in the same boat as me... or cell, as it were... so I climbed off the cot and stepped gingerly nearer to the body. I poked it with my toe and it didn't move. I moved closer and peered over their back to try to see their face. The light was way too low in the cell to see details, especially as the face was turned away from the light and in shadow. Stepping over their legs, I knelt down, placed my hand on their shoulder and pushed. Nothing really happened except a small movement, and the body then rocked back to its original position. I hated being this weak. If I had my strength, it would not have been a problem. Taking a deep breath, I braced myself the best I could in the cramped quarters and shoved the upper part of the body so it would roll over, and the person moved over onto their back.

Surprise made me stare at the person on the ground. They had taken a beating, that was for sure, but I could still easily recognise him. Max lay unconscious on my cell floor with a huge black eye and a swollen cheek. There was a trail of blood that had run down from his split lower lip and it had dried on his chin.

"Max?" I said and nudged his shoulder. "Max, can you hear me?" This time I remembered what I was taught in basic first aid at school and I rubbed my knuckles over the upper part of his chest, in the centre, and just under the collar bone. It worked. He began to groan and tried to open his eyes.

"Shhh... it's okay, it's Kate. You are in my cell. What happened? Who beat you? Why did they do it? Oh, and ouchy, it looks like your eye is swelling up."

Max groaned again, tried to sit up and put his hand to his forehead, in pain.

"Here, let me help you. You can rest on my bed," I said, and helped him slowly to his feet, and sat him on the cot. "I suggest you heal your face before the bruising closes that eye."

"Can't... they... injected... me," he said in a disjointed voice.

"Oh, right. Sorry. What happened to you?" I said and sat on the bed next to him.

Max didn't answer, he began to shiver and rub

his arms, the black t-shirt he was wearing was no defence against the cold of the cell.

I pulled the blanket up from under us and spread it over us both. We had to sit close together for it to cover us, and within a few minutes our body heat warmed us both, and the blanket helped to keep it in. Max hadn't spoken for some time, and seemed to be concentrating on something.

"Now that you are warmer, can you tell me what happened?" I said.

"I'm an idiot," he said, as if that explained everything.

"Highly likely, but that doesn't explain anything." I said, and grinned at him.

He looked at me, firstly in shock and then humour spread over his face like the warm sun coming out from behind the clouds and he raised an eyebrow.

"Really?"

"Yup," I said. "So c'mon, spill it."

He looked serious again. "I was caught listening to Jonas' plans by Grigori, and he was all for killing me on the spot as a traitor to their cause, but Jonas said I could die with the others and... well, here I am."

"Oh, crap," I said, unsure of what to say exactly.

"Yeah, exactly," he said, and laid his head down on his drawn-up knees. "Ow! Shit." He lifted his head up again.

"Yeah. Mind that, it looks pretty nasty. If you

can stand it, put your bruised cheek against the cold wall, it may bring the swelling down," I said, and readjusted the blanket so it covered him as he moved.

"I feel so weak. I'd kinda gotten used to being a Chameleon. I was enjoying it," he said.

"Yeah, me too. Hey, what day is it? How near are we to the Evolution Ball?"

"It's Monday. You have been in here one night. There are five days left, not including today, why?"

"Just wondered. There's no way of counting the time here," I said.

"Well, they will bring food around twice a day and will inject us once each day, so use those things to gauge when a day has passed," he said and pulled away from the wall.

"Did that help?" I said looking closely at his cheek in the dim light.

"Yeah, a bit, thanks. It's kinda numb now," he said, gently touching it.

A strange but comfortable silence fell over us and we both sat on the cot, our upper arms and hips touching, to allow the cover to reach over us both. I could feel him against me. It was odd to be so close to someone I didn't know, and until only just recently hated with all my being.

"How's my dad?" I said, and then wished I hadn't.

"He's okay, he and my mum are so wrapped up with Ben that I rarely see them, and when I do, they argue with each other all the time, so I stay away a lot."

"Who's Ben?" I said, and looked at him.

"Yeah, right... Benjamin Henson, my brother... and, well, your half-brother, too."

"Oh... yeah. Right. I didn't know the baby's name nor that I had a... half-brother." I looked away as my eyes filled with tears. There was no way to stop them now, and again I wished I had my abilities, so that I could control my body.

"Sorry, I didn't intend to..." Max said.

"It's okay." I said, and angrily brushed the tears away.

This time the silence between was uncomfortable, as neither of us knew what to say, and the thought of spending several days and nights together in the cold, almost dark cell was not a pleasant one.

The hours dragged onwards so slowly that there was nothing to do but talk to each other and, although we avoided the topic of family, we talked about everything else, from places we had lived (and he had lived in so many), to the things we liked to do, eat and read. We even discussed our favourite movies and were amazed to find we had very similar taste in many things.

At last, the door opened and two burly-looking guards stood in the doorway. Dinner was served. Well, when I say served, I mean a tray with two paper plates on it and two Styrofoam cups was carried into the room and placed on the cold stone floor opposite the bed. The items were then placed directly onto the floor and the tray was taken away. This time the Asian woman walked in at the same time and the two men held us still while she injected us, and then left without a word. The door slammed shut and it was all dark and quiet again.

Max threw back the blanket, climbed off the cot and bent down to pick up the food and drinks.

"Madam, dinner is served," he said, with a big grin, as he handed me a plate of bread, cheese and cold meat and a cup of lukewarm coffee.

"Why, thank you kind sir," I said and laughed at the absurdity of it all.

"You are most welcome," he said, his smile genuine and kind as he climbed back under the cover and began to eat.

I sat and ate the meagre meal and pondered about just how wrong I had been about Max. I guessed that first impressions weren't always right, and that pleased me greatly, considering we would be spending so much time together in such close quarters.

As I imagined, the night began to creep on steadily around us, I started to feel the temperature drop even more and I yawned loudly. It was getting harder to keep my eyes open in the cold. What a strange sensation it was to feel tired again. Definitely not what I had gotten used to recently.

"We should sleep. Our bodies are struggling

with the absence of the Chameleon abilities," Max said.

"Yeah." I said and a thought came to me. "How come they have these injections? Where did they come from, do you know? What's in them?"

"I have no idea; when Jonas arrived here, he had the supply with him, and then some others brought more, earlier today," he said, as he laid down on the cot. "This cot is just big enough for us both, if you don't mind sharing. We will have to lay on our sides and cuddle up to keep warm."

I could feel my cheeks burn in a familiar blush. Thank goodness the room was dimly lit.

"Yeah, sure. Makes sense, I guess," I said in a businesslike tone, but couldn't help but feel excited by him as I laid down next to him, the small cot forcing us to lay close to each other.

"No point doing this half-hearted," he said, and put his arm around me and pulled me close. "The only way to survive the cold is to cuddle up. This okay?" he said.

"Yeah," I said, my voice barely a whisper as it came out. I felt him relax beside me when I agreed, and I placed my hand on his chest. "Sorry, gotta put it somewhere."

"No worries," he said as he pulled the blanket up to our necks.

I could feel his chest rising and falling as he breathed, the warm air from his breath stroking my cheek as it floated by and out into the cold air of the cell. My stomach lurched with excitement and I tried hard to think of something to talk about, to help take my mind off his warm body so close to mine, even if it was fully clothed. I was shocked by my traitorous mind, how could it think of him... him of all people... like that? Finally, I thought of something to say that would keep my mind off him, I hoped.

"So... you said there were others down here, locked up. Who else is here?"

"The surviving members of the Council, the Council's upper staff. Sadly though, they killed most of the guards and the castle's household staff when they took over. They were very loyal to the Council, to the end."

"Oh my God. He really did it this time, didn't he?" I said.

"Who, Jonas?"

I nodded.

"Yeah, he did."

"What will happen to us all?" I said, as a deep cold fear climbed down my spine and set up camp in my stomach.

"Honestly, I don't know, I can't see a way out of this, not for any of us," Max said.

"Yeah, neither can I."

We lay in silence for a while. I could almost hear his brain ticking over with thoughts. just as mine was.

"What are you? I mean what type of Chameleon

are you?" I said, already knowing the answer.

"I'm a Bleeder, but I refuse my nature and my urges. I don't want to hurt humans or kill them just so I can feed, but Jonas wanted me to change all that," he said and waited for my reaction.

"I thought so," I said. I felt sad that he was and knew we would've lived two very different lives, if we hadn't been trapped here, waiting to die. I began to wonder why I felt it was sad for us, perhaps even to think that there was something between us, a spark of some kind. I dismissed the thought as crazy and continued to listen to what he was saying.

"That's the only reason why I wasn't in the room with you and the newly evolved after the interment. Jonas seems to only trust Bleeders. But if Jonas has his way... he will completely remake our society into a Bleeder one, and, even though I am one, I don't think I want to see what that would look like."

"Me neither," I said.

Despite the fact that if he wasn't drugged, he could feed off me right here and now, and that I barely knew him, I cuddled in closer to his warmth. His presence gave me some comfort, as my mind tumbled over possible outcomes of this ongoing nightmare... a nightmare that included the inevitability of our deaths.

TRUTHS

The days and nights passed slowly. Max and I unexpectedly became friends, and although we were living in extremely close quarters, he was an absolute gentleman, and oddly enough, we didn't disagree once. As being held hostage in a cold, small cell went, it was somewhat pleasant, if I didn't think about the possibility of dying soon. We had, of course, counted the days down, and I sat on the cot, snuggled up in the blanket next to him when the door opened and flooded the room with light. I blinked and shaded my eyes until they adjusted, and felt my stomach lurch as I realised this was not a food delivery nor an injection visit: this was it.

The last visit.

I glared at the two Chameleons standing in the doorway, as did Max, both of us waiting on the next moment, the one that would set in motion our final time on this planet. My breathing came more rapidly as panic began to set in again, and no amount of concentration could stop it. I felt Max's hand slip into mine as we stood up together and followed the guards out of our room and down the brightly lit corridor, our collars beeping at the movement, but thankfully stopping at four. Honestly, I didn't even flinch at the beeping because one way or another I knew I was going to die today.

As we followed them, a strange calm came over me. One very similar to when my powers worked, but this time , I think it came to me out of the absolute certainty of events and their outcome. At least, I had been able to enjoy my gifts for a while, and I had been lucky enough to have fallen in love with Joshua before I died. I thought about him then, and prayed to whomever was listening, in the God or Goddess department, to not let him have come to the Evolution Ball, and make him still be safe at home.

I heard voices behind us as we climbed the stone stairs out of the dungeons, and I turned to see who it was. Briefly, I saw more of Jonas' guards escorting the remaining members of the Council. All of them had collars on, and each of them were complying with the guard's orders. Assuredly, they were drugged too, and had no way of escape.

We were led through the castle and past the Council's inner chambers to a new part of the building where I hadn't been before. Down stone corridors we walked until we came to a halt outside two enormous doors with ornate ironwork on them. Here we waited for some time, and I swear I could hear music and laughter. It seemed weird under the circumstances, and not what I had expected at all.

We were all arranged in a line, two by two, and flanked by guards as the doors were slowly, and, for their size, quietly opened to reveal a ballroom full of decorated tables, dancing Chameleons in formal wear, and a huge raised dais with the nine empty throne chairs of the Council. The music came to an end, and the dramatic sound of drums drew everyone's attention toward the dais, and away from seeing us at the back of the ballroom.

The drum beats died down and there was utter silence as the distinguished guests patiently awaited the entrance of the Council of Nine.

It was not what happened.

The silence was broken by gasps and colourful swear words as Jonas walked out onto the dais with Grigori and several others of his most trusted allies. His guards appeared from every shadow and doorway to surround the surprised guests.

Jonas stood in his jeans and t-shirt, arms crossed and smirking, not caring for the formality of the occasion, his sword swinging threateningly from its leather sheath at his hip. He walked to the centre of the dais and held his hands up for silence. The noise ceased immediately and he had the full attention of his audience, even if it was a captive one.

"Greetings, friends," he said in the gentle voice of Nathan, his alter ego, which he had adopted to try to kill me and my mum only a few months ago.

I cringed hearing that voice.

"No one here is your friend!" a man shouted from the crowd and other voices agreed.

Jonas ignored the comment. "You were invited here to celebrate the newly evolved members of our illustrious society, but instead you will be celebrating the newly reformed society without the corrupt and tyrannical leadership of the Council."

Angry words flooded over him from the audience and a few struggles broke out with the guards, who easily overpowered the guests. Confusion spread amongst the people as the panic and fear built in them, I could almost taste it from where I stood.

"What have you done?" A woman shouted from the crowd with a confused and angry look on her face.

"I have ensured that I have your complete attention. By now you will realise that you no longer have your powers. All the celebration drinks you have been freely drinking for the last twenty minutes were drugged. You are all now as helpless as the inferior humans are."

The crowd exploded with shouting, swearing and angry words but, try as they might, no one could overpower the guards that surrounded them. Jonas stood watching their reactions with a pleasant smile on his face, as if he had just announced the winner of a book award and not that he had just drugged, and made as weak as lambs, the most powerful and important members of the entire Chameleon society.

Eventually, the noise died back down.

"What do you want?" A voice came from the crowd.

"Simple, I want you all to know the truth behind the facade you have been shown and what you have been seduced into supporting for centuries, and then I will have justice," Jonas said, and looked straight down the ballroom to the door where we stood and gave a brief nod to his guards.

As our guards moved us all into the room, those around the guests separated them down the middle and opened a pathway through for us. I could hear cries of joy and fear combined as the guests saw their sponsored newly evolved and the remaining Councillors were alive, as we were ushered past them and onto the dais. We all stood with our collars beeping, looking bedraggled and filthy from our incarceration. This was the first time I had been able to see all of those Jonas had locked up in the cells alongside Max and I. I was horrified to see both Daniel and Amanda in the group. Daniel had a massive bruise on his forehead and around his right eye. Amanda, who was a newly evolved from last year, stood absolutely still. She looked like she was so terrified that it rooted her to the spot. At the far end, I could also see the rest of the newly evolved, including Peter. They huddled together, not having a clue what was happening. At least I'd had Max to fill me in on the little he knew.

I glanced at Max who stood next to me and surprised myself by reaching out for his hand. It was the only way that I felt I could cope with my fear and nerves. I discovered his hand was a little sweaty, like mine, from fear. I squeezed it and he squeezed mine in return. It gave me a small measure of comfort.

I looked up at the guests of the ball, all beautifully dressed in ball gowns and tuxedos. They would have looked beautiful to me if this all wasn't so bloody scary. I looked from face to face, praying and hoping not to find... my stomach lurched again as my eyes found Joshua in the crowd, staring right back at me. I instantly let go of Max's hand, feeling guilty, as a blush came to my cheeks.

Why was I bothered if my ex saw me holding hands with someone when we were all probably about to die? I tried to shake the thoughts out of my head, and I forced my eyes away from Joshua, but next to him was his mum, Helena who was staring in shock at her husband and next to her were Tara, Wil, Michael... and my mum!

Oh God, they had brought her.

Oh. My. God.

My mum was here. Now. To see this.

She had obviously come with the Marstons. I wanted to shout out and tell her to run away as far and as quickly as she could, but I knew it would do no good. She was a human, after all, and would have no chance of escape against Jonas' Bleeders.

Tears welled in her eyes as I looked directly at her, begging the universe to make her vanish, make her not be here... make her be at home safe.

Why the hell did they bring her? I knew the answer, of course. They had brought her because they wanted her to celebrate with us all when I graduated into Chameleon society. This is not how this night was supposed to go, not at all.

"Standing before you are the last of the newly evolved to be tested under this corrupt regime, and I give them back to you as a gift of my sincerity and belief that what you will discover here this evening will make you see how I've only ever wanted the truth for our people," Jonas said and gestured for the huddled group of newly evolved to be released.

I watched the guards remove their collars and escort them to their waiting sponsors in the audience, who greeted them with joy and hugs, but then that same audience soon became wary and distrustful of Jonas once again.

I looked at Jonas and frowned. So he had changed his mind about converting the newly evolved into Bleeders, but why? Did he truly think that he was some kind of hero on a mission of good? Did his demented mind actually think he was doing the right thing for us all?

Similar thoughts were given voice by members of the audience, and then someone said, "What of the others?"

Jonas looked across the dais at the remaining people and turned back to the guests, "Each of these Chameleons is a traitor to our true society and as such, they are condemned to die."

Outrage poured forth as the audience surged forward. Unfortunately, they were held in check by the guards and could do nothing but say how they felt.

Jonas waited patiently for the noise to die down.

Once again, I grabbed Max's hand and felt him move next to me so our arms were touching. It was a comfort to me just as it had been in the cell over the past few days. This time, I didn't care what Joshua thought of me holding another guy's hand: nothing really mattered now.

"I, of course, don't expect you to believe what I'm saying to be true, so I will indulge you with a bit of the lesson, if you don't mind bearing with me for a moment?" Jonas said.

"And if we do?" A man shouted.

Jonas ignored the question and moved along the line of his prisoners to the middle where the Council members stood. He paused in front of Ramy, who merely looked at him with indifference, as if this was the daily life of the Council's leader.

A guard walked across the dais and gave a scroll to Jonas, who nodded his thanks and turned back to his audience.

"Here is one of the many examples of evidence I have discovered over the last few years. Here in my hand is a list of newly evolved Chameleons who failed their interment and testing," Jonas said, watching the confusion on the faces of his audience. He then pulled a piece of paper from his jeans' pocket. "And this is a list of the ones I have been able to trace for the last 100 years, although it's not the full list, as you can see by its size when compared to the other. I can now tell you what has happened to our young ones at the hands of these megalomaniacs," he said, looking at the Council.

Utter silence descended on the hall as each and every one present wanted to know what Jonas would say next and what the truth was about the age-old mystery.

"My friends, we have been fed nothing but lies. The Council, our so-called leaders, have covered up the fact that every single Chameleon who failed their post-interment testing was shipped off to several human governments for experimentation and vivisection."

The roar of anger was so profound and so loud, I had to cover my ears.

"How can we believe you?" a woman said as the noise began to abate.

"How did I know you would ask that Victoria, as

you yourself lost the newly evolved you sponsored a few decades ago, did you not?" Jonas said.

Victoria nodded, her piled-up blond hair, neatly arranged on her head for the ball, shaking with the movement.

"If you give me a moment, I can prove all I say to be the truth," he said, and walked off the dais and out of the nearest door.

The crowd murmured amongst themselves, their discontent growing, as did their voices.

"Be at peace, my friends. He cannot substantiate what he claims. He is a crazy fool. His blood lust has made him so," Ramy said in a calm, authoritative voice.

"What should we do?" a man called to Ramy.

"Remain calm. I have a contingency plan in action from our last encounter with Jonas. All will be well, my friends." Ramy's voice and face remained impassive.

I looked at him and wondered if anything ever got through that stony exterior. He was, after all, drugged and collared like the rest of us and in a line up waiting to die, but he was acting and speaking as if nothing out of the ordinary was happening at all.

Jonas reappeared at the edge of the dais. "Are you finished yet, Ramy? You're so predictable. Couldn't resist trying to control them one last time the second I was out of the room, huh?" Jonas had returned with his arm around a frail-looking woman, with long blond hair, who walked slowly by his side.

A few gasps sounded from the audience as they saw the woman, but I did not recognise her at all. "Who is that?" I whispered to Max.

Max shrugged his shoulders and shook his head.

"Some of you clearly have recognised my guest, for those that haven't this is my beautiful wife, Lucy, or as most people know her, Lucrezia Borgia. She went missing after she went in search of our sponsored newly evolved when he failed his testing and the Council ruthlessly removed him from our society. I have been searching for her for decades, but it wasn't until recently that the full and traitorous truth was revealed to me, when I finally found her." Jonas gently placed the woman on one of the Council's empty chairs and then walked back to the edge of the dais. "For years, she has been held by the humans, drugged so much that her powers now lay dormant, possibly never to return, and experimented on in the most foul manner possible. The humans have used her and many others of our kind to research immortality. Our people were used as guinea-pigs by the humans and fed to them by Ramy and his cohorts," Jonas said, the last few words escaping through his gritted teeth as his anger rose.

"How do we trust what you say is the truth?" a woman from the audience called and others agreed with her.

"Not only can Lucy verify all I say, there are others still locked in various secure facilities around the world and held in secret by the humans. I have a paper-trail from one such facility where I found my wife, and I have visual proof in the form of security surveillance tapes from that very facility, which you are all welcome to watch."

As the shocked comments and noise from everyone in the hall erupted again and then began to quieten down, a disbelieving voice could be heard. "What of the others up there with you, what do you want us to believe an archivist and his assistant have done against our society?"

Jonas walked over to the end where Daniel and Amanda stood. "These two, as you know, are our archivists, and they have endeavoured to conceal the truth behind the Council's rulings, from hiding the true fate of our comrades to falsifying records and leaving a trail of lies to hide the crimes of their masters."

"You are the liar, and you will pay for this, you twisted sadist," Daniel said, his human rage obvious by his red face and bulging eyes. "I have never heard of such atrocities, never mind having falsified any records pertaining to them."

I had never seen Daniel so angry, nor so human. He was usually a very calm person about all things. I guess when you threaten a man's family, friends and even his society's ruling body, who knows what human emotions would bubble to the surface.

Amanda stood next to him completely still and said nothing at all. She just stared ahead and I wondered if she was in shock.

Jonas walked away from Daniel and Amanda and came to stand in front of me and Max. "This boy deceived me and lied to try to save this girl from a traitor's death, showing himself to be an unworthy traitor, too."

Surprised, I looked at Max. He had told me nothing of this. He looked directly at me, fear showing on his face. I squeezed his hand again, in what was rapidly becoming a pointless gesture, as there was no hope for either of us.

Jonas roughly grabbed my arm and pulled me forward towards the edge of the dais. "This is Kate, who you probably all remember from the Evolution Ball last year, and who I spared until now, due to the fact I believed she was important to my plans. Now, I understand I was lied to and she was important to another's agenda. Kate has broken our first rule: thou shalt not kill a fellow Chameleon."

The audience gasped.

"I have never killed a Chameleon!" I said, not understanding his accusation and outraged by it.

"You took Ramla's life with your own hands, you even admitted it to me in front of witnesses," he said, and tightened his grip on my arm, bruising it instantly in his anger.

"I..." Horrified that what he'd said might have been true and the fact he'd just told everyone I knew, and cared for, that I had killed someone. All the words stuck in my throat. I didn't dare look up and out at the assembled Chameleons and my mum. Oh God, my mum.

"See! She has no rebuttal. I have also just received word that my security cameras caught her doing this very deed," Jonas said, and glared at me.

If looks could kill, I would have been done, there and then. My brain, at last, kicked back into gear and I looked directly at him.

"Ramla was not a Chameleon, she was a human seer. I know because she had no Chameleon colours."

"You are wrong. She was in the middle of evolution when the car she was driving crashed and killed her entire family, leaving her in an unconscious state and stuck between human and Chameleon. Although she was in a coma her Chameleon ability came forth, and she was the strongest seer I have ever known, and I've known a few since the blessed Oracle of Rome," Jonas said.

"I... I didn't know," I said, as my voice trembled and tears ran freely down my face. All the hideous emotions of that one fateful moment came rushing back to me as I fell to my knees, sobbing in front of them all, not daring to look up at the condemnation in their eyes.

"Well, now you know. You killed a Chameleon and must die for it," he said ruthlessly, and nodded for a guard to drag me onto my feet and back to the line-up.

Max saw my legs wobble, and grabbed me from the guard to hold me tight against him.

I leaned into him, sobbing in Max's arms and refused to look for my mum or anyone else in the crowd, terrified and ashamed to the very depths of my soul.

Without waiting for further conversation, Jonas returned to the line-up and stood in front of the Council members. He instructed them to kneel before him. Most refused and were forced to their knees by the guards.

Jonas pulled out his sword from the sheath at his waist, and held it at Ramy's throat.

"Tell the truth, traitor, or die here and now," he said with a voice of steel.

Ramy looked up at Jonas with no expression at all on his face and then looked directly at the crowd.

"I know nothing of these lies and allegations."

Jonas grabbed Empusa, one of the two closest members and dear friends of Ramy, and dragged her forward, forcing her to stay on her knees. He took a step back, swung and held his sword up above his right shoulder, ready to swing it down on her neck, while a guard stepped forward and removed her collar. "Admit your guilt, Ramy, or watch your fellow traitors die one by one," he said.

Ramy continued to look straight ahead and said nothing.

The sword swung down in a blur and removed the head of the woman in a fraction of a second. Her head dropped to the floor and rolled away as screams and anger filled the room, her body flopped to the floor with as much grace as a sack of bricks.

Lamia, Empusa's closest friend, screamed: "No!" She tried to move forward, but was easily grabbed and held still by Grigori. Other Council members tried to stand and move towards Jonas, but they were all held in place by the overwhelming strength of the guards.

"Admit it, or she will be next," Jonas said, and pointed to Lamia, knowing full well she was Ramy's favourite and sometime lover.

Again, Ramy said nothing and looked ahead. Jonas grabbed the woman and dragged her forward, next to the bloody corpse and severed head with glazed over eyes of her friend. Again, a guard removed the collar as Jonas positioned himself ready to strike.

"Last chance to save your woman," Jonas said.

Ramy said nothing.

Again the sword began to fly through the air.

"Wait!' Ramy shouted and looked at Lamia.

Jonas' blade stopped mid-flight, only because he used his Chameleon strength to stay the blade.

"I admit I made a deal with the humans, but it was to save us not destroy us," Ramy said in a voice that sounded so defeated that everyone was shocked by it as much as his words.

The audience paused from their angry objections at Jonas' behaviour and stared in disbelief at their leader. A few moments passed as the news sunk in before they surged forward again. This time Jonas' guards let the crowd get closer to the dais, although they were still surrounded and could do no real harm.

"You see, my friends, he has lied to us all and sold us out to the humans, and for what? Now they have developed these collars..." Jonas said with disdain as he gestured to the rest of us who were still wearing them. "And some kind of serum that negates our abilities, making us as weak and as vulnerable as they are. I say he is a traitor to our kind and should be executed."

There was an angry roar of assent from the audience, with just a few dissenting voices which were drowned out by the sudden lust for Ramy's death.

Jonas nodded with pleasure as the majority of the crowd agreed with him and at last understood what he already knew to be the truth. Moving over in front of Ramy, he raised his sword. "Do you have any last comment, before I can finally get my justice?" he said, and nodded to the guard to remove Ramy's collar.

"I did nothing wrong," Ramy said, and looked utterly disinterested as his mental walls went back up and he closed off all traces of emotion.

It was impressive to watch Ramy close down his emotions so efficiently, considering that he was presently human and not doing it with his abilities.

Without further words, Jonas swung the sword down with his full force.

"Halt," a voice echoed around the room with surprising strength.

Jonas' arm and sword were just millimetres away from Ramy's exposed neck, and no matter how hard he tried, he could not force the weapon forward to slice through the flesh.

Instinctive fear spread round the room like a ripple on a pond.

"Cease." This word was less loud but just as powerful.

Jonas was shaking with effort as he tried to hold the sword but it flew from his grasp and into a stone column behind the thrones.

CONTROL

Everyone looked across the room to the massive wooden entrance doors and utter silence descended on the ballroom.

There stood a slight figure dressed in a light grey robe with a deep hood over their head, shadowing their face. The person walked very slowly down the hall, as if they were out on a summer's stroll.

A sudden noise to my right made me look at the Council members who were all on one knee with their heads bowed and their right hands held out before them. I had never seen them behave like this, nor had I seen such a subservient reaction to anyone before. I turned back towards the strange figure and watched as it stopped in the middle of the room near the guest hostages.

"The Hermit," someone said in a hushed and irreverent tone.

To my utter surprise, the small whisper ran through the crowd and then they all went down on one knee and held out their right hands in the same way as the Council had. Only the Trusted Humans remained standing, and they looked as bewildered and as confused as I felt. I saw my mum standing there, looking at the stranger and then she looked at me. I looked away, unable to bear her questioning gaze in my shame, but not before I saw Michael pull her down onto her knees.

All the other humans were grabbed by their masters and mistresses and pulled down too, and instructed to hold out their hands in deference.

I looked around and saw that everyone except Max, Jonas and I were on their knees. Max lowered himself too and pulled me down with him.

"Who is that?" I whispered in his ear.

"Dunno, but if they can make everyone here react like that, I'm not going to argue," he said.

I carefully gazed up past my eyebrows and saw Jonas finally and defiantly become the last one to kneel. He did not look like he meant it, and it was as if he was forced to.

"My Lord Anu... we did not expect you," Ramy said, his voice shaking with a deep, cold fear.

The fear welled in my stomach. Whoever this was, they were capable of making Ramy afraid, and that in itself was a truly frightening thought.

"It is my Lady Sarpanit, at present, and no, I do not suppose you did expect me," the stranger said in a voice that was neither male nor female.

"Apologies, my Lady, I had not known of your

change," Ramy said as he remained in the kneeling position.

"Not many do, but it pleases me to be this way when I want, just as it pleases me to be Lord Anu, too." The woman threw back her hood to reveal a beautiful and perfect olive skin, deep dark eyes and luscious, long black hair.

She looked along the line-up of prisoners on the dais and, with a mere flick of her hand, the collars detached and fell from all of us, as if they were nothing but feathers on a breeze.

I looked over at her, utterly stunned. The power that radiated off her was palpable, and it strangely drew me in. The sharp intake of breath reminded me there were other people in the room. This woman, or whatever she was, demanded attention, so much so that all thought of others had left my mind as I looked upon her.

"I leave you, my young ones, to rule in my stead, to be my truth and word. But what do I hear in my faraway lands? You all fight and disassemble from each other, like human younglings. I thought I had made it clear for you to ensure peace and harmony so we could ride through the ages together so I might go forth and be with all my children."

"I... we... have endeavoured to do your wishes, my Lady. However, our way has been barred by dissenters of late," Ramy said, and looked over towards Jonas.

Lady Sarpanit climbed up onto the dais and

walked over to the grandest throne, which was, of course, Ramy's and sat down. She slowly arranged her cloak about her and then looked up again.

"I know exactly what you have all been doing and that is why I am here," she said, as she looked out to all her subjects.

Ramy, still on one knee, swivelled around to face her, but remained in the deferential position.

"You may all rise," Sarpanit said in a gentle voice as if she was speaking to a kindergarten class.

In silence, everyone obeyed. They stood up and continued to look at her like rabbits in the headlights.

"Set them free." She gestured towards the guests.

The guards hesitated, but only for the briefest of moments, and stood back from the guests, freeing them all.

"Jonas, Ramy, Lamia, Grigori and Kate, stay where you are. The rest of you can leave this platform. You are all now cleared of any wrong doing," Sarpanit said and inclined her head, as everyone quickly moved off the dais, including the guards.

I watched as the remaining followers of Jonas now joined the guest and guards below the dais and waited to find out what would become of their leader. It seemed strange that they all stood together as one group now and were not trying to kill each other.

Max turned to look at me with worry in his eyes as he stepped down from the dais. I hated watching him leave my side. I felt strong next to him, but he had been freed and I was pleased about that. However, I was not, and a cold fear spread through my body, making me sweat and bite my lower lip with anxiety.

"Kate," Sarpanit said.

My eyes darted toward her in fear and I was rooted to the spot, unable to do anything other than quiver and drench myself in cold sweat.

"You did what you knew to be right, and I am aware that you had no idea Ramla was a Chameleon, which she was. I have spent many hours with her, in her mind, as she showed me the happenings of my children."

I was shocked by her words. I had actually killed a Chameleon after all, and by all appearances, a friend of what looked to be the most powerful one of all time. My throat dried, and even if she ordered me to speak right then, I would not have been able to.

"She knew much and could see far. She will be greatly missed," she said and nodded to herself. "You are not guilty of breaking our first law, for you truly believed Ramla was human. You may go," she said, and dismissed me with a wave of her hand as if I was a naughty child.

My knees buckled in relief and I collapsed down onto the wooden platform, as my vision became spotty and blurred. I felt strong hands on me as I was lifted down and placed on a chair.

I could hear my mum's voice telling me to concentrate on breathing in and out, but the voice seemed strange, as if it was far away or muffled somehow. My vision became clearer with every breath I took, and I had the strangest feeling of coming back to myself. At last, I began to feel better and, as my vision cleared, I looked up at those around me. So many familiar faces looked down at me with concern. My mum knelt before me and I looked down into her eyes as she reached out to hug me. Tears streamed down my face as I was enveloped by her love.

"Kneel," Sarpanit said. Her voice had changed and became deeper, with such power behind it that it commanded all attention in the room to snap back to her.

The four left standing before her knelt quickly.

"Jonas, Ramy, Lamia and Grigori, you have all done things that have upset the balance. Not only the balance I had created in my domain but also out there with my other children, the humans. I understand the trouble they cause as they know no other way, but you all should be wiser. You are not, and that is why I have returned from my faraway lands. For I must now conquer all and set in motion deeds to restore the balance."

"But, my Lady..." Ramy said.

"Silence!" The sound boomed around the room

and, as she lifted her hand, Ramy's body rose off the ground and floated a foot off the dais.

Ramy's hand flew to this throat; he gasped for breath as he hung there.

She watched him for a few moments, and with another small movement of her hand, she lowered his body and released him from her grasp. "You will only speak when asked, understood Ramses?"

Ramy coughed and spluttered, trying to gain his breath again and nodded. He returned to the supplicant's position without another word.

"Lamia, you have done nothing to stop the atrocities of Ramy and Empusa. You may not have collaborated, but you also knew of their deeds and still did nothing to save my Chameleons who failed the testing. For this, I banish you from my society for the entirety of your long life. You will remain separate, from both my Chameleon and my human children, and you will no longer feed as you like. You will feed from now, until the end of time, without taking a single life or I will stop yours."

"Wait, I can explain... I..." Lamia said on both knees, her hands held out in front of her begging to be heard.

Sarpanit tilted her head towards Lamia and she ceased speaking, her voice lost forever.

Lamia tried to make sounds but not a single one came out of her mouth.

"Now you will learn what remaining silent really means. Remove her from my presence," she said to no one in particular, but her will was done instantly.

The guards that were once Jonas' knew who was really in charge now and did Sarpanit's bidding without a second look at their old master.

"Grigori Yefimovich Rasputin," she said, and her gaze turned on him.

Grigori visibly wilted under the look.

"You took the life of my present companion, when I am in this form, as you endeavoured to overthrow my Council in Croatia. Not only did you break my highest law but you also deprived me of the great soul that was once Marduk. For this you will die, do you wish to say anything first?" she said.

Grigori, who was not usually a particularly verbose man at any time, shook his head and remained silent. He knew his life was forfeit and there was nothing to be said as he accepted his fate because he also knew there was no one strong enough to save him, not even his friend Jonas.

"So be it remembered," she said and held two fingers in the air.

The sword freed itself from the stone pillar and flew across the room, severing Grigori's head from his body in the blink of an eye. The weapon came to rest, point first, in the wooden platform at Sarpanit's feet.

The entire room of Chameleons staggered backwards in surprise and fear as Grigori's head rolled off the dais and came to a stop with his eyes looking vacantly up at the vaulted ceiling.

I stood at the edge of the crowd, watching justice finally being carried out, with one arm around my mum and standing next to Max. I was shocked by the power of this Chameleon. Not only could she change sex at will, but she was also able to control anything around her. I had never imagined one could get to be so powerful. I tapped Daniel, who stood in front of me, on the shoulder, "Who is she?"

"She is Lady Sarpanit and Lord Anu," he said over his shoulder as if that explained everything.

"Okay," I said, hoping for a little more than that.

From behind me came a voice I recognised instantly.

"She is the first and oldest Chameleon. She built our society and has ruled it from the beginning of time," Joshua said.

He spoke right near my right ear, making me jump. I hadn't realised he was standing directly behind me. It was lovely to hear his voice again, but then I remembered Ramla's warning and hardened my heart to it. "So, how come I have never heard of her before?"

Helena leaned in toward me and spoke very quietly. "She rarely comes out in public. That is why she is known as The Hermit. No one has seen her for hundreds of years. Some younger Chameleons in our society believe she is a myth and nothing more than a story," she said in reverent whisper.

"Wow. Well, I guess she isn't a myth after all, and that 'story' has one hell of a bite to it," I said. I couldn't help but be impressed by her.

"Shh..." A tall, thin woman hissed at me and looked back over the heads in front of her with a look of profound awe on her face.

"Ramy and Jonas, my children, you are both such disappointments. You have caused more trouble with my children than any others have over my many years. Now you have created a hatred for us by my other children and the hatred has coalesced as a force to be troubled with. You must be sentenced to death for your crimes against your brother and sisters," Sarpanit said and paused as she smoothed a lock of her dark hair.

The entire room stilled, and not a murmur could be heard. As I looked at the kneeling backs of Ramy and Jonas, I noticed that neither of them moved a millimetre as they awaited their sentences to be carried out.

"My lady, you have it wrong, I was trying to save our... your people," Jonas burst out, unable to contain himself further.

Sarpanit simply looked at him, raised an eyebrow and tilted her head, like a dog would when trying to work something out.

"You seem to think you are a good child, but you are wrong. You have purposefully killed many of your brothers and sisters in your pursuit of vengeance. Your original search for your love was a noble and justified one, but you became warped by your hatred of my society and became the very thing you despised: a tyrannical monster, just as Ramses here has become. You are both the same now," she said in a gentle tone, as if trying to explain something to a small child.

Jonas just looked at her, shock and realisation dawning on his face as he understood the truth of her words and he said no more.

Sarpanit looked out at all her subjects. "For our way forward, which I have seen thanks to my dear friend, Ramla..." She paused with a look of sadness on her face.

A fission of guilt ran down my spine and Max reached out to touch my arm in a welcomed gesture of support and friendship.

The look of sadness on Sarpanit's face was swept away and replaced with one of sheer determination. "I will need you all, and indeed both of you, Jonas and Ramses, as we will be using your individual resources as one to help me restore the balance. For what is to come, I will unite my children, and you two will work together or your sentence of death will be carried out here and now. Do you understand?" she said, using that hard, forceful voice again.

Both men nodded in agreement, knowing full well they would have to step very carefully during every moment of every day now, or lose their lives in an instant at her hands.

"Once we have achieved the balance again with my human children and all of my children are at peace with each other, then I will choose who will lead in my stead, so that I may return to my faraway lands. At such time, I will revisit your punishments again, should you survive what is to come. Tell me you understand. Speak now."

"Yes, Lady Sarpanit," Ramy said in a wavering voice.

She nodded and looked at Jonas.

"As you wish, my Lady," he said in his smooth voice, the one he uses to placate someone while plotting behind their back.

"It would be a mistake to think your childish charms would work on me, Jonas," Sarpanit said. "Now, leave me, all of you, and take your petty arguments with you. I must think upon the way forth, for there is not much time left."

Without a single word amongst us, we all filed out of the ballroom as if we were of one mind. For now we had a truce, but I couldn't help but wonder how long this truce between the factions would last. I glanced back as I left the ballroom and saw Sarpanit sitting on the throne, utterly alone. A small, but oh so powerful figure who held the future of Chameleon society and possibly the world in her hands. Dread and fear rippled through my tired body as I turned back and followed my friends out of the ballroom in a stunned silence.

***

After the drama of the Evolution Ball that wasn't, my family, friends and I gravitated towards each other and it was decided to go to the reading room, to relax and discuss all that had happened to us. As we sat in the comfy chairs, a strange, uneasy silence settled over us all. I looked round the room and saw Daniel and Helena sitting with Tara, Wil and Peter at the far end, while Michael sat next to my mum, who in turn was next to me. Joshua was on his own, behind his parents, and Amanda was vaguely looking at the books, as if she was not really seeing them. I stared at her as her golden blond hair caught the early morning light from the huge, ornate window opposite her and I suddenly realised that she was the one I'd seen kissing Joshua in Ramla's vision. Why had I not recognised her before? I replayed the scene in my mind for maybe the hundredth time and realised I'd only seen a glimpse of her face from the side and a good shot of her golden hair. Well, as I couldn't be with him, to save his life, at least he would be with a good person. I knew Amanda from last year at Joshua's testing, and we had gotten on very well. She was smart and funny, and I approved, even if I had no say in the matter. I felt I could let him go more easily now, knowing this, and a weight lifted off me.

"Hey?"

A voice called me back to the present and I looked up to find Max standing in the doorway of the reading room. He hesitated as he looked around the room and saw who was in there.

"Come in, Max," I said, pleased to see him.

"What's he doing here? He worked for Jonas," Joshua said, while staring hard at Max, in a voice that sounded both sulky and angry.

"I never worked for him," Max said defensively as he stood and stared right back at Joshua, unfazed.

"He did what he did to survive and probably saved my life too," I said. "Sit here, Max." I gestured to the seat right next to me.

"Yeah, right," Joshua said, and continued to glare at Max.

"It matters not who worked for whom now, and if that's what Kate says happened, then that is how it will be, Joshua," Daniel said to his son in a firm voice.

"Oh, I almost forgot, with everything that is going on: congratulations, Kate," Helena said.

Everyone spoke at once and joined in with the congratulations.

"What for?" I said, confused as I looked around at them.

"You were just accepted into Chameleon Society, of course," Helena said.

"But I... we..." I looked at Max. "We were only in the ground... interred... for a few days, and we didn't do the final testing with the humans in a public place."

"No, but you were just accepted, as one of us, by our highest and most important Chameleon, our ruler, Lady Sarpanit. There is no higher way of confirming your evolution and entering our society," Daniel said.

"Oh, yeah. Right." I looked back at Max. "I guess we were." I relaxed a little, at least I wouldn't have to go through all that again.

He smiled and nodded.

How different he seemed now, and my heart swelled at his smile. I never thought I would be attracted to a Bleeder, never mind that in a million universes would I have guessed it would have been him, either. For a while, my brain pondered, in the silence of the room, on how much had changed in such a short time.

Everyone sat quietly. They were all going over what had happened in the ballroom and were wondering about the future.

"What will happen now?" I said to the room, looking around at anyone for an answer.

"I honestly don't know, I was not alive the last time Sarpanit came out of her seclusion. I do not know what she is capable of," Daniel said.

"I was," Michael said, but added nothing more.

"I didn't like what she said about the future,

sounds to me like something really bad is about to happen," Tara said.

"I agree, that did sound bad," Wil said and put his arm around Tara protectively.

"I guess we'll have to make sure we all look after each other. We can only wait and see what the future will bring and deal with it as and when," Mum said. She was the single, reasonable voice of a human in a room full of concerned Chameleons.

None of us now knew what our future held, but it did mean that Jonas and Ramy would now be working together under the orders of Lady Sarpanit and I couldn't help but think that was a bad idea.

A very bad idea indeed.

EPILOGUE

A nna followed Jonas and his wife as he and his remaining followers headed dejectedly to one of the guest floors of the castle to find and claim rooms for themselves. It seemed that they would all be staying for a while.

Jonas hadn't spoken since his confrontation with Lady Sarpanit, and seemed very subdued, probably because he was refused the revenge he wanted against Ramy, who he wanted to kill for his crimes. He and his wife, Lucy, took a room and closed the door behind them without even a single word or look toward his loyal followers who stood in the corridor outside.

The followers looked at each other and dispersed, all the fight drained out of them. Where they went, Anna neither knew nor cared, but she could feel their profound confusion as to what was happening, and what would become of them.

Everything had changed now that Sarpanit had

arrived and spoiled Jonas' plans. Anna's mission must have changed too, she reasoned. She needed to contact her boss and relay everything she had seen and heard.

She wandered the corridors and found a room for herself. She bathed, then sat by the fire, wondering how she could connect with her boss without Jonas, or anyone else for that matter, overhearing. After all, she was surrounded by Chameleons, all of whom had excellent hearing. Then she remembered she'd seen the Northman Mikkel, or rather Michael as he went by now, in the group of guests at Evolution Ball.

"Oh, that's just excellent," she said to herself, and smiled. She sat and plotted how to get him to help her and to use his ability to cloak her conversation with her boss. "Ah, Mikkel, how fortunate for me you are here, but you might not think it is so." She disliked having to use her intimate knowledge of someone for her own needs but, in this case, it was for the good of all Chameleons everywhere, and that was why her mission was so important.

***

The woman looked out of her high-rise window. She did not see the glorious view of the city before her. Instead, she stood there annoyed about the latest mess her staff had made.

"Honestly, sometimes I think I should do everything myself," she said, and stalked over to her desk, jabbing a button on her phone as she sat down.

"Yes, Miss Borden?" A young man's voice said through the intercom.

"Get me Fletcher on the line, now."

"Yes, ma'am."

Within moments her phone rang. She snatched it up impatiently. "Yes?"

"Miss Borden, Mr. Fletcher for you," the man said and connected the call.

"Lizzy, how are you, my lovely?" the Australian accented man said.

"Don't 'my lovely' me, you mediocre little prick of a man. I understand we have a disaster on our hands and the Board is most displeased. Heads will roll for this," she said to him, while feeling the need to reach down the phone and punch his stupid little face in.

"I can only apologise for this mishap..."

"Mishap? Is that what you call it? The entire bloody Chameleon world now knows the Iridescent Project exists, and they have freed some of our test subjects, not to mention they've got their hands on our collars and the serum. It's not a mishap, it's a complete fuck up!"

"I... well, I..." Fletcher said.

"Oh, do stop blathering you imbecile, and clean this atrocious mess up or I will come out there and clean it up for you, and then I will clean your house too. Do you understand me?" she said as she lifted up her shapely legs and put her Louboutin-clad feet upon her desk.

"Yes, Miss Borden," he said in a rather deferential tone.

"Good. Inform me when it's done and you had better be quick. My patience is wearing more than a little thin, and so is the Board's."

"I'll get right on it," he said.

"You do that," she said, and slammed the phone down. "Asshole."

There was a knock at her door.

"What?" Lizzy barked out as an instruction to enter.

Her young, handsome assistant entered with a file in his hand and placed it on her desk directly in front of her. "It's the file you requested from the medical examiner's office on Stefan Watts."

"Right. Thank you, Timothy," she said as she took her feet off her desk and immediately opened the file.

"Oh, and the nursery called, your son is ready to be picked up when you are."

"Good, are all the arrangements made? I would like to get home without any idiotic delays tonight."

"Yes, Miss Borden, your helicopter is fuelled and awaiting you and your son on the roof as we speak," Timothy said, confident he had anticipated all his boss's needs.

"Good, I need a good night's sleep and a weekend at home, before I break the world and start World War Three," she said, rose, put the file in her Gucci leather briefcase and walked out of her office to enjoy some family time at home.

The last instalment of 'The Chameleon Sagas':

IMMORTAL LIGHTS

As the world plummets unknowingly into a battle between Chameleons and humans, Kate blossoms into her new life and finds out what her Chameleon gift is, however, she struggles to comprehend where it came from.

Can she use this gift to stop an all out war and create a lasting peace between humans and Chameleons? Or is it too late for us all?

From England to Turkey, chaos rages until the final truth is revealed, one that will change all life on the planet until the end of time.

IMMORTAL LIGHTS

The battle for supremacy begins.

Author Bio

J.E. Marriott is an internationally acclaimed author of paranormal mysteries, supernatural thrillers and magically enchanted tales.

In 2008, she permanently moved from her home in Lincolnshire, in the UK, across the pond to Ontario, Canada, where she has happily, and permanently, made her home and is working as a full-time author.

She is a university accredited historian and avid reader of a wide spectrum of genres. She brings her unusual English lilt and humour to all of her writings, no matter the genre.